W9-BRJ-645

WINTER AND THE GENERAL

WINTER AND THE GENERAL

Julian Jay Savarin

This first world edition published in Great Britain 2003 by
SEVERN HOUSE PUBLISHERS LTD of
9–15 High Street, Sutton, Surrey SM1 1DF.
This first world edition published in the USA 2003 by
SEVERN HOUSE PUBLISHERS INC of
595 Madison Avenue, New York, N.Y. 10022.

British Library Cataloguing in Publication Data

Savarin, Julian Jay
    Winter and the general
    1. Müller, Hauptkommissar (Fictitious character) - Fiction
    2. Police - Germany - Berlin - Fiction
    3. Suspense fiction
    I. Title
    823.9'14 [F]

    ISBN 0-7278-5992-7

Typeset by Palimpsest Book Production Ltd.,
Polmont, Stirlingshire, Scotland.
Printed and bound in Great Britain by
MPG Books Ltd., Bodmin, Cornwall.

One

The old man was dying, and he knew it.
He reclined on a Corbusier replica in his conservatory,
right hand dangling. His throat was cut. Gripped tightly in the
dangling hand was an opened razor. Directly beneath the tip
of the blade a small, neat pool of dark red blood in a perfect
circle had collected on the otherwise pristine floor.

The sharp blade gleamed, as if from scrupulous polishing;
and the blood that slowly trickled down the arm to the hand
and on to the razor seemed in a hurry to get off that gleaming
blade. It was as if the blood itself dared not stay on the metal.
Closer scrutiny would show a tiny speck that stubbornly
refused to move. But this was not fresh blood, and did not
belong to the old man.

Rügen, the largest of the German islands and just off its
far northeast coast, was in the grip of the Baltic winter.
Connected to the mainland by the bridge at Stralsund, it lay
peacefully beneath a brilliant white carpet of snow, its fields,
roads and houses under the crystalline blanket making it the
perfect, imagined Christmas postcard. Its many sea bridges –
long, fairytale piers – poked like snow-encrusted fingers into
the petrified sea. The cold fire of the low sun threw golden
shafts that gleamed off the impacted crystals. The waters of
the Baltic, still as frosted glass, gave the impression that the
entire island was mounted upon it, a centrepiece in some vast
display hall. It looked as if it could be carved out of the
setting and put on a box of chocolates. Anything disturbing
this tranquillity would seem like the worst of sacrileges.

The old man, and the brutal manner of his dying, was one.

The house where the old man lay had its genesis in the eighteenth century. Originally built as a manor house, it was perched upon high ground with a sheer drop some distance beyond its large garden, to the stony beach below. Modernized to meet the requirements of the twenty-first century, a huge conservatory which the old man called his winter garden had been added between two of the building's four turrets. A palace of glass and well stocked with thriving plants, it looked out upon the cold Baltic beyond the snowbound garden.

On a low table was a chess set. The large board was of polished marble, its tall medieval figures fashioned from the same material. A game was in play.

A young man, face expressionless, was sitting in a cane armchair looking at the dying old man. He stared, as if mesmerized, at the strange pattern of the wounds in the cut throat. The first, horizontal, appeared to reach from ear to ear. The second went from the base of the neck, to end at a point close to the chin. At the centre of the cross thus formed, the wounds peeled slightly outwards, allowing a small bloom of red to grow, then spill into a continuing trickle.

A low, unearthly sound came out of the old man. It reminded the young man of another sound: one he'd once heard on a visit to a Pacific island. The people on the island killed sea turtles for food, by slitting their throats. He'd seen it happen. One big example had made a groaning noise that was almost human as it died. The sound the old man now made was just like that.

The young man was dressed in outdoor clothing that was all white: multi-layered, all-weather hooded jacket, scarf, trousers. The hood was thrown back, revealing hair that was so blond, it was itself very close to being white. On his feet were sturdy, cleated boots. They too were white; even their soles. He looked like a soldier kitted out for winter combat, and seemed to be waiting for something.

He watched clinically as the old man's mouth moved but now no sound was heard. The young man remained seated, continuing to watch, pale eyes surveying the old man with all the compassion of a predator.

He turned his head to glance briefly outside. The sky was perceptibly darker.

'For just a while there, you sounded like a turtle I remember,' he said to the old man conversationally. He paused. 'More snow on the way. Time I should be leaving.'

He got to his feet unhurriedly and walked over to the dying man, stopping directly before him, blocking out the view from the fading eyes.

'Many people live for quite a while,' he went on in the same conversational tones, 'even after their throats have been cut. I personally know at least one person who survived, and of one who didn't. You won't . . . but you'll have plenty of time to remember, and to understand why this is happening to you.'

The eyes moved frantically. There was fear, rage, and hate in them. The mouth quivered once more but again no sound issued out of it save for a low, bubbly wheezing. The steady trickle of blood welled from the neatly ugly wound.

'You're filling up with your own blood,' the younger man continued. 'That's why there's not so much of it outside. You'll probably drown.'

The old man had a strangely demonic face. His weather-burnished skin looked like tanned leather, and the thin wisps of hair on his head gave him a bald look. The wide positioning of his eyes and the almost vertical arch of his eyebrows gave him a striking air of malevolence, even as he reclined helplessly before his tormentor. He was a tall man and despite his age looked remarkably fit.

'But you will still bleed like the pig you are,' the man in white said with a thin smile. 'Soon, your nice expensive sweater, and your nice expensive trousers will be soaked.' He brought the hood up, securing it in a snug frame about his face. He glanced at the chess set, but did not touch it. 'Your last game, and you're losing. I haven't yet found what I've been looking for,' he continued, 'but I'll be back for another look . . . in time. You'll be long gone by then. Enjoy the journey to whatever hell you're going to. I'll probably meet you there someday.'

He turned away, went to the huge French window and slid a panel open, then paused to look back.

'Leave it open, shall I? It's so nice and warm in here, you won't feel too cold. But it should help you to remember.'

His German was perfect, but he was not German.

He went out, and did not look back as he crossed the garden, vaulted a low gate, and disappeared. A light snow was already falling, covering the tracks he had just made.

At about the same time in Berlin, *Hauptkommissar* Jens Müller, Graf von Röhnen, was looking forward to a quiet day. His immediate boss and bane of his life, Police Director (Probationary) Kaltendorf, was away on one of his interminable conferences which tended to be talking shops, and networking forums. For the politically aspiring and ambitiousKaltendorf, they were the very stuff of life itself. For Müller, they were bliss, and promised hassle-free days. He hoped this would prove to be one of the longer conferences.

He made his way along the corridor towards his office and, despite the cold outside, was feeling immensely pleased with the world. Today, he could concentrate on his ongoing investigation into the mystery of Romeo Six. Only Pappenheim knew he was doing so. Kaltendorf would have several fits, if *he* knew.

Müller entered his office with a sigh of pleasure, and looked forward to the start of his working day.

He had barely shut the door and was removing his coat when one of the two phones on his desk began to ring. The black one. He paused and stared at it furiously.

'No, no, *no!*' he said. 'Not so early, Pappi!'

The phone was a direct connection to *Oberkommissar* Pappenheim, his deputy.

The phone kept ringing.

Sighing, coat still half-removed, Müller went across to his desk and picked it up.

'I came in quietly, Pappi,' he began. 'How did you know . . . ?'

4

But it was not Pappenheim.

A vaguely familiar voice said, 'Sorry . . . not Pappi. Something has happened to General von Mappus, on Rügen. You should look into it.'

The line went dead.

Müller slowly put the phone down. 'Why does your voice sound familiar? And who the hell is General von Mappus?'

On Rügen, the old man gripped the razor tightly. His slowly dying eyes were focussed on a white distance that was far beyond his garden. His mind travelled to that distance, to a point in time where the razor belonged.

The winter of November 1942, near Stalingrad.

Hell on earth tore the cold day with its roar of destruction. All around, the air was streaked with the fire trails of barrage after barrage from Katyuskha multiple-rocket launchers, their erupting explosions, their dark billowing clouds, the screams of fighting, dying, and wounded men, the thunder of artillery, the chatter of machine guns, the bark of rifles, the hoarse yells of mainly futile orders. The world was witnessing man's greatest insanity so far.

In a makeshift snow trench reddened by the blood of the dead and dying, the remnants of what had been a Waffen-SS battalion pressed themselves hard against the sides as they tried to find cover from the vengeful Russian bombardment. Bodies lay in grotesque postures, some head-down along the sides of the trench; others without heads or limbs. Some had neat holes in their helmets, where Russian snipers had taken their own toll.

Then abruptly, the barrage shifted. In the sudden, unnerving silence, no one even whispered, for fear that even such a low sound would zero the fire back down upon them.

Haggard faces with beards made grey-white by clinging frost stared tentatively at each other. Once-pristine winter combat gear was now ragged and soiled. Some wore white combat helmets, others soft forage caps kept secure by dirty strips of cloth, makeshift hoods that were knotted

5

beneath their stubbled chins. Every word, every breath, it seemed, steamed its way out of mouths ravaged by the cold.

The most senior officer still alive, a captain, stared back at what was left of his command with eyes that had long been robbed of feeling; but strangely, his expression carried a trace of sympathy.

'Well, Max? Nice mess, eh?'

Maximillian Holbeck, a sergeant, and at twenty-five a year older than the captain, gave a grim smile. 'Which one? This insanity of a campaign that the private named after Friedrich the Redbeard? Or our immediate situation?'

'Both.'

'Look around you, Captain. Once, we were a battalion then very quickly, Ivan turned us into a company, then a platoon, and now . . .' Holbeck peered cautiously round a bend in the trench. 'If there are no crazy Ivans infiltrating at the other end, I would say your command is less than a troop.'

'What about von Mappus?'

'That kind never die,' Holbeck replied with contempt. 'He'll be around somewhere. He's an Iron Cross chaser. I've watched all the better ones go . . . but he's still breathing. Sometimes, I think the Ivans like him.'

The captain gave a sour grin, glancing at their own Iron Crosses. Each had an Iron Cross First Class.

'They give these out like sugar,' the captain said. 'Come to think of it, it's a lot harder to get sugar . . . here, or back home . . .'

'Aah . . . sugar,' Holbeck said with longing. 'I heard it existed . . . far in the past . . .'

'Just be careful of von Mappus,' the captain went on. 'As a lieutenant, he's your superior officer. I would rather have just had the replacements they finally sent us . . .'

'And who are now all gone.'

'Who are now all gone,' the captain agreed, looking grim as he thought of the rapid decimation of his unit. 'But if anything happens to me, he has command. You are better suited to take over, but he won't let you . . . if he is still alive. His kind is not smart enough to listen to sergeants. And better not let him

6

spot that little camera you liberated in Latvia. I don't have to remind you that only official photographers are supposedly allowed cameras. The High Command would not like some of the pictures I've seen you take.'

'You saw?'

'I saw. How many film cassettes have you exposed?'

'Three. The fourth is in the camera. It's my last one until I can "liberate" some more.'

'Better keep them safe.'

'I've got them – and the camera – in a weatherproof pouch in my pack. They're as safe there as anywhere. No damage as yet since Latvia.' Holbeck looked at his superior officer searchingly. 'Why didn't you stop me?'

'We need a record of all this. When this stupid war . . . which we'll lose . . . is over, many will deny what has happened here, or try to rewrite history. You can imagine the stuff . . . we were only soldiers . . . hard, efficient, elite . . . but never criminal.' The captain spat. 'Many will want to believe that. Your little camera will show the true record.'

'If you feel like that, why are you in the Waffen SS?'

'Why are *you*?' the officer countered. 'You were a teacher. Someone like you should have stayed back home, to teach the young ones . . . if there'll still be a home to go to, after this. Ivan will have his revenge for what we have done. I would . . . in his place.'

'And what would I have taught at the time? The crap from the Party? The Party took away most of my books . . . anything they deemed unsuitable for the Reich . . . Darwin, Hemingway, Mann, Remarque, Twain . . . In their eyes, this made me some kind of deviant . . . worse, a deviant *teacher*. Very bad for the *Volk*, you see.'

'Who pointed the finger?'

'Someone close . . . as always. We have become a nation that spies on itself. The pointer in my case was a colleague at the same school. He was also the local Party man . . . probably still is, busy building his own little empire . . .'

'And going after all the women he couldn't get before he had power . . .'

7

'That too.'

The harshness in Holbeck's voice made the captain say, 'I'm sorry. I didn't mean . . .'

'Nothing to be sorry about. My ex-fiancée set her sights high . . . she wanted to be with the real holders of power . . . like so many people these days. She left as soon as she spotted which way the wind was blowing. Her choice was a young *Standartenführer* . . . not Waffen SS, of course. *He'll* never get close to the Eastern Front,' Holbeck added disparagingly.

He shrugged, closing down the bitter memory.

'Anyway,' he continued, 'my former colleague was outraged that I wanted to tell the kids about Darwin. *Evolution? Treason!* So I got smart. I did a fast turnaround. In a world gone mad, I decided to join *the* most privileged armed force – the chicken farmer's creation – before someone decided to dragoon me into a pioneer unit, the Labour Corps or, God help me, a penal battalion. I passed selection with flying colours. I spouted all the rubbish expected. Not very noble, but practical. What better place to hide than in the praetorian guard? Survival.'

The captain looked about him. 'You call *this* survival?'

Holbeck bared his teeth in a grin that was of the damned. 'Here, I can shoot back. The irony is that he came to me before I left on this travel adventure, and asked if I would speak at the school. Now that I was in the Waffen SS, I was a true German who had come to his senses. Before the transformation, he looked upon me as *un*-German. Now he respected and envied me. I don't know which is worse. He would have given anything to be in the Waffen SS, but he has a weak lung . . .'

'So? Did you speak?'

'I spoke . . . and betrayed all my principles.'

The captain was silent for a while. It was hard to tell what he was thinking. Perhaps he was wondering about what would become of his own family by the time the war ended; whenever that might be.

'Look at it this way . . .' he eventually began. 'You could

8

hardly have taken the kind of pictures you have in any of those units.'

'That is how I try to give myself absolution.'

The captain looked about him again, and gave a weary sigh. 'You're a subversive, Max . . . *and* in the Waffen SS. Have you any idea what would happen to you if . . .'

Holbeck gave a low, harsh chuckle that was as totally devoid of humour as his grin. 'You mean they could give me a fate worse than this? I'm starving, and I'm freezing. Death and its stench is all around me, and will never leave my nostrils. Like everyone else, I've even eaten the horses we brought out here as load pullers, or mounts. I stink worse than a wild boar wallowing in its own shit . . . and my humanity is nearly gone. The Ivan snipers pick us off and in all this noise, they bring their own silent death . . . but not to von Mappus . . .' Now it was Holbeck who spat. 'The devil's own. I'm certain his parents were thinking of old Redbeard when they gave him his name. Friedrich, *Freiherr* von Mappus. No wonder he's chasing Iron Crosses.'

Holbeck spat once more then glanced quickly round, as if expecting to see von Mappus materialize out of the winter twilight.

'So *you'd* better not get yourself killed, Wolle,' he went on to the captain. 'If anything happens to me, you must take my films and camera. I also have a diary . . .'

'You also keep a *diary*? You must like living dangerously . . .' The captain paused to look about him once more. 'Living dangerously . . .' he repeated drily.

They both laughed at the insanity of it.

'As for von Mappus,' Holbeck said, 'I don't trust a man who still manages to remain clean-shaven in all this. Every day, he scrapes at his face with his damned cut-throat razor. He has a handsome face, but it looks evil. Have you seen his combat gear? You'd think he was on parade in front of the Austrian . . .'

'Watch out for von Mappus,' the captain said, repeating his warning. 'You're a teacher . . .'

'I *was* . . .'

'That matters little to von Mappus. You were a teacher,

9

and therefore an intellectual subversive. The way he thinks, it would not surprise me if he accused you of being a member of the White Rose. The White Rose,' the captain went on quietly. 'When history judges us for the criminals we have become, these people, whoever they are, will at least be remembered as custodians of what little is left of German honour. One tiny flash of light in our darkness . . .'

'Which will soon be extinguished when the Gestapo have caught up with them. One of their leaflets calls the Führer a subhuman.'

'Nice choice of words. So what does that make those of us who follow him in deed, if not in spirit? Or those like von Mappus to whom the spirit is the Grail itself?'

'Sub-subhuman?' Holbeck responded.

The captain peered at the sergeant. 'Don't tell me you *are* one of them . . .'

Holbeck shook his head. 'I'm not. But months ago, I found a leaflet in my kit. I have no idea how it got there . . .'

'And you've *kept* it?' The captain was aghast. 'I take back what I said. You don't like living dangerously. You're suicidal!'

They stared at each other, then gave rasping laughs, the captain's body shaking with the effort.

'Suicidal,' he muttered weakly, as their laughter subsided. 'What else can a man be out here?'

They were about to go into another round of bitter, maddened laughter when, as suddenly as it had stopped, the barrage returned with a vengeance, brutally ending their brief moment of peace. They huddled against the cold earth as hell pounded at them once more. For what seemed like years, they shrunk themselves into the unforgiving snow.

Then at last, there was abrupt silence once more.

'I think the bastards are playing with us,' Holbeck said after a while.

There was no reply.

Holbeck looked. 'Captain?'

The captain did not move. His eyes were open, but there was no life in them. No obvious wounds were visible; not even a trace of blood.

10

'Shit, Wolle,' Holbeck said with weary resignation. 'Why did you have to go and die?'

'Is he dead?'

Holbeck whirled, machine pistol coming up. The clean-shaven von Mappus, standing at full height, was grinning ferally down at him.

'If I were a Russian, *Scharführer, you'd* be dead too.'

Despite the general disregard in the Waffen SS of Himmler's insistence that they use SS ranks instead of the widespread practice of employing Wehrmacht terminology, von Mappus followed it to the letter.

'Well?' he barked at Holbeck. '*Is he dead?*'

Wishing a Russian sniper would find von Mappus a tempting target, Holbeck was reluctant in his reply.

'He's dead.'

'He's dead, *what?*'

'He's dead, Herr *Obersturmführer.*'

'And don't you forget it next time! He was weak! An old mother hen treating you all like his brood. Not fit to be an officer in the Waffen SS! *I* am now in command, and things are going to be very different!' Von Mappus moved a little way back down the trench. 'Get your gear and on your feet!' he shouted to the remaining soldiers, as if the Russians were not all around them. 'Move! You are not old women! You are Waffen SS! *Move!*'

He turned back to Holbeck. 'You too, *Scharführer*! Let's go!'

'Sir . . . the captain . . .'

'The *Hauptsturmführer*,' von Mappus corrected with a savage glare. 'Although he does not deserve the rank . . .'

'But we can't . . .'

'Holbeck,' von Mappus said very quietly.

'Sir?'

'Don't *ever* interrupt me again. *Leave him!*'

The me-officer-you-NCO attitude favoured by von Mappus was very different from the dead captain's closeness to his men, and the respect he showed them. Von Mappus, Iron Cross chaser and fanatical believer in Himmler's policies, was all of twenty-one.

Berlin in the present.

Müller had hung up his coat, but was still looking warily at the phone as if expecting it to jump off the desk at him.

Just as he was about to sit down, it rang again. This time, it was Pappenheim. The fluting sound of his draw on his cigarette was clearly heard.

'First one of the day, Pappi?' Müller asked.

'Don't be ridiculous. Some of us start *really* early.'

Müller smiled tolerantly. 'So . . . what's the call for?'

'Checking to see if you were in.'

'Well, I am . . . and I was looking forward to a few quiet days during our master's absence.'

'"Was"?'

'I just got a call on this phone. I thought it was you, at first.'

'But?'

'A vaguely familiar voice with a strange message.'

'On a supposedly secure line.'

'Just what I was thinking. I thought we'd made it all secure since the last time.'

'It *is* secure. Herman Spyros put Hedi Meyer, his goth genius, on it. We both know how good she is.'

'Well someone's beaten her system.'

'I'll check on it. So what was the message?'

Müller had a question of his own. 'Ever heard of a General von Mappus?'

'When I was a boy, I read somewhere about an *Obersturmbannführer* – that's lieutenant-colonel to you and me – von Mappus, Waffen SS. Ferocious combat veteran. Very young for the rank . . . accelerated promotion in the field. Went up a rank almost after every firefight. Enough Iron Crosses to rebuild the *Graf Spee* . . .'

'I think I've got the picture, Pappi.'

'Anyway,' Pappenheim continued, unabashed, 'he died somewhere around Stalingrad, adding his bones to that monstrous graveyard.'

'Do you believe in reincarnation?'

'Not the last time I looked.'

'Well . . . your von Mappus was reborn to become a general, and something's happened to him . . . possibly died again.'

Pappenheim said nothing for a few moments as he sucked at his cigarette. 'Where?'

'On Rügen.'

'*The* Rügen, up there in Meck–Pomm?'

'Unless you know of another one.'

'Curious. What did your mysterious informant say?'

'"Sorry . . . not Pappi. Something has happened to General von Mappus, on Rügen. You should look into it." That's an exact quote. The voice was male.'

'He knows about me too. Very, very curious. A hoax?'

'Someone who's able to get through to this number, making a hoax call? I doubt it.'

'Me too. So? What do you want to do?'

'I suppose I'd better follow it up. So much for quiet days.'

'Can't stand the heat, shouldn't have joined.'

'Thank you, Pappi. I really needed that.'

'Want me to do some checking?' The timbre in Pappenheim's voice betrayed he was grinning.

'In your own time.'

'I'll be back yesterday.'

They made their way out of the snow trench with its smears of blood and dismembered corpses. Von Mappus, the only one walking upright, was leading. They had taken off the dead and dying all they could carry: extra ammunition, weapons, meagre rations, even items of clothing. There were just nine of them left.

'Look at him,' someone grumbled from behind Holbeck. 'Strutting as if he owns this piece of hell. There's never a sniper when you want one.'

A sudden, crunching sound made Holbeck turn. The man behind him was toppling from his crouching stance.

'*Sniper!*' Holbeck yelled, dropping to the ground.

Even von Mappus dropped.

13

'You don't think you're so invulnerable, after all,' Holbeck muttered into the snow as he pressed himself as flat as he could and lay unmoving. 'Please don't hit my camera and my films,' he continued in a whispered prayer to the distant enemy sniper.

Then the barrage from the multiple-rocket launchers recommenced. It went on for what seemed like centuries, until the entire area where they cowered was covered in a thick cloud of dense smoke.

'*On your feet!*' von Mappus bawled above the noise. '*Use the smoke! Move! Do you want to die like chickens?*'

They stumbled upwards and staggered into the acrid gloom, barely able to see each other. The nightmare barrage continued.

Then once more it switched to another sector. The smoke began to thin out. They ran at the crouch. They followed von Mappus who was running upright, and moving in a swift zigzag.

They reached the base of a high mound that was covered with remarkably clean snow. It looked as if it belonged to another place where there was no war. There were no dead bodies; no pockmarks from shells. Nothing at all to show that it was in the middle of a war zone. The rumble of the barrage was a seemingly distant thunder.

They dropped thankfully into its cover and looked about them, probing their bodies for unfelt wounds. No one still alive had been wounded.

Holbeck felt for his secret pouch. There were no new holes in it.

'Not many of us left,' someone said. 'Kallert and Hofberg didn't make it.'

Holbeck looked round to check. Including von Mappus, they were now down to six. The other two had simply vanished, as if they had never existed. There had been no sounds of their passing: no screams of unbearable pain; no frightened whimpers for their mothers. Nothing. Their lives seemed to have come to an end in a manner that was as abrupt as the switching of the barrage.

It was as if having fed, Holbeck thought, the barrage

14

had decided to move on, in search of other victims to consume.

Von Mappus had got out his binoculars and was working his way up the mound. He made only the barest attempt at staying low.

'Look at him,' the one who had spoken continued. He was a former amateur boxer who was now their machine-gunner. 'He thinks the Ivan bullets won't touch him.'

Walter Nagel was a methodical northerner from near Hamburg. A large man, he carried his machine gun as if it were made of plywood.

'Perhaps he knows something we don't, Walter,' Holbeck said with pointed dryness. 'No bullets seem to have hit him as yet.'

'That won't last forever,' the other retorted hopefully. 'Why did the captain have to die?' he went on. 'Why not that walking propaganda machine?'

'You've been out here too long, Walter,' someone else remarked in a voice that was at once sarcastic and world-weary. 'You've forgotten our mission . . . to purify the Bolsheviks, and their Jew political commissars. That is, wipe them all out.' His laugh was a rasp that, like the captain's and Holbeck's previously, was scarcely human.

'Something that has always confused me . . .' Holbeck began with a straight face. 'How can the Jews be capitalist criminals, *and* communist criminals at the same time, Hube?'

'They're Jews,' Konrad Hubertus, the one with the inhuman rasp, answered, as if that explained everything. 'They were put on this planet to be our prey.'

Holbeck stared at him. 'I see. Now it's all clear. That's a deep thought, Hube. I never believed you could think that far.'

'Come on, Sarge,' Hubertus said. 'You're pulling my dick.'

'Not if I can help it.'

They all laughed, but not loud enough for von Mappus to hear.

'Well, *they* seem to be doing a better job of exterminating

15

than we are,' Nagel said. 'Look at us! I remember when the unit rolled across like nothing could stop us. We crushed everything in our path. The unstoppable Waffen SS . . . Now, we are . . . six . . . My God. *Six!*'

'There must be more of our boys out there . . . somewhere. They can't all be dead . . .'

'Or taken prisoner,' a new voice said with a shiver of horror. 'I once heard someone say they tie SS prisoners against the muzzles of tank guns, then fire them.'

Holbeck looked at the speaker, a youth of less years than von Mappus. Despite the privations of the winter and the fierceness of past combat, he still managed to look like Himmler's mad ideal of the perfect Aryan. He was one of those who seemed unable to grow a beard, no matter what. It was a tribute to his fighting skills that he was still alive. He seemed far too young and innocent to have survived while older, more experienced, hands had long since joined the ranks of the dead.

'You can expect a lot worse, Johann,' Holbeck said with calm brutality. 'They will not forget the things we have done in the name of our glorious Reich, and will pay us back many times over. Before he died, the captain said as much. He would do the same in their place. He was a realist. Not like that man up there trying to claim this little hill for the Fatherland.'

Johann Moos glanced uncertainly upwards. Von Mappus was almost at the top and had decided to crawl up the rest of the way. He was now inching his way to the summit.

'If there is a God,' Holbeck said fervently, 'a sniper will soon have a perfect shot.'

'Forget God,' Nagel said. 'We've long turned our backs on him. The devil's brood, we are.' He gave a dirty-sounding cackle.

They were all looking up at von Mappus, waiting for the sudden eruption of blood and bone from the officer's helmet that would tell them a Russian sniper had found another target.

'One shot from a Mosin–Nagant,' Hubertus said, a prayer in itself, 'and goodbye, *Leutnant* von Mappus.'

The Russian sniper rifle had innumerable kills to its name.

'Don't call him that,' Holbeck advised. 'He wants to be addressed by his Waffen-SS rank.'

'Oh I'm so sorry to upset Himmler's little darling.'

They kept looking up at the hill, hoping for a sniper.

Nothing happened. Von Mappus was still in one piece as he cautiously raised his head.

'Shit!' Nagel swore. 'The devil's own.'

Von Mappus now had the binoculars to his eyes. He remained in position, unmoving, for long minutes.

'Perhaps he's already dead,' Hubertus suggested, hope rising. 'Perhaps a sniper got him through the binoculars, right through the bridge of his nose, and he's already a stiff. Some snipers are so good, they really can do that . . . even through a scope and into another sniper's eye, I've heard. Then you'd be in charge, Sergeant. You could get us out of here.'

But von Mappus was making his way back down.

'*Shit!*' four of them cursed in low voices.

Holbeck kept his own counsel.

They waited expectantly as von Mappus made his way almost jauntily back down to them, the snow rising in a fine wake off his boots. They watched him all the way, pack animals on their guard, waiting to see what would happen next.

Machine pistol slung across his chest, von Mappus came to a halt, facing them, legs slightly apart, hands on hips.

'The way is clear for a great distance beyond this hill,' he began, looking at each in turn, challenging them to disagree. 'There is open ground, but plenty of cover beyond it. Some woods . . .' He paused, looking at Holbeck. 'Yes, *Scharführer?*' he continued impatiently. 'You've got something to say?'

'The enemy could already be using the woods, sir . . . or the ground ahead could be mined . . .'

'I am aware of that!' von Mappus snapped. 'I did not plan a headlong rush out in the open. There's a snowstorm approaching. We'll move under its cover. If the enemy is in there, we'll take him by surprise. We are six Waffen SS. We

17

are equivalent to a company of these bolsheviks. Is *that* alright with you, *Scharführer?*'

'I await your orders, sir,' Holbeck said diplomatically.

Von Mappus gave him a cold stare. 'I am a very dangerous man to play with, Holbeck. See that you remember it.' Before Holbeck could say anything, von Mappus began to address the others. 'I will make the situation clear. The Wehrmacht has a class-ridden officer corps. We of the Waffen SS do not. The Wehrmacht looks down upon Waffen-SS officers as little more than commissioned thugs.

'I have a title, and this may lead you to the mistaken belief that I am like them. Wrong. I am a lot worse. My title is not mine by direct succession. It was passed on to me as a last resort, because there was no other male family member to receive it. I am very distantly related to that family, and I have scandalized them by joining the Waffen SS. I went to visit them in full uniform. They were horrified, as well as frightened of me. It was a good feeling.

'I have told you this little story so that you will understand something about me. Unlike your last commander, I will not tolerate any refusal to obey my orders, nor have them debated over. And . . .' von Mappus fixed Holbeck with a hard gaze, 'I will not tolerate interruptions when I am speaking.'

A silence descended, then the big man from near Hamburg raised a hand.

'Yes?' von Mappus snapped.

'The captain never gave orders we didn't follow,' Nagel said calmly.

'The *Hauptsturmführer!*' von Mappus corrected with a snarl. 'From now on, you will *all* use Waffen-SS ranks, and address me accordingly! *Is that clear enough for you, SS Unterscharführer?*'

'*Jawohl, Herr Obersturmführer!*'

Von Mappus glared at each in turn. 'See that you all remember it. I don't like repeating myself. Now . . . weapons check.'

As if in preparation for a parade, von Mappus began to meticulously inspect the weapons carried by each man. All wore sidearms, irrespective of rank.

In addition to his MG 34 light machine-gun, Nagel carried a Belgian Browning Hi-Power automatic pistol. Ammmunition belts for the machine gun hung from him in a criss-cross. He seemed able to carry them with little effort. He could change the gun barrel faster than Holbeck had ever witnessed. Johann Moos doubled as his loader and carried more spare ammunition, but with less ease.

'Why the Browning?' von Mappus demanded of Nagel.

'It is a very good weapon, sir. Many people carry it . . . Waffen SS, as well as Wehrmacht. We've been using the factory since we occupied Belgium . . .'

'I am very well aware that certain members of our armed forces see fit to use foreign weapons. I do not! However, there is little I can do at this time about the collection you all seem to have with you. As soon as we rejoin our unit, I will see to it that this is rectified.'

He looked at Moos, almost kindly. Perhaps he saw an aryan mirror of himself. Moos carried a Mauser 98K rifle, and a Walther P38 similar to von Mappus's. He was an excellent shot with both, and all who fought alongside him considered him to be at sniper level with the Mauser.

'Good German weapons,' von Mappus said with approval. He gave Moos's weapons a cursory inspection before turning to Hubertus.

Hubertus also carried a rifle . . . and a Thompson sub-machine gun with a thirty-round box magazine fitted. His sidearm was another Browning.

Von Mappus stared at the Thompson. 'This is an American gangster weapon! Where did you get it?'

'I worked in America for a while. This was my working tool. I was able to . . . er . . . take it with me when I came back to fight for the Führer. It is a great weapon for close quarters.'

'You *worked* with it? You were a *gangster*?'

'I was an enforcer, sir . . .'

'Police?'

'Er . . . no, sir . . .'

'A gangster,' von Mappus snapped. 'Have you ammu-nition for it?'

'Plenty, sir . . . although I wish I could get hold of one of those fifty- or hundred-round drum magazines.'

'Where from?'

'Dead Russians,' Hubertus replied. 'They seem to have supplies of tommy guns from somewhere . . .'

'Your *Ami* gangsters, perhaps,' von Mappus suggested, face hard.

'Yes, sir. Perhaps.'

Von Mappus gave Hubertus a cold stare. 'Your rifle!'

Hubertus handed it over. Von Mappus checked it minutely.

'Clean,' he said, apparently surprised to find it so.

'I learned a lesson about dirty guns a long time ago,' Hubertus said.

'Where?'

'America. A pistol jammed. I took two shots in the gut before I managed to unjam it and kill the person who shot me.'

'Another gangster?'

Hubertus smiled thinly. 'A policeman.'

Without another word von Mappus threw the rifle at Hubertus, who, despite the chill in his bones, caught it easily.

Hubertus kept his thin smile as von Mappus moved on to Villem Grootemans.

Grootemans, the least talkative member of their depleted little group, was a tall, naturally thin man, with dead eyes. His physique belied his fierce strength which was fuelled by a hefty, but oddly clinical dose of fanaticism. He did not believe in impossible goals. Privately, he considered the Third Reich to be already on its last legs.

'Grootemans,' von Mappus began with some curiosity. 'You are Dutch?'

'No, Herr *Obersturmführer*. I come from the Cape.'

'The Cape?'

'South Africa.'

Von Mappus looked pleased. '*Afrikaner*. Good. Good. One would expect someone like you would be with the *Tommis*.'

Grootemans' mouth turned down. 'The *English* South Africans, and some Afrikaners. But others of us do not like the British. We share the ideals of the Führer on racial purity. Before I went to the Cape, I was in South-West Africa . . .'

'Ah. Our former colony. We will take it back when we win this war.'

If he thought von Mappus was raving mad, Grootemans gave no indication.

'Yes, sir,' he said.

'How did you get to the Reich?'

'Our people had contacts. I came over in thirty-eight.'

'Excellent,' von Mappus said with approval, as if Grootemans had just won a race. 'It is always good to have dispersed aryans among us.'

Grootemans, kitted out with German weaponry, handed one of his two MP40 sub-machine guns over. He carried one across his back, the other across his chest. By taking reload pouches from the dead, he had stocked up on plenty of ammunition.

Von Mappus gave both weapons an almost casual inspection.

'Excellent,' he repeated as he returned the weapons with a surprising degree of civility. 'Excellent.'

He ignored Holbeck and, hands back on hips, began to address the ragged group.

'As your superior officer I can promote, or demote, in the field.' He looked at Grootemans. 'Grootemans, you are now *Scharführer*, and Moos is promoted to *Unterscharführer* . . .' He paused, frowning. 'You don't seem too happy, Grootemans.'

Grootemans waited so long before replying that von Mappus grew impatient.

'Well?' he barked.

'With respect, Herr *Obersturmführer*,' Grootemans began at last, glancing at the others, 'we five are the last of the originals. We have been together from the very beginning. We know how each other thinks. We react instinctively. The captain . . . er *Hauptsturmführer* . . . was one of the originals too. We had begun to believe he was immortal. Very strange, his dying like that.'

21

Von Mappus looked as if he felt he were being betrayed by a fellow aryan. 'Are you *refusing* my order?'

'No, sir. I am trying to point out that we are more efficient as we are. Nagel and Moos, for example, work so well, they don't talk in combat. Nagel never has to ask for ammunition. Moos *always* knows when it's time to feed more. I'm trying to say, Herr *Obersturmführer*, that we are already an efficient, *aryan* team.'

Grootemans stopped abruptly, as if all that talking had suddenly worn him out. But his dead eyes looked upon eyes that were as dead as his.

Neither man blinked. Long moments passed.

Then the silence was raucously broken by a Russian artillery barrage. No one dived for cover. The unfortunate, targeted area was well away from where they were. Even so, the noise was appalling. A growing cloud of darkness enshrouded the near distance.

As suddenly as on previous occasions, the barrage stopped.

'We should get out of here soon,' Holbeck said into the ensuing silence, 'before they find us.' He did not seem to mind that von Mappus had just unceremoniously attempted to demote him.

Von Mappus, concentrating on Grootemans, did not turn to look at Holbeck.

'Very well,' he finally said. It could have meant agreement with Grootemans' reasoning, or Holbeck's advice to move on. 'We move in five minutes.'

Two

Pappenheim stared at the plain buff folder on his cluttered desk.

He took a final, satisfying draw on his inevitable Gauloise, before stubbing it out in the already full ashtray; then he picked up the folder, and opened it.

A single sheet of paper with two paragraphs – one hand-written – was all the information it contained. The first paragraph had obviously been copied from an original. The second was the handwritten note. Pappenheim read the details quickly.

'Hmm,' he said, when he had finished. He tapped twice at the sheet of paper with an index finger. 'Hmm,' he repeated.

He picked up one of the phones on his desk, the direct line to Müller.

'Your room, or mine?' Müller said even before Pappenheim could speak.

'Yours. I want to get out of this smoke for a while.'

'Since I know this is like saying I hate lobster, you must have discovered something interesting.'

'Strange would be a better word.'

'Then come on over.'

Pappenheim walked along a corridor festooned with no-smoking signs, towards Müller's office. The signs, decreed by Kaltendorf, were at times ignored by Pappenheim when he felt like it. On this occasion, he behaved himself.

A big, round man, Pappenheim moved with an economy of energy that gave the impression he was in no hurry to get anywhere. This was a serious misjudgement, as many had found to their cost. In reality, Pappenheim was an astonishingly swift mover, very light on his feet. His wife had once said to him she had never been partnered on the dance floor by anyone better. In his quieter moments, Pappenheim would remember her words with a deep fondness and longing.

The five years since her death had not dulled the memory, nor the freshness of her presence.

'It's open!' came Müller's voice in answer to Pappenheim's knock.

'You know,' Pappenheim began as he entered and pushed the door shut with his behind, 'every time I come in here it's like a breath of fresh air.'

'If I thought you meant that, I'd consider it a compliment. But I know better. You love that smog in your office.'

'How well you know me,' Pappenheim said as he placed the folder on Müller's desk.

Müller glanced at it. 'It's very thin.'

'Forget quantity. Quality is the thing.'

Müller picked up the folder, and paused. 'Do I want to know where this came from?'

'No.'

'Just thought I'd ask.' Müller opened the folder, and stared at the single sheet of paper. 'I see what you mean. In *Polish*?'

'Very conveniently translated, as you'll see.'

Müller looked at the handwritten note. 'Very convenient. "Waffen-SS *Obersturmbannführer* Friedrich, Freiherr von Mappus,"' he began to read, then paused, raising an eyebrow. 'A *Freiherr* . . .'

'The minor nobility,' Pappenheim said with a straight face, 'as our unloved boss on his better days likes to describe you, get everywhere. As for his *bad* days . . .' Pappenheim paused for effect. 'But as you can see, we sometimes even find them in the police, *Herr Graf* von Röhnen.'

Müller glanced at Pappenheim. 'That was humour, wasn't it?'

But Pappenheim had decided to choose that moment to study the wall directly across from Müller's desk. A painting hung there.

'That's new,' he remarked. 'What happened to the Mondrian?'

'Neat change of subject. It is back in my apartment. I thought it was time for Monet.'

Pappenheim stared at the painting. 'Appropriately, a snowy scene . . . and on the broken gate, a lone *Elster*, thief of time.'

'I think Monet meant that magpie to be sunning himself.'

'You see what you see . . . I see what I see . . .'

'When you're quite finished. Now, may I continue?'

'Be my guest,' Pappenheim said with a fleeting smile, as he turned round.

'Thank you. "Killed in action on the Eastern Front,"' Müller continued to read, '"July 1943. Awarded Knight's Cross for outstanding action in December 1942, when, with a small complement of Waffen-SS troops, he attacked and completely destroyed a secret Russian ammunition and supply dump. Though greatly outnumbered, von Mappus never faltered. The dump, and its personnel, were completely wiped out. Also recommended for, and given, accelerated promotion from Obersturmführer to Sturmbannführer – major – for this action."'

'Skips a rank to the equivalent of a battalion commander,' Müller commented without looking up. 'Quite the hero. Then it lists his decorations. As you said, enough to rebuild the *Graf Spee*.' He shut the folder. 'Who brought in this little gem?'

'A taciturn man in a dark coat, with a Silesian accent. As hard a face as you're likely to see. Mouth no softer.'

'A German Pole? Or a Polish German?'

'That's my line,' Pappenheim said with a grin.

'After all these years with you, something's bound to rub off.'

'Such nice things, the man says.'

'Well?' Müller urged.

'He arrives at the desk downstairs,' Pappenheim went on, 'and says to Dirk Schaefer, the *Meister* on duty: "I have something for *Oberkommissar* Pappenheim." Schaefer doesn't like his manner, but stays polite.'

'Now *that's* news. Schaefer can be the most impolite

police sergeant on the planet when someone rubs him the wrong way.'

'You should have seen the Silesian. I think poor old Schaefer was in shock and quite fascinated, in a morbid sort of way. Couldn't believe what he was seeing, or hearing. He looks at the envelope the man is holding, and offers to take it. "This will be handed to *Herr* Pappenheim by myself!" the man in the dark coat barks . . .'

'*Barks?*'

'Schaefer's very word. He picks up the phone and calls Berger. Before he can say much, the man barks again. "*I said Pappenheim!*"'

'Demotion was swift,' Müller commented. 'First your correct rank, then *Herr*, then plain Pappenheim.'

'For my sins. In the end, I had to go down. He looks at me as if I were a tick on a cow's behind, then hands me the folder as if giving me military orders. I half expected a click of heels and a right arm shooting out.'

'So . . . Waffen SS, do you think?'

'He's the right age to have been. But he *seems* much younger. Thinnish, and fit. No fat on him. Must have been those Stalingrad rations . . . if he was there.'

'Did you expect someone like that?'

'Not from the contact I made. The Silesian comes from a source which – for the moment – I don't know of . . .'

'That must hurt.'

'Not for long,' Pappenheim retorted cheerfully. 'But it is all rather strange.'

'Anything from our colleagues on Rügen?'

'Had a chat with an *Oberkommissar* from there . . .'

'There are times, Pappi, when I believe there's no one on the entire national police force you don't know.'

'Don't be ridiculous. There are a few people, and some things, I don't know . . .' Pappenheim again gave a twitch of a grin. 'Including where our Silesian came from. So far,' he continued, 'the Rügen boys have no evidence of anyone registered as a General von Mappus up there and, further, they have no indications as yet that anything's happened to excite their interest. They're still looking.'

'Hmm,' Müller said.

'That's what I thought.'

'Ideas?'

'Either von Mappus really died all those years ago near Stalingrad, and your vaguely familiar voice on the phone got it all wrong . . .'

'Or?'

Pappenheim turned again, this time to face the huge window that gave an almost panoramic view of the city. 'Looking through this every day would give me vertigo,' he remarked. 'I think I'll stick to my cell of an office.'

'Lucky for me.'

Pappenheim ignored the comment. 'Or,' he went on, still looking out on the city, 'someone, somewhere, wants us to *believe* von Mappus did die in the Russian slaughterhouse . . . which raises plenty of new questions.' He turned back to Müller. 'Perhaps what our goth found out might shed a little daylight . . .'

'She managed to trace the call?'

'She did better than that. She hacked into a transmission satellite . . .'

'She *hacked* a *satellite*? Can she really do that?'

'And without leaving a trace of her visit. Your informer called you from somewhere in the Caucasus . . . not a million miles from Chechnya . . . That young woman's a true genius. The Intelligence mob would kill to have her working for them.'

'One branch did try to recruit her. Remember?'

'And she turned them down. I well remember. Most definitely an angel. So? Any memory jog?'

'I was saving that till later,' Müller replied. 'I think it was Grogan.'

'*The* Grogan who sometimes calls himself Vladimir?'

'The same. It was his voice. I'm certain of it. We had a brief phone conversation last August.'

'Then given he has already supplied us with information that even the Great White has no idea we've got . . .'

'And many others besides . . .'

'Among whom are those who would love to have us

suspended . . . and I don't just mean from duty. If it is Grogan, he would not make such a call just for fun.'

'And if he really is out there in the Caucasus,' Müller said, 'our American benefactor who may be a Russian, or vice versa, might have taken a deliberate risk to make it.'

'And he'd know we would attempt a trace.'

'Which he could easily have dodged.'

'His way of telling us his information is genuine.'

Müller nodded slowly. 'Exactly.'

'So where does that place our grim Silesian?'

'Not among the angels.'

The snowstorm whipped and howled about them, a demented thing that seemed to be an ally of the enemy. They had wrapped their tattered battle scarves about their heads, leaving only slits for their eyes. By covering their mouths, they minimized the intake of the chill air into their lungs. Strange, shuffling figures, they looked like snowbound mummies, and spoke as little as possible.

Some time before, Moos had found two pairs of goggles near the bodies of a combat motorcyclist and his sidecar occupant. Both had been riddled by machine guns fired at close range. Of the attackers, there was no sign; their footprints long obliterated by the whirling snow.

Moos and Nagel now wore the goggles.

Ahead of the short column, von Mappus – barely visible – strode almost upright, as if defying the storm to knock him down.

'This storm is fighting for the Russians,' Moos said in a muffled, gasping voice that Nagel just managed to hear above the noise of the wind.

'What do you expect? It's a Russian storm, and Russian snow. Of course it's fighting for them.' Nagel sounded cheerful. Whipped snowflakes spattered against the goggles, causing him to wipe at them every so often.

Behind them, Hubertus was suddenly loud as he spoke. 'I think it's easing!'

'You're right!' Moos said, listening for a few seconds. 'It is easing! How far do you think we've come?'

'Be quiet!' came Holbeck's voice in a fierce whisper ahead of them. 'Do you want to tell the Russians where we are?'

They shut up, and plodded on.

But the storm had only been pausing for breath. It gathered itself and lashed at them again.

They struggled on for about another hour, seemingly making the barest progress. At times, those with rifles used their weapons as makeshift walking sticks to lever themselves on. The snow, in the air and on the ground, made every step a supreme effort. The only good thing about the situation was that they made no contact with the enemy. The snow was protecting, as well as battering them.

Ahead, von Mappus trudged on, a man possessed. He would not be defeated by mere snow. He never looked round to check if they followed. He expected it of them.

It was Moos who first caught sight of a shadowy movement in the gloom, on their left flank.

He tugged briefly and urgently at Nagel's sleeve. 'I've seen something!'

Nagel was just able to hear the words. He kept on walking, but glanced at Moos. 'Where?'

'Over to our left, and a little behind.'

Nagel paused to peer into the grey-white gloom. 'I see nothing. It's the hunger. You're hallucinating. Come on, unless you want to freeze where you stand.'

'I saw something!' Moos insisted as they trudged on.

'He's right,' Hubertus said after a while. 'There is something. Keeping pace with us.'

Nagel forgot the storm and the cold. He brought up his machine gun. Moos and Hubertus could not both be hallucinating. Moos, perhaps. The hardbitten Hubertus, never.

Then, abruptly, they entered a small area of utter calm. The storm whirled about them, but they were no longer within it. They stared wonderingly as, in an almost perfect circle, it continued to rage on the perimeter of their strange oasis.

'We're in the eye,' Holbeck said. The transition was so complete, he was able to speak at normal levels.

'Will it move?' Nagel asked.

'It is moving.' Holbeck pointed. 'See over there?' Their

29

calm circle was shifting; infinitesimally, but definitely. 'It's coming towards us. We'll be back in there soon enough, unless we move with the circle.'

Von Mappus had stopped, turned round, and was coming towards them purposefully.

'What's this?' he asked sharply as he came to a halt. 'A hen's committee? Why have you stopped?'

'Sergeant . . . *Scharführer* Holbeck suggests if we stay within the circle, we can keep out of the storm, sir,' Nagel answered.

Von Mappus turned malevolent eyes upon Holbeck. 'What can you expect from a man who was a teacher?' he snapped at Nagel. 'Do we now leave it to a snowstorm to decide where we go?'

'I saw movement, sir,' Moos put in quickly.

'He's right,' Hubertus said. 'I saw it too.'

Von Mappus stared at them. 'Movement? Where?'

Hubertus pointed at the whirling snow. 'In that. There!' he added urgently. 'It's coming through!'

They all turned their weapons to face the threat, von Mappus included.

First an indefinable shape, then a firm, bulky silhouette; then a recognizable figure stumbled out of the shifting whiteness, and into their oasis of relative calm.

'*Don't shoot!*' Holbeck yelled. 'He's ours!'

No one fired, but all remained ready to do so as the figure approached. The winter camouflage, and helmet, were definitely German.

The newcomer did not hurry as he came towards them, apparently undisturbed by the weapons turned upon him. As he drew closer, they discovered he was a Waffen-SS major from their own division. They stared at him disbelievingly.

He stopped, and slowly loosened the scarf that protected his face, to reveal features that were slightly less haggard than their own. His dark eyes, those of a man who had gazed upon too many nightmares, appeared to look through them.

'Six little romeos,' he began in weary amusement. 'Where to, boys? Looking for girls?' The breath steamed out of him.

They loosened their own scarves, and continued to stare at him.

'Can't speak? I'm not surprised. So much for the great conquerors of the Bolsheviks.' The major peered at Holbeck. 'You're Max Holbeck, aren't you?'

'Yes, sir,' Holbeck replied in astonishment.

'Don't be surprised. Wolle was a friend of mine. He spoke about you. Best sergeant he ever had, he told me. He always considered you to be officer material. I suppose he's dead?'

'Yes, sir. I'm sorry.'

'Don't be,' the major said again. 'We'll all be following him before much longer, if my fellow Austrian back in Berlin has anything to do with it. I'm Heinz Gaegl.'

The soldiers all gave von Mappus surreptitious glances as Gaegl so openly disparaged their supreme leader.

Stiff-faced, von Mappus looked at the major, rigidly deferring to the superior officer while at the same time making no effort to hide the outrage in his eyes.

Gaegl turned to him, ignoring the look. 'And who are you?'

Von Mappus actually tried to click his heels in the snow. '*Obersturmführer* von Mappus, Herr *Sturmbannführer*!'

Gaegl stared at him. 'Good God, *Leutnant*. You're not on parade. You're in the middle of a hellhole that your Führer has sent you to. You're in a meat grinder, and what will come out at the other end will only be good for fertilizer! Wake up! I've heard about you too,' he added. Gaegl did not sound as if what he'd heard had been pleasant.

Von Mappus stiffened even further, but said nothing.

Gaegl turned back to Holbeck. 'There's a village out there. Plenty of food. The war does not seem to have touched it . . . yet. As Berlin seemed unable to maintain the promise of keeping us supplied, I sent a sidecar patrol out to forage; but they never came back . . .'

'I think we found them,' Holbeck said. 'Well, Moos did,' he corrected, jerking a thumb at the youngest among them. 'They'd been ambushed.'

Gaegl gave a tired nod. 'I expected something like that.

31

None of what's left of my men can walk properly,' he went on. 'Not even the officers. Apart from myself, there are just two left . . . and one's got a bad wound in his right leg. The other is trying to cope with frostbite. He's got the command in my absence. So when Klemp and Heuer failed to return, I went out to see what I could find. I've been gone for what seems like days. Now I can . . .'

'Forgive me for interrupting, sir,' von Mappus said in his stiff voice. 'A *village*? Out here? And they did not shoot at you?'

'Strange as it may seem to you, von Mappus, they did not. And neither did I . . .'

'But sir . . . they are *Russians*.'

'So?'

'We are at war with them!'

'There are just women and children out there. I don't shoot women and children, especially when they don't shoot at me first . . .'

'Sir!' von Mappus again interrupted. 'Those women and children *are the enemy*! These women and children kill us just as their men do . . .'

'Ours will be doing the same when we are invaded.'

'The Reich will *never* be invaded!'

The major stared at the lieutenant in amazement. 'Von Mappus,' Gaegl said with the weariness of centuries.

'Sir?'

'Do you really believe that?'

'Yes, sir!'

'A wise officer, von Mappus, knows how to recognize a military reality. Only fools have not yet woken up to the fact that the Reich *will* be invaded, *and* devastated. And that includes the man in Berlin, who sowed the wind. We shall all reap the result.'

Von Mappus was staring at Gaegl, aghast. 'That is defeatism, and disrespect for the Führer!'

Gaegl gave a laugh that was not fully sane. 'What are you going to do, you parade dummy? Shoot me?' He turned once more to Holbeck. 'The village is about a day away when you

32

get through this giant snowflake . . . to the west. If you make it without running into Ivan, you'll find plenty of food. Now, I must be getting back to my men.'

'They may all be dead by now,' Holbeck said gently.

'Then I should be with them.'

Gaegl rewound his scarf, gave Holbeck a farewell pat on the shoulder, and began to move past.

'You're running away!' von Mappus shouted. '*Coward!*'

Gaegl chose to ignore the insult, and headed towards the perimeter of whirling snow.

'*Stop!*' von Mappus shouted again.

Gaegl did not even pause.

The sudden chatter of the MP40 shocked everyone as von Mappus fired a long burst into the back of the Waffen-SS major.

Gaegl arched backwards, stumbling to his knees. Then he fell heavily forward on to the snowy ground. Everyone watched in amazement as he forced himself to his feet, and staggered towards the snowstorm. Bright red leaked out of him, but he kept moving. He did not utter a sound, nor did he look back.

The soldiers all stared at the major in horror, then at von Mappus.

Holbeck began to go after the wounded officer.

'*Holbeck!*' von Mappus snarled.

Holbeck paused, and looked round. The MP40 was pointing at him.

'I'll use it on you too!' von Mappus promised. 'Leave him! The coward can die out there!'

'Sir . . .'

'You are not indispensable, Holbeck. Don't try me!'

The concerted click of weapons being cocked diverted Holbeck's attention. The others were pointing their own weapons at von Mappus.

Von Mappus had clearly not considered this, even in his wildest imaginings. His eyes widened to their limits as he looked at the snouts of the four guns aimed at him.

'Just give the word, Sergeant,' Hubertus said quietly.

Holbeck raised a swift hand to stop them. 'Hold it! No

one I outrank murders an officer while I am around,' he said pointedly, staring hard at von Mappus.

'Go see to the major, Sergeant,' Hubertus said. 'If the *Obersturmführer* kills you, then you won't be around to stop us.'

'Don't do anything stupid,' he said to them. He turned to look for the major, but Gaegl had vanished. 'He's gone!'

They all looked.

'Perhaps we saw a ghost,' Moos said.

Nagel pointed at the ground. 'One that bleeds?'

Von Mappus was looking at them ferally. 'You have all made a very big mistake. I repeat. A *very* big mistake! I will *not* forget this!' He reserved his hardest stare for Grootemans. 'I am disappointed in you, Grootemans. I thought we had an understanding.'

Grootemans said nothing.

'*You will all be court-martialled!*' von Mappus raged. 'I make you this promise . . .'

'And you too . . . *sir*?' Holbeck said with deliberate harshness. 'You shot Major Gaegl . . . in the back. That is bad enough. If he dies . . .'

'I will have executed a deserter! I am within the code of conduct. This was cowardice in the face of the enemy. But you five, have *mutinied*. There is a difference! You did not believe that ridiculous story, did you?' he snarled at them. 'A *village*? In this wasteland? The man was a *coward*. He was running away from the enemy! He abandoned his men!' He glared at Holbeck. 'And as for you, Holbeck . . . don't believe that because a cowardly *Sturmbannführer* calls you by your first name, or treats you as he would an officer, this means something to me.

'Anything from such a coward is *nothing* to be proud of. And, furthermore, don't expect any favours from me because you stopped these mutineers. In all probability, you are one of those seditious intellectuals who belongs to the White Rose. We know some of you pollute the army of the Reich; but we execute traitors, wherever we find them. I am watching you, Holbeck! Now, all of you! Secure your scarves and *move*! Put all thoughts of this mythical village out of your minds. We will rejoin the division. Gaegl cooked up that story to save his own neck . . . but it didn't work! Now *move!*'

He turned his back upon them and stamped through the snow towards the storm, expecting them to follow.

'Just one squeeze on the trigger,' Hubertus said in a pleading, low voice as von Mappus moved out of earshot.

'Shut it!' Holbeck said to him as he secured his own scarf.

'I just hope we don't live to regret it,' Nagel said.

'I just hope we don't live to regret it,' Pappenheim said.

Müller looked at him. 'Regret what?'

Pappenheim pointed at the thin folder. 'The Silesian's gift.'

'A Trojan horse?'

'Perhaps.'

'A Silesian bearing gifts. I'll be suitably wary of gifts. What about your contacts? It is quite possible – in a roundabout way – that the Silesian did come from them.'

Pappenheim shook his head. 'No. The Silesian comes from somewhere else. I'd stake my last cigarette on it.'

'That's a high price. I'm suitably convinced. So?'

'So I'd better poke a few ant nests. See what rushes out.'

'Don't get bitten.'

'My heart is pure. I won't be.'

A smiling young woman in her mid-twenties, on the dangerous edge of being plump, with dark, wavy hair tied loosely in a ponytail reminiscent of Müller's, walked briskly along the corridor, carrying a small pile of mail. She wore a shoulder harness with an automatic pistol in the holster. Her smile widened as she saw Pappenheim leave the *Hauptkommissar*'s office.

Lene Berger, a police sergeant, had a secret crush on Pappenheim. It was, however, hardly a real secret. Müller knew. Her police partner, Reimer, knew; as did many of her colleagues. And Pappenheim himself knew. Both pretended the crush was non-existent.

'*Obermeisterin* Berger,' Pappenheim greeted cheerfully

as they met outside the door to his office. He glanced at the mail. 'Anything interesting in that lot?'

'I wouldn't know,' she said, handing the pile over. 'I just intercept the stuff.'

Pappenheim darted a look around to check if anyone was within earshot. 'In,' he ordered, holding the door open.

He shut the door quickly as she entered, and made a beeline for his desk. He snatched at his pack of Gauloises, lit up with the desperate urgency of a drowning man grabbing for a lifebelt, and took a deep pull as he sat down behind the desk. He leaned back, and blew a pulsing ring of smoke at the ceiling.

'Aah!' he sighed, the satisfaction oozing out of him. 'One more minute in Jens Müller's smokeless zone, and I'd have fainted.' He squinted at her. 'Nothing to say?'

'If you mean about your smoking, your –' she glanced critically about the untidy office – 'er . . . office . . . no, sir.'

'Good. I wouldn't have paid any attention. Others have been trying for years. And you shouldn't be rude to your superiors.'

'No, sir.'

Pappenheim began sorting through the mail. 'So. Anything at all of interest in this bunch? I know. I know. You've no idea what to look for.'

'I would . . . if you'd told me.'

'Don't be petulant,' Pappenheim said, taking another drag and blowing a second smoke ring at the ceiling, where it joined the first, which, though dissipating, was still floating in perfect shape.

He admired his handiwork dreamily.

But Berger decided to drive home her point. 'Since the end of August, I've been intercepting all incoming mail addressed to you and the *Hauptkommissar*, and bringing it directly to you. Frau Krottke is dying of curiosity.'

'I'll bet she is. But as I'm sure you've long told her that this is to do with a very special investigation and she should mention it to no one, our civilian postal lady will have to live with her curiosity.'

'And Reimer is making jokes.'

Pappenheim paused. '*Reimer?* What kind of jokes?'

Berger hesitated.

'Now come on, Lene,' Pappenheim said. 'If you start it, finish it. What does Reimer find so amusing?'

'He, er . . . asked how many apples I was taking to teacher today.' Berger stopped, looking wary.

'He did, did he?' Pappenheim remarked with a softness that was a certain warning of danger.

He said nothing more for such a long time, Berger began to feel anxious. She watched as he smoked the cigarette with a deliberation that clearly indicated he was planning something.

'Boss?' she began tentatively.

'I know a *Kommissar* in Hamburg,' Pappenheim at last said, 'who's looking for people to man a special team. The team is to operate in St Pauli. So far, he's not getting many volunteers. One would have thought he'd be turning them away. Reimer is one of our best people, but if he's not very careful, he could find himself on indefinite detachment to the red-light patrol.'

'Boss, you wouldn't. *St Pauli?*'

'Boss, I would . . . if Reimer keeps thinking he's a comedian. Anyway, you all know my bark's a lot worse than my bite.'

'No, it isn't,' Berger said. She pointed to the letters. 'Another smelly one from France is in there.'

'I know you mean *perfumed*, so I'll let it pass. The *Hauptkommissar* is enjoying a little hero worship from a seventeen-year-old. Ever since what happened last August, she's been sending him little billets doux every now and then . . .'

She arched her eyebrows at him. '*Billets doux?*'

'You know the sort of thing . . .'

'Never tried it myself.'

'Well,' Pappenheim said, ignoring her mild barb. 'The young lady seems to find our esteemed Graf a bit of a hero.' Knowing a lot more than he was letting on, Pappenheim continued, 'He could do with it now and then . . . especially as her father, our wonderful boss, frequently wishes him to

37

perdition. I love the irony. Besides, he's safe. She's far too young for him.'

'Sounds like an old song,' Berger said as she quickly went out.

Pappenheim lit a fresh cigarette and squinted at the closed door. 'And as I keep saying,' he remarked quietly, '*you're* too young for me.'

In the corridor, though she had not heard his words, Berger instinctively knew what he was thinking.

'No, I'm not,' she said to herself.

In his office, Pappenheim said, 'Hmm,' and blew a fresh smoke ring at the ceiling, then began sifting through the pile of letters once more.

He picked up the one from France, sniffed at it, and smiled. 'Ah, Miss du Bois.' He sniffed at it again. 'Concentrate on your studies and leave my poor superior alone. When he rescued you from that madman last August, he was only doing his job . . . even though you are the Great White's daughter.'

He turned to the other letters, searching through them with an almost manic diligence. 'And what about you?' he continued. 'More to the point . . . *who* are you? One note in August, then nothing.'

He checked each item minutely; but none was similar to the mysterious note in the sealed envelope, whose edge he had spotted peeping out from beneath Müller's door. Müller had been away at the time, in the south of France, and Pappenheim had pulled it out. The single word 'Müller' had been the only writing on the envelope; and no stamp had been there to betray a postmark.

After much deliberation Pappenheim had opened it, to be greeted by the shock of its contents. It had concerned Müller, and had been devastating in its revelations. The writer had intended to cause maximum pain, and severe damage to all that Müller believed about himself. Protective as ever, Pappenheim had never told the *Hauptkommissar*, and had been intercepting the mail ever since.

Pappenheim well knew he was skating on thin ice. Even so, he was prepared to take the risk. He needed to trace the anonymous note-sender . . . before another of the poisonous missives eventually succeeded in reaching Müller.

But the note-sender – someone apparently capable of breaching the building's security defences in order to get that first, and so far only note to Müller's door – had been conspicuously inactive over the passing months. This inaction filled Pappenheim with foreboding.

He looked at one of the phones on his desk, and picked it up. 'Time to poke at a few nests to see what comes crawling out.'

But before he could dial a number, the second phone rang. He put down the one he'd picked up, and grabbed the other.

'Alright. I give up.' Nothing in Pappenheim's voice betrayed the turmoil going on within him.

'Confessing already?' Müller said lightly.

'You know me. Guilty until proven innocent.'

Müller gave a short laugh. 'We're the police, Pappi. We're supposed to do it the other way round.'

'Now he tells me. And what's burning in that fine cranium of yours?'

'An idea.'

'Always good to have one.'

'Meet me in the rogues' gallery . . . and bring the goth along.'

'Will do. Give me a few moments to poke at a particular ant nest, and I'll be right there.'

'Fine.'

Berger entered the large office she shared with five other sergeants and senior sergeants. Reimer was at his desk, talking urgently into his phone. His expression clearly showed it was a personal call.

He ended the call just as Berger reached him.

'You should be careful with those calls to your girlfriend,' was her opening gambit.

His face clouded over. 'God. Sometimes, I give up on women.'

'Trouble?'

Reimer gave a sigh of great weariness. 'She's complaining

again that I work too many long hours. And she doesn't like it when I go undercover. I mean . . . we don't have a bad life . . . better than many, in fact. We eat very well, we have a great apartment, we have fantastic holidays . . . Last time, we went to Hawaii . . .'

'Reimer . . . I can see your problems,' Berger said with heavy irony. 'Well, you've got more . . .'

He stared at her. '*More?*'

'Have you been upsetting the *Oberkommissar*?'

'Pappenheim?' Reimer was horrified. '*Me?* Do you think I'm suicidal?'

'You tell me. Anyway, you know his bark is worse than his bite.'

'No it isn't,' Reimer countered in a manner born of long experience. He continued to stare at her. 'What . . . what did you hear?'

'He mentioned something about detaching you to Hamburg. Indefinitely . . .'

Reimer paled. '*What?*'

'He knows a kommissar there who's setting up a task force for St Pauli . . .'

'Is this a joke?'

'Why don't you ask Pappenheim? You can always refuse.' Berger was the picture of innocence as she looked at Reimer. 'Don't tell me you're afraid to go.'

'It's not St Pauli I'm worried about. It's my girlfriend. Have you any idea what she'll say? She already believes that police who work undercover sooner or later become corrupted by what they're working on.'

'Smart woman.'

'To her way of thinking,' Reimer went on in an aggrieved tone, 'an art investigator can be bought off . . . someone working with robbers can become one . . .'

'And those working in red-light districts sleep with the prostitutes. As I said, smart woman. Every police force in the world is vulnerable. But you're not like that, Reimer . . .'

'Tell that to my girlfriend. She thinks men are weak. She even said to me once that if Adam had offered the apple to Eve, *she*'d never have eaten it.'

'As I said . . . smart woman.'

Reimer quickly stood up. 'Look. I'm going out to make a call. Will you cover for me?'

'OK.'

Berger watched with a ghost of a smile as he hurried out.

One of the *Obermeisters* entered seconds later, glancing back along the corridor as he came into the room.

'You look happy,' he said to her. 'And Johann looks harassed. You two are like a divorced couple. Woman happy, man unhappy. What did you do to him?'

'I didn't do anything to him. I just mentioned that he might be sent on a special job to St Pauli . . .'

'And he's *unhappy*? Lucky bastard. Wish I had that chance.'

'I rest my case,' Berger said.

As he went up to his own desk, the senior sergeant glanced at her with a mixture of suspicion and uncertainty.

Berger concentrated on some paperwork, and said nothing further.

Müller found the gothic Hedi Meyer waiting alone by the solidly gleaming, black door of the documents room. This was the 'rogues' gallery'. Within that room were secrets Müller and Pappenheim had stored, that even Kaltendorf knew nothing about; and which many outside the building itself would do anything to get their hands upon. Including murder. A keypad was in place where a knob would normally be.

Hedi Meyer was a tall, ethereally pale individual who gave an impression of fragility that was totally misleading. She was dressed in black jeans, black shoes and a black, lightweight polo-neck sweater. Jet black hair, her natural colour, gleamed healthily. She wore blue eye shadow, but no lipstick. Though a fully-fledged police officer with the rank of sergeant, she did not normally carry a weapon. She was, however, an excellent shot with the standard-issue automatic pistol.

Müller glanced at Hedi Meyer's hands. 'Miss Meyer, you've got blue fingernails on one hand, and green on the other. Any particular reason?'

She held them up in display. 'I'm in my blue-green period.'

41

'You mean like a painter. Say, like Picasso . . .'

She smiled at him. 'You don't know what I'm talking about, do you, sir?'

'Er . . . no.'

'Blue for calm, green for fertility. I'm calmly fertile. Look at my eyes. One is blue, and the other green. Come on, sir. Look.' She opened her eyes wide.

Hesitantly, Müller peered at them.

'Not like that,' Hedi Meyer admonished with mild impatience. 'You can't see anything if you stay a hundred kilometres away. Closer . . .'

A mild cough behind them caused Müller to look round. 'There you are, Pappi,' looking relieved. 'Miss Meyer was about to show me her one blue, and one green eye.'

'So I see,' Pappenheim remarked with a straight face.

'It's not really one blue and one green,' Hedi Meyer explained. 'It's just that sometimes, one turns a little green. Green for fertility.' She was quite serious about it.

'I see,' Pappenheim repeated. He glanced at Müller, face giving nothing away, but eyes lively. 'Are you going to tap at that keypad? Or am I?'

'You've got an affinity with it. You do it.'

'Flattery will get you everywhere.'

Pappenheim had moved round and was tapping rapidly at the keypad as he spoke. The familiar red pinprick of light flashed once, turned green, then the lock hissed and snapped open. He pushed at the door. Bright lights came on automatically as they entered.

Pappenheim was last in, and he pushed the door shut. It gave a soft but powerful click. A gentle whirring betrayed the presence of an air-conditioning and filtration unit in the large, windowless room.

The entire space on every wall save one was taken up by banks of steel cabinets that went from gleaming floor to high ceiling. Every drawer in each cabinet had its own keypad. Though having similar cabinets stacked against it, there was also space left on the last wall for a wide computer desk, with a very powerful machine on it. Its monitor was a wide plasma screen big enough for a home cinema. A mighty sound system was connected to it and at the desk itself was a leather-bound swivel chair with a high back.

Pappenheim glanced about him. 'Aah. Home. The air in here is so *clean*, I sometimes almost feel it's poisoning me.' Müller's office and this room were the only places in the entire building where Pappenheim would discipline himself sufficiently to avoid putting a cigarette to his lips. He turned to Müller. 'And the idea that's roasting your synapses?'

Müller pointed to one of the stacks. 'In there. Grogan's minidisc, and the CD copy that Hedi made.' He looked at Hedi Meyer. 'You do remember, don't you?'

She nodded, and a brief shiver appeared to pass through her. 'I'll never forget.'

'I'd be surprised if you could. It still amazes me how calm you were when you disarmed that tiny bomb the Romeo Six madman had buckled round Solange du Bois' waist.'

She gave him a weak smile as she turned the computer on. 'You should have been where I was.'

The machine was so quiet as it hummed to itself, only the tiny running light betrayed that it was working. The screen flicked into life almost within the same instant that she had pressed the button.

'This,' she began with eager enthusiasm as she sat in the chair, 'really impresses me. The last time I was in here, I couldn't believe how fast it was. I can make it faster, though, and do some seriously invisible hacking if you need . . .'

Pappenheim was opening one of the drawers. He paused in the act of taking out the CD to look over his shoulder at her. 'Miss Meyer, we didn't hear that, did we?'

'Hear what, sir?' Focussed on the computer, she did not look round.

'I thought so,' Pappenheim replied with a sideways glance at Müller as he handed the CD to Hedi Meyer.

'Thank you,' she said, again without taking her eyes from the machine.

Müller smiled tolerantly at the back of the goth's head.

Hedi Meyer put the CD into the already extended tray, and slid it home. Müller and Pappenheim stood on either side of her, to peer at the screen.

'What are we looking for?' she asked.

Pappenheim threw Müller another glance. 'What *are* we looking for?'

'You'll know when we see it.'

'*I'll* know?'

'Patience is a virtue.'

'Hmm,' Pappenheim said.

The Grogan CD was an information goldmine, containing as it did a collection of clandestinely and dangerously taken videos – the various clips recorded over many years, and seamlessly edited together. It was the record of an infection – long planned and executed – of the nation's body politic; so invisible its presence was, to all intents and purposes, virtually undetected. Had it not been for his recent experiences, and the disc, Müller would never have imagined the extent of such an infiltration. But much of its reach was still beyond his knowledge. The infection had a name: *Romeo Six*. Most of the people in the recordings – some known, others complete strangers – were the architects of the infection, and their activities had spilled into the lives of Müller and Pappenheim, the previous August.

But Romeo Six had been running long, long before that.

Müller and Pappenheim now watched as the recording came onscreen. No one spoke as familiar scenes went by. Every so often, Müller would glance questioningly at Pappenheim, but Pappi continued to stare at the screen without comment.

The material on the CD came to an end.

Müller was looking at Pappenheim. 'Run it again,' he said to the goth.

'Yes, sir.'

Hedi Meyer restarted the CD. Again it ran; again nothing from Pappenheim.

'A third time,' Müller said to her.

As the CD began its routine once more, Müller glanced at Pappenheim, who was now frowning at the screen.

'Stop!' Müller ordered the goth.

She froze the image. It was of a lavish banqueting scene.

'The A-list crowd again,' Müller remarked, a dry edge to

his voice. 'Politicos, *promis*, military, and a few spooks who would not like to know we've got this.'

'Or how we got it,' Pappenheim added.

'Quite.' Müller glanced at Pappenheim, looking hopeful. 'Something?'

Pappenheim was uncertain. He briefly reached forward to touch the screen with a probing finger. He had touched a standing figure, partially obscured by a neo-classical pillar. The person was in conversation with someone in full view. The man in view was a well-known political aspirant.

'Behind that pillar,' Pappenheim said to Müller. 'Hedi,' he went on to the goth, 'can you zero on it?'

'No problem.'

The man Pappenheim had indicated was in a neat suit, and had an erect stance. The rear half of his body was showing, and only the left side of his head – from the ear – was in view.

She put the mouse cursor on the man's head, clicked, then moved the scroll wheel with her index finger. The scene at that point enlarged to fill the screen, but the image of the person behind the pillar had become slightly blurred.

'Can you give it more definition?' Pappenheim asked her.

'No problem,' she repeated.

This time, she tapped rapidly at the keyboard, then paused. On screen, magic was happening. The image first brightened, then sharpened in contrast, before settling into a perfect enlargement.

'Very good,' Pappenheim told her with approval. 'Now for the hard part. I need to see more of his face.'

'No problem,' Hedi Meyer said for a third time. She began to fish into a deep pocket, and brought out a CD in an unlabelled jewel case.

'What's that?' Müller asked, looking at the CD doubtfully.

'A little program of mine. When you asked me to come here, I brought a few things with me, just in case. I've got two more of these, with other programs. All mine.'

'Miss Meyer, this is not our computer. It's the taxpayer's. Don't crash it with untested programs.'

She held up the CD, and looked at each in turn. 'This can help. I can make the pillar disappear, and give the man a face . . .'

'Do it!' they both said.

Hedi Meyer smiled, turned back to the computer, and put the CD into another drive.

'There are many picture-manipulating programs on the open market,' she began conversationally as the CD started, 'but none like this. Don't worry. This won't cause a crash. It's very stable. No bugs. OK,' she added. 'It's ready.'

'Nothing's happened,' Pappenheim said.

'Plenty has happened.'

To prove the point, Hedi Meyer placed the cursor on the pillar, and clicked once. The pillar vanished, leaving the half body of the obscured man as a surreal image.

'And who says the camera cannot lie,' Pappenheim murmured.

'The camera still does not lie,' she said. 'It always takes what it sees. It's what happens afterwards that lies. Now, I'll click once on the half body, and the program will do the rest. It will work from what's left there and, based on that, will try to construct a full image. It will then give us a series of suggestions.'

She clicked, and a red outline surrounded the image of the man. A blur of images followed, then froze. The man was complete, his suit a perfect whole. A percentage bar had appeared at the foot of the image.

'Eighty per cent,' Hedi Meyer said. 'Just the first try.' The screen was busy again. 'It will keep this up until I stop it, so just tell me when to.'

The program turned up eight more possibilities, but none got a response from Pappenheim.

The bar had reached 98 per cent, when Pappenheim said, '*Stop!* That's it,' he went on softly. 'That's it.'

Hedi Meyer froze the now complete image of the man. 'I can rotate him to get the full face.'

Both Müller and Pappenheim were staring at the screen.

'Let's see what he really looks like, Miss Meyer,' Müller said.

Using the mouse, Hedi Meyer slowly caused the figure to rotate, until it was looking directly at them, it seemed.

Pappenheim gave a soft intake of breath. 'Well, well, well.'

Müller glanced at him. 'The Silesian?'

'The Silesian.'

Hedi Meyer gave an expressive shiver. 'I'd not like to meet *him* on a dark night.'

'I would think many people have,' Müller said, continuing to stare at the image of the Silesian, 'but did not survive the encounter. Especially if they were near Stalingrad in the forties.'

'Not only Stalingrad,' Pappenheim added with certainty. 'And not only in the forties.'

Three

They stumbled unexpectedly upon a meandering snow trench.

The ground was no longer generally flat, but had evolved into a more undulating landscape. As they thankfully scrambled down the steep sides to get out of the ferocity of the persistent wind, it seemed as if they could abruptly hear better, and felt less cold. The difference, in reality, was minimal, but to them it was a huge relief.

'Don't relax,' Holbeck paused to caution. 'We may not be the only ones taking shelter in this trench. Grootemans and Hubertus, take the rear. Nagel and Moos, I want you two in the middle, to cover the sides. I'll be up front with the lieutenant.'

The lieutenant was striding back towards them, eyes furious. 'Did I order a halt?'

'Sir,' Holbeck began, 'I was just setting up fluid firing positions in case . . .'

Von Mappus gritted his teeth. It was not just against the cold. '*Holbeck!*'

'Sir?'

'*I* give the orders here!' Von Mappus glared at the sergeant. 'You really are pushing me to my limit, *Scharführer*! You . . .'

'*Ivans!*' Hubertus's shout came with the simultaneous barking and stuttering of his and Grootemans' weapons.

Von Mappus had no choice but to respond to the imperatives of sudden combat as, like the others, he flattened himself against a side of the trench to face the threat. He seemed to have at last learned to stop striding into battle like some kind of invincible Siegfried.

As abruptly as it had begun, the firing stopped. No one moved from his position.

They waited, tense, eyes searching upwards and along the trench, in both directions.

'If they throw grenades from the top,' Moos whispered, 'we've had it.'

No one made comment. Only the wind continued its howling; but at least the savagery of its passage was broken somewhat by the curves of the trench, and the steepness of the inclines.

'Sir,' Holbeck began in a low voice to von Mappus. 'May I send Hubertus and Grootemans to check?'

Von Mappus stared through him, but gave the slightest of nods.

Holbeck inched his way past Nagel and Moos towards the rear. 'Go and see if you've hit anything,' he said to Hubertus and Grootemans. 'But don't stick your necks out. Watch your backs, and ours. We've got enough dead aryan heroes turning into ice out here.'

Hubertus grinned without humour. 'On our way. Come on, Grooty.'

The two of them vanished beyond a bend in the trench.

Another few minutes passed tensely. Everyone braced himself for another outbreak of firing; but the guns remained silent.

Then Hubertus and Grootemans were back, unceremoniously carrying a small, struggling creature between them: a girl of about ten. She made no sound.

Hubertus gave another of his weird grins. 'Our Ivans. All one of them.'

They all stared at the child. She was well clothed against the elements, and did not appear to be starving. Hubertus and Grootemans hung on to her, keeping her suspended. Her legs propelled themselves frantically, giving the impression that if they were to let go, she would set off as if from a catapult. Throughout, she continued to utter no sound. It was uncanny.

'Is she hurt?' Holbeck asked.

'Not a scratch,' Grootemans replied. 'So much for our shooting.'

'She was fast,' Hubertus said with some amusement. 'Round one of those bends like lightning. But we found her hiding behind a pile of snow. I think she's lost.'

Von Mappus had been staring at the child like a predator that had unexpectedly come upon prey.

'Don't be ridiculous!' he snapped. 'This is her territory. She knows her way around. The Bolsheviks use children as runners. She is probably on her way to a unit with a message. Look at her clothes. She's better dressed for this weather than we are. And she does not look hungry. That speaks volumes.'

'Should we search her, Herr *Obersturmführer*?' Hubertus asked with exaggerated deference.

Von Mappus gave Hubertus a suspicious glance, before returning his attention to the child.

'No. Who knows enough Russian to interrogate her?' Von Mappus was now looking at Holbeck. 'As a former teacher, *Scharführer*, do you know Russian?'

'I can get by . . .'

'As I thought.' There was a distinct sneer in the lieutenant's voice. 'Go on. Interrogate the little Bolshevik.'

'Any Russian I may have is very bad . . .'

'Interrogate her, *damn you*! Don't give me excuses! And keep hold of her!' von Mappus snapped at Hubertus and Grootemans. 'She's writhing about like a little snake!'

Holbeck approached the dangling, struggling child.

'We are not going to hurt you,' he began in halting Russian.

The child stared at him, and suddenly went still. Then she fired a stream of Russian at him.

'Whoa!' he said. 'Not so fast. I am very bad with your language.'

Unexpectedly, she began to giggle. 'You are like the other German.'

Holbeck stared at her. 'The *other* German? What other German?'

'The one we gave the food to. He couldn't speak our language, either.'

Holbeck was dumbfounded. 'The one . . .' he began at last,

50

then stopped. It must have been the major. He was suddenly very frightened for the child. He had to protect her from von Mappus.

'What is she finding so funny?' von Mappus demanded.

'My Russian,' Holbeck said.

'That does not surprise me. Even I can hear by your useless efforts how bad you are. And I can't understand a word of that savage tongue. Teachers!' The word was full of contempt. 'Mind-corrupters when not controlled! Well? What did she have to say?'

'Just childish nonsense so far.'

'Keep trying! We haven't all the time in the world. And neither has she.'

There was a chill in the last remark that filled Holbeck with foreboding.

Before Holbeck could speak, the girl was again throwing a burst of Russian at him. 'What does he mean . . . I don't have time?'

Holbeck felt himself going pale. 'You . . . understand *German*?' he asked in his struggling Russian.

'Yes. My father can speak it. He spoke to the other German officer. Shall I speak to you in your language . . . ?'

'*No!*' Holbeck was appalled. If von Mappus found out, the child would soon be just another corpse joining the countless others in the snow.

The child's eyes grew wide. 'You are frightened of that one?'

'No. I am not frightened of him.'

The eyes were wise beyond her years. 'Then you are frightened for me.'

'I . . .'

'Come on, *Scharführer*!' an increasingly impatient von Mappus urged. 'Get on with it! We're not here to have a conversation with that disgusting little Bolshevik! Find out who she's taking her message to.'

Despite her apparent maturity, she was still a child and she responded to the lieutenant's impatience with her own.

'*I am not taking a message to anyone, you stupid man!*' she shouted at him, mercifully in her own tongue.

51

Von Mappus glared at her, then at Holbeck. 'What was that? What was that she said?'

'Hubertus and Grootemans are hurting her,' Holbeck lied quickly.

'Good. Don't you two let go of her,' von Mappus warned them.

'No, sir,' they said.

The child was again looking at Holbeck. 'You lied to him.'

'Yes . . .'

'"*Da*",' von Mappus interrupted. 'That means "yes". Even I know that. And a while ago you shouted "*niet*". Meaning "no". What did you refuse her, and what did you say yes to?'

'She wanted to be released,' Holbeck said. 'I refused.'

'Good. And the "yes"?'

'I told her she would be freed if she answered us truthfully.'

'Very good,' von Mappus said. 'After all, as a teacher, you should be good with children. Continue.'

The child looked from Holbeck to von Mappus, then back again.

'What are you doing out here?' Holbeck asked. 'Have you no family?'

'My father, my mother, my brother. They are in my village. We are far from the war.'

'But what are you doing out here in a trench?'

'This is not a trench. It is a small stream that sometimes has water in the spring and summer. It goes through our village. In winter, we use it as a road. We sent the German officer this way, but I think he got lost. My father said he was a little crazy because of the war. He said he had to get back to his men.'

'We are all a little crazy,' Holbeck said. 'Some more than others. And he is with his men now,' Holbeck added, though the child could not possibly understand.

Holbeck wanted to laugh at the craziness of it. Their 'snow trench' was no more than a dried-out watercourse which led to the village the major had spoken about; a village that really existed.

'And they sent *you* to find him?' Holbeck asked.

For the first time, the child looked uncomfortable, as if she had been caught stealing. 'They don't know . . .'

'They don't *know*? Are *you* crazy? *Don't you realize how dangerous . . .*' Holbeck stopped. The child was shrinking from him. Only then did he realize he had been shouting.

'Good, *good!*' von Mappus said, looking at Holbeck in surprise. 'That's the way to treat them. Now she's frightened of you. I have perhaps been underestimating you, Holbeck.'

'Now do you see?' Holbeck said to her, his fear for her safety making him shout even louder.

'I . . . I can take you to my village. There is food . . .'

'*No!*' Holbeck shouted. 'That man will kill your people. All of them! I must find a way to let you go. We will not go to your village.'

'But the other soldier was nice . . .'

'Not all soldiers in this uniform . . .' he began.

'What was that?' von Mappus interrupted again. 'Why did you shout "no"?'

'She wants Hubertus and Grootemans to put her down.'

'Don't you let go!' von Mappus warned them a second time.

'We won't,' Hubertus assured him.

'Well, *Scharführer*?' von Mappus went on to Holbeck. 'Any daylight out of that little savage?'

'Nothing, sir. She knows nothing. I think she's playing truant.'

Von Mappus looked exaggeratedly about him. '*Truant?* Out *here*? I think it must be the teacher in you. You are soft in the head, Holbeck. God knows how you made it into the Waffen SS. *I'll* take over this interrogation.'

Von Mappus drew his pistol and came forward. He looked down upon the child with eyes that were totally devoid of the slightest vestige of humanity. He put the pistol against the child's forehead.

'*Talk*, you little animal!'

'If I may suggest, sir,' Holbeck began quickly. 'This will frighten her even more. Then we won't get a thing out of her.'

53

'*Wrong, Scharführer!* Fear is the key to these creatures. They must learn to fear us more than death itself. It is the only way.'

But the child's reaction was not what von Mappus had expected. Far from being frightened, she displayed the sense of invulnerability of the very young. Her outraged eyes glared back at von Mappus from beneath the snout of his pistol.

'*I am not an animal, you stupid man!*' she yelled. Unfortunately, this time she spoke German.

In the minds of the soldiers, time was suddenly still. Even the wind seemed to have drastically abated. Holbeck felt a chill that went beyond the winter's grip upon his bones. Von Mappus was staring at the bold child in stunned disbelief.

The five soldiers waited for the shot that would end the child's life.

Then, abruptly, von Mappus withdrew the pistol and put it back into its holster. He gave a feral smile.

'Do you see, *Scharführer?*' von Mappus gloated. 'I just got more out of her than you with your weak attempts at sweet talk in her wretched tongue. She speaks the language of her masters, if perhaps worse than you do her own. For a little animal . . . Sorry,' he added with grim courtesy to the child. 'For a little *Bolshevik*, she shows courage. I can appreciate that. Now tell me, child, which unit were you going to . . . and where is it positioned?'

'I was not going to any unit, stupid man!'

'I am not the *Scharführer*, child,' von Mappus admonished very softly. 'Don't make that mistake. If you call me stupid once more, I *will* shoot you.'

The girl shot Holbeck a swift glance and saw the pleading in his eyes. She said nothing.

'Very good,' von Mappus said. 'You're learning. And don't look to the *Scharführer*. *I* am in command here. Now, I will ask you again. Where is the unit?' he demanded, emphasizing each word.

'My arms hurt. Tell them to put me down.'

'Not until you answer.'

'There is no "unit". My village is not far from here.'

Holbeck shut his eyes briefly in despair. The countdown to the destruction of the village had begun.

'*Village?*' Von Mappus stared hard at the child. 'What village?'

'*My* village,' she replied, as if to someone slow to learn. 'You are standing in a stream that runs in spring and summer. It will take us to my village. We have plenty of food. We gave some to the other German. *He* was nice.'

'She means the major!' Moos exclaimed. 'He was telling the truth!' His eyes, full of reproach, stared at von Mappus.

Von Mappus looked quickly at them in turn. 'She is lying! There *is* a unit out there, waiting in ambush. How can you believe . . . ?'

'She could not have known about the major, unless she had seen him . . . *sir*,' Nagel said.

Hubertus and Grootemans abruptly let go of the girl.

'Off you go, kid,' Hubertus said to her. 'The *Obersturmführer* won't shoot. *Will* you, *sir*?' he added to von Mappus, teeth bared in challenge.

With a last glance at Holbeck, she ran off in the direction she had said would lead to her village.

Von Mappus stood absolutely still for some moments; then he slowly turned his head to survey them, an animal at bay.

The gaze finally settled upon Holbeck. 'If you want command, Holbeck, you will first have to shoot me. But as your moral rectitude prevents you from doing so for the time being, let us see if that village really exists.'

Von Mappus turned, and began to walk in the direction the child had gone.

The others looked irresolutely at Holbeck.

'What now, Sarge?' Hubertus asked.

'We follow. If there *is* a village, I must prevent that madman from destroying it.'

'And if there's no village but a bunch of Ivans waiting in ambush, just as the lieutenant said?'

'We're Waffen SS. We fight.'

Hubertus grinned. 'Something I understand.'

Müller and Pappenheim studied the image of the Silesian.

'As you said, Miss Meyer,' Müller remarked, 'definitely not someone to meet on a dark night.'

'At least,' she said, 'not without a weapon.'

'I could not agree more.'

'Can you make me a full-colour print?' Pappenheim asked. 'Size . . . A5.'

'Yes, sir. Easily.' Hedi Meyer started the printout.

'And prepare two copies of that image for sending by encrypted email, separately.'

She nodded. 'If you don't want me to see the email addresses, I can set everything up and you can finish up . . .'

'You can see the addresses,' Pappenheim told her, 'but you tell no one . . . not even your boss. And don't you worry. If the need arises, I'll fix it with him.'

'Yes, sir.'

Müller glanced at his deputy, but said nothing as Pappenheim dictated a short message to each recipient of the email.

Hedi Meyer gave a soft gasp when she was given the email addresses, but made no comment as she prepared them.

While she worked, the printout of the Silesian flopped on to the printer tray. Pappenheim picked it up, and showed it to Müller.

'A good likeness?' Müller asked.

'He was perhaps two . . . or three years younger when this was taken,' Pappenheim said. 'Hard to tell. But it's a very good likeness. Excellent work, Hedi,' he added to the goth.

'Thank you, sir.' She paused to swivel the chair round to look at them. 'When we're finished, I can play around with the computer to make more efficient use of its memory, and firewall it in such a way as to make it hack-proof. I can do that with my programs.'

'This is already a very secure machine,' Müller said. 'Herman Spyros has made sure all our machines are hardened.'

'I know, sir. I've worked on them. But this is the most important machine. I can add a better layer of security.'

'Better than your boss?'

'I would not put it quite like that, sir.'

Pappenheim tapped at the printout of the Silesian as he

glanced at Müller. 'This is really good stuff. I'll talk to Herman Spyros about the machine.'

Müller nodded, then peered at the screen.

He studied it for so long, Pappenheim was moved to ask, 'Am I missing something?'

'The man the Silesian is talking to,' Müller said.

Pappenheim looked at the figure, who was right-side-on to the camera. 'What about him?'

'A spark of light is on his little finger.'

'Must be a ring,' Pappenheim suggested.

'Then let's see. Hedi . . . could you zero on that spark, please?'

She nodded, and brought it up until it filled the screen.

It was indeed a ring; but a very special one. It was a seal: a doctored variation of one of the ancient seals of the Knights Templar. The familiar two knights on the one horse was there; but over this was superimposed a jagged X.

'Any jangling bells?' Müller asked Pappenheim.

'A whole cacophony.'

'Did you notice whether your Silesian was wearing one?'

'Now he's *my* Silesian? He wasn't,' Pappenheim went on. 'I checked.' He absently touched his own wedding ring. Despite being a widower for some years, he still wore it. 'Not a single item of jewellery on any finger.'

'A man like that,' Müller commented with mild scepticism. 'Given what we know so far, don't you find it strange? These kind of people always wear something to identify their peer group. It's a must.'

'He didn't want me to see it.'

'A possibility.'

'So? Shall I also send this on to my contacts?'

Müller shook his head. 'I'd rather wait. See what the Silesian's photo brings rushing into the daylight. But let's have a printout of it. Hedi? Could you let us have one, please?'

'Coming up as you speak.'

The printer again began its soft hum.

'Alright,' Müller said to Hedi Meyer as he took the result out of the tray and studied it critically. 'I'll hang on to this.

Do your stuff after we've gone. Make certain you shut the door properly when you leave. The security system will arm itself once you are clear. Open up to no one. This is without exception. Anyone who has to knock should not be coming in here without permission in the first place; and anyone else has the access code.'

'Yes, sir.'

'If someone does come in while you're still here, you are to refer that person to me.'

'Including *Polizeidirektor* Kaltendorf?'

'Including him.'

'Yes, sir,' Hedi Meyer repeated, expression giving nothing away as she turned back to the computer.

'Alright, Hedi,' Pappenheim said to her. 'Send those mails.'

She clicked on the button to despatch the emails to the addresses he had given her, then closed down the Grogan CD. She removed it from the drive and handed it back to Pappenheim.

He returned it to the cabinet, then pushed the drawer shut. The light on the keypad blinked once as the drawer code reset itself.

'We'll leave you to it,' Müller told her. 'You'll be OK in here by yourself?'

'Of course I will. I'm in a police building, in the safest room.' She smiled at him. 'You won't believe the speed of the computer next time you see it at work.'

'Just don't crash it. Please. It's my neck.'

'Then your neck is safe with me, sir.'

'"Then your neck is safe with me, sir",' Pappenheim mimicked as they walked along the corridor, back towards their offices. 'She has a crush on a certain *Hauptkommissar*, I think. That's three.'

'*Three?* What are you talking about?'

'Let's see,' Pappenheim began solemnly. 'Solange du Bois, Hedi Meyer . . . and, of course, not forgetting most of all, Miss Carey Bloomfield of the CIA. Yes. That's three.'

'She's *not* CIA . . .'

'She tells you . . .'

'If you keep going on about it, I'll keep nagging you about Berger.'

'You drive a hard bargain. I'd better move on to the Silesian.'

'That would help. Where are you taking the picture?'

'To the den of hard-faced individuals from countries east – including Russia – in Neu Kolln.'

'The Death Strip. Luigi Bocca's pizza restaurant.'

'He doesn't like hearing pizza and restaurant in the same breath. Some of his clientele,' Pappenheim went on, 'might make even the Silesian blench. You never know. One of them may know him, or of him. Perhaps even Luigi himself. That was a good idea you had,' he added. 'How did you know?'

'I didn't. It was just a hunch. Grogan made the call. And from what we know about him . . .'

'Which is a lot less than what we *don't* know . . .'

'A lot less,' Müller agreed. 'I decided on a long shot. That material he gave us is like an ongoing puzzle. Every time you look, you find something new. I hoped we – or you, in this case – might spot something.'

'Well, we spotted two. A regular little gallery of rogues, and potential rogues, he's presented us with.'

'One wonders about his motives.'

'One certainly does . . .'

'Let's have another look at the Silesian.'

Pappenheim handed over the printout.

'Do the eyes match?' Müller enquired as he took it.

'Not exactly, but they're very close to the real thing.'

'As a policeman, I've looked into some mean eyes,' Müller commented, studying the image of the Silesian. 'But these are quite something. Slate dead.'

'More so than the bastard's who caused us all that trouble last August?'

'Oh yes.' Müller returned the printout.

'Then I'd better get over to Luigi's,' Pappenheim said as he took it back. 'Find out what I can.'

'Still nothing from our colleagues on Rügen?'

'Nothing as yet. No one's reported anything to any police

unit. And even if they did, it's heavily snowed-under up there. It will take them forever to find out if something has happened. Notice I haven't mentioned that seal.'

'You just did.'

'I remember an envelope,' Pappenheim began, unabashed, 'with a blue seal exactly like that on the back. There was a note in it from Grogan, which he gave to Miss Bloomfield to pass on to you, last August.'

'Just what I was thinking,' Müller said. 'Anything else about that seal to excite your interest?'

'The jagged X does remind one of the SS runes, crossed.'

'What a relief to know I'm not hallucinating.'

Pappenheim grinned. 'Would you say we were pointed to it?'

'I would definitely say that.'

'What other treasures, I wonder,' Pappenheim said, 'has our friend Grogan hidden in there for us to find?'

When Müller remained silent, Pappenheim studied him closely.

'What?' Müller demanded.

'You look twitchy.'

Müller frowned at him. 'What are you talking about now?'

Pappenheim glanced at his watch. 'Still early over there. She'd probably chew the head off anyone calling her at this hour . . . but I'm certain she wouldn't mind if *you* did.'

'You're talking in riddles, Pappi.'

'Riddler, that's me. Ah! Here's my door. Work to do.'

Pappenheim escaped into his office before Müller could make a suitable response.

Annandale, Virginia.

The phone in the bedroom rang twice.

'Jesus!' she exclaimed as she came awake, voice soft with sleep. 'Who the hell's this?'

At the third ring, the answering machine next to the remote handset clicked on.

'Hi,' she heard her voice say. 'You got me. Leave a message, and I'll get back to you.'

'I'm assuming you're away . . .' the caller began.

She picked up the phone quickly and pressed the connect button. The answering machine immediately stopped.

'*Müller!*' Carey Bloomfield said in her sleepy voice. 'It's three thirty in the *morning*! Are you *nuts*?'

'It's nine thirty out here . . .' Müller was infuriatingly calm.

'Hah, hah! Next joke.'

'Sarcasm becomes you,' Müller said.

'Not the right time to make with the jokes, Müller. I didn't get to sleep till midnight.'

'It must have been a very special party . . .'

'I wish. So why the call after three months of silence, Müller? Missing me?'

'Sarcasm continues to become you.'

'Are you going to tell me why you called? Or are we going to burn the transatlantic wires in small talk?'

'You sound cranky.'

'I'm always cranky at three thirty in the morning, damn it.'

'You'll feel much better on this side of the pond,' Müller said mildly.

There was a long pause as electronic connections hummed to themselves almost below aural level.

'I think I'm still asleep,' she said. 'I didn't just hear that. There's a tree outside my bedroom window, Müller. Last time I saw it, which was just *three and a half hours ago*, there was glaze on it. In February, we nearly had the hottest day on record. Now the weather people say Lake Barcroft could freeze. That means *winter*, Müller. And I'm betting you've got winter too. Now me, although I wasn't born in any of those places, I'm a California babe, a Florida babe, a Hawaii babe. I love places where it's *warm*. Now if your offer was to, say . . . the Caribbean, I'd be on the next plane in a heartbeat . . .'

'If you're quick, you can be over here by this evening.'

'One of us is definitely asleep. As I'm awake now, it can't be me.'

'I'll meet you at Berlin–Tegel.'

'Listen, Müller . . . *Müller?*' Carey Bloomfield stared at the receiver. 'I'm talking into space.' She hit the cancel button to close the connection. 'Damn that man! Who the hell does he think he is? I'm going back to sleep.'

She lay down in bed determinedly. After a few minutes of lying there irresolutely, she got up once more and picked up the receiver. She dialled a number.

'Didn't wake you, did I, Toby?'

'Is this a joke, Carey? It's past nine thirty out here.'

'Don't remind me.'

'So what are you doing awake?'

'I just got a call.'

'Pregnant pause.'

'From Müller.'

'Ah!'

In Berlin, Müller was looking at the phone he had just used.

'If I know my Miss Bloomfield,' he said to it, 'she'll lie in bed for a few moments, then pick up the phone to talk to someone she works for.' He stood up, and went over to the window to look out upon his city. 'Then she'll find a way to get over here quickly. Her unpredictability makes her predictable. Sometimes.'

He smiled to himself.

Luigi Bocca's restaurant was the sort of place that silent men with hard, watchful eyes frequented. Many of them came from countries that had previously been part of the Soviet Bloc. It was definitely not the kind of establishment that police officers – if given the choice – would tend to visit, even in squads of four.

Pappenheim was not your average policeman. He breezed in like a respected customer which, indeed, he was. Pappenheim looked about him. The restaurant was doing good business. The men with the hard eyes pretended not to see him.

Luigi Bocca, a small man with an outrageously deep voice, greeted him warmly. 'Ah, *Commissario*! Nice to see you again.' Bocca made a show of looking beyond Pappenheim.

'Your friend, the other *Commissario*, he is not with you? I remember him from last August. Very quiet.'

'He's the strong, silent type. My friend, *and* my boss. He won't be coming today.'

'Well he is always welcome.'

'I'll tell him.'

Filled with entrepreneurial zeal, Bocca had come to the former East Berlin soon after the fall of the Wall. In a moment of gruesome humour, he had named his establishment the Death Strip, after the DDR's infamous killing field behind the Wall. He tended to speak German with a heavy Italian accent; a joke in itself, considering he was born in Bremen. His Italian was on a par with Pappenheim's, which was saying very little.

'So, *Commissario*,' he went on to Pappenheim, full of bonhomie, 'what can Luigi prepare for you today?'

'You shouldn't look so happy to see me, Luigi. People might talk.'

Bocca frowned slightly, then brightened. 'Ah. You are making with the jokes.'

'Yes, Luigi,' Pappenheim confirmed with leaden gravity. 'A joke. Today, I'll have your excellent espresso.'

'And to eat?'

For reply, Pappenheim fished a cigarette out of a nearly empty pack.

'These things will kill you,' Bocca admonished.

'Of course.' Pappenheim lit up, and inhaled with unashamed pleasure.

'Would you like the usual room?'

'No. Today . . .' Pappenheim slowly looked about him, and spotted a free table in a far corner. There were no windows close to it, and it afforded a full view of the entire dining area. 'This will do.'

'You are looking for someone,' Bocca said, glancing in the direction of the table.

'Very sharp, Luigi.'

Trailed by Bocca, Pappenheim began moving towards the table. When they got to it, Pappenheim took the corner chair.

He looked up. 'You seem a little stressed-out all of a sudden, Luigi. What's wrong?'

'This table . . .'

'Yes?'

'Well, usually . . .' Bocca's words faltered as Pappenheim's baby-blue eyes fastened upon him.

'This table . . . ?' the *Oberkommissar* prompted.

But just as suddenly, Bocca brightened again. 'No matter. It will be OK.' He hurried away to get the espresso.

Pappenheim kept his eyes upon Bocca, until he went out of sight beyond the bar.

'Hmm,' Pappenheim said. 'Twitchy.'

As she ran along the snowbound bed of the stream she saw a figure, well clothed against the winter, hurrying in her direction. She knew instantly it was her brother, Andrei.

'Galina!' he said, short of breath as he drew up. 'Are you crazy? You could have got lost!'

He grabbed her by the shoulders and shook her, fear for her safety mixed with anger made his grip rougher than he had intended. Like his sister, he had matured well beyond his years. He was just two years older, and was tall for his age.

'Let go!' she scolded. 'You're hurting me! And I can't get lost. You know that. I'm better than you!'

He released her. 'Well? Did you find your German major?'

'No. I think *he* got lost. But I found some more.'

He stared at her. '*More?*'

'One of them is not as nice as the major, but the others are OK . . . especially the sergeant. He's nice.'

Despite her outward maturity, she was still a child, and she spoke of Holbeck as if she had found a replacement for the major.

Andrei again placed his hand upon her shoulders. 'Galina, the major was like . . . a miracle. Others will not be like him. We cannot defend ourselves against people like that. Where are they now?'

'But we are not in the war. We are too far from . . .'

'To these people, *everywhere* is in the war. *Where are they?*'

'You're hurting me again!'

'Galina . . . *where* are they?'

'Behind me. And let . . . *go!*'

Again, he did so. 'Behind you? How far?'

'I ran very fast . . . even in the snow, and they think our soldiers are waiting . . . so they will be very slow. It will take them a day to reach our village.'

He sighed. 'Galina, you must stop this. Every time you go away, I have to come and find you . . .'

'You don't have to!' she sulked. 'I never get lost . . .'

'I know, but father always sends me . . .'

'He doesn't have to. Mother knows I cannot get lost . . .'

'I know,' Andrei repeated. 'But you know how it is. Come on. Let's get back. I found your horse . . .'

'You didn't find Babi,' Galina retorted with some asperity. 'She *never* gets lost. I left her on top to wait for me.'

'Mine is with her. Are you hungry? I have food.'

She shook her head. 'I still have some.'

He sighed again as they set off. 'Galina, you must stop looking for lost people. They are not harmless little animals like those you find in the woods. People, especially these kind, are very dangerous animals. Let us hope we will still have our village when they leave. Hurry. We must warn everyone.'

They hurried along the bed until they came to a point where Andrei's footprints zigzagged down the left slope, some distance from where he had met her.

'When I saw Babi, I guessed you had come down here . . .'

'I didn't come down this way . . .'

'Whichever way you came down,' Andrei interrupted with some impatience, 'up you go! We must get to the village quickly.'

They ploughed up the incline to where the horses were patiently waiting in the now much-abated snowstorm. Galina's 'horse' was more of a pony, and she climbed aboard without difficulty.

Andrei's was a bigger animal, but he too was able to easily

get into the saddle. Both horses were farm animals with large hooves, enabling them to operate in the snowy terrain without difficulty.

They started at a walk, then Andrei and Galina urged their mounts into as fast a trot as the snow would allow.

The six Waffen-SS soldiers trudged along the bed of the stream, moving cautiously, for fear of ambush.

Then von Mappus came to a sudden halt. Holbeck nearly stumbled into him. Von Mappus glared at the sergeant.

'Watch where you put your feet, *Scharführer*!'

'Sorry, sir. Why have we stopped?' Holbeck added.

Von Mappus pointed. 'For a while, we have been travelling in a straight line. Now, what do you see?'

Up ahead, the bed of the stream curved tightly to the left.

'A bend, sir,' Holbeck replied with neutral weariness.

'A bend, sir,' von Mappus repeated. 'An ambush position, sir!'

'With respect . . .'

'With *respect*? Despite being a teacher, you don't know the meaning of the word, *Scharführer*! Go forward and check it out!'

'Yes, sir.' Holbeck turned to select a man to go with him.

'Alone, *Scharführer*!' von Mappus ordered.

'Yes, sir,' Holbeck repeated, turning round to move on ahead.

Hubertus came forward. 'I can accompany . . .'

Von Mappus stared at him. 'When I need your suggestions, Hubertus, I'll ask for them! Stay where you are!'

Hubertus stayed put.

The others followed Holbeck with anxious eyes as the sergeant moved closer to the bend. They watched as he paused to carefully check his surroundings, then disappeared round the corner.

Tense minutes passed in complete silence, save for the subdued howl of the wind above them.

Then Holbeck reappeared.

Their collective sigh of relief was loud enough to cause von Mappus to tighten his lips.

Holbeck came up to von Mappus. 'All clear for some distance, sir,' he reported with absolute correctness. 'No ambush positions, as far as I could check. I climbed a slope to make certain. Nothing, and no one at all out there.'

But that did not satisfy von Mappus. 'And your little Bolshevik?'

'Gone, sir.'

'Of course she's gone! Did you think she would wait for you? She has joined up with the patrol she was scouting for, or the unit for which she is a courier. She is not a harmless child. Get that into your head! We have all heard the stories of children rolling grenades into foxholes. The Bolsheviks will be waiting, somewhere out there, for us to walk into a trap. I am not a fool, *Scharführer*. You may want to believe the little savage, but I do not!' Von Mappus raked the others with blazing eyes. 'Move on!'

He turned and headed for the bend, machine pistol held ready for use.

As they followed, Hubertus raised his Tommy gun and mimed an aim at the lieutenant's back.

Holbeck censured him with a look.

Hubertus gave a thin smile as he lowered the weapon.

Pappenheim was nursing his second espresso, and third cigarette.

Some of the Death Strip's customers had left, while new ones had come in. All still pretended not to notice Pappenheim. He had removed a plain brown envelope from his coat and placed it on the table, next to his coffee. Now, he slowly opened it, removed the printout of the Silesian, and laid it face up on top of the envelope.

No one appeared to take notice of his actions, but he sensed an immediate electrification of the atmosphere.

He smiled to himself and took a sip of coffee, followed by a long pull on his cigarette, and waited. It was not a long wait.

Luigi Bocca came to the table within seconds. 'My grandmother,' he began, 'knows you are here. You know how she likes you. She says she can prepare a very special fettucini for you, if you have the time.' His eyes flicked once, twice to the printout. He paled visibly.

'And how is the old fascist?' Pappenheim enquired, studying Bocca's expression with detachment.

'Going as strong as ever. She will outlast you or me.'

When he chose to admit to it, Bocca's political leanings took a definite left slant. His grandmother's irredeemably hard-right views, stemming from the era of Mussolini, sometimes made for interesting discussion within the Bocca household.

'That would not surprise me,' Pappenheim remarked, 'but alas, I must turn down the invitation. Time is not on my side today. But thank her, and give her my regards.'

Bocca nodded. 'I will.' He could not resist a third glance at the Silesian's image. 'How did you know?'

'How did I know what?' Pappenheim queried, remembering how his own recent conversation with Müller had followed a similar route.

'He comes here . . . sometimes. He always sits where you are.'

'Well, well. Wonders never cease. I didn't know, Luigi. I came here, hoping something would turn up. Your establishment is such a popular crossroads, you see.'

'This is a very dangerous man, *Commissario*,' Bocca warned in a low voice. 'Even the people in here keep away from him.'

'Recommendation indeed, for a man in his seventies or eighties.'

'He does not look it. He comes in here with two bodyguards. Russians.'

'*Russians*. Interesting choice of bodyguards. As I just said, wonders never cease.' Pappenheim took a last swig of his coffee, and got to his feet. He put the cigarette between his lips, then picked up the envelope and the printout. 'When you see him again, you will let me know, won't you, Luigi? You know how to contact me.' The cigarette bobbed up and down as Pappenheim spoke.

Bocca seemed less than happy at the prospect. '*Commissario*, we have an agreement, you and I . . . and I have

68

always been helpful . . . and *discreet*. This would not be very discreet.'

Pappenheim glanced around the room. 'You seem frightened, Luigi. These people don't normally frighten you.'

'They don't. They know this is neutral territory . . . if you understand me.'

'Perfectly.'

'But the man in that picture would not respect territory.'

'I know what you mean,' Pappenheim said, remembering the Silesian's attitude to Schaefer. 'He never did . . . even years ago.' He took a final drag on the Gauloise and killed it in the ashtray. 'Alright, Luigi. You're off the hook. I have another idea. See you later.'

Before the other could respond, he moved to the nearest table of diners, and placed the printout on the table. The two men sitting there did not even glance at it.

'I'm looking for this man. If you don't know who I am, Luigi can tell you.'

Pappenheim repeated the routine at each occupied table. No one seemed to look at the printout, but he was certain they all knew it was of the Silesian. When he had visited the last table, Pappenheim made his way to the exit, and paused to look round.

'Enjoy your meal,' he said, loud enough for the entire room to hear, then went out.

Müller's phone rang.

He stared at it for some moments, before picking it up. 'Müller.'

'Where did you get my picture?' the arrogant voice demanded.

Müller paused. 'As I have no idea who you are, this is a rather difficult question to answer. And where did *you* get this number?'

'Don't take me for a fool, Müller!'

Müller stared at Monet's magpie. 'As we're strangers, it's *Hauptkommissar* Müller . . .'

'You're playing with fire, Müller . . .'

'How many times have I heard that in my career . . . ?'

'One day, it could be the last . . .'

'Is that a direct threat to an officer of the law?' Müller asked evenly. 'If so, it could be construed as a criminal offence. But I think you're smarter than that . . . whoever you are.'

The line clicked, and Müller found himself listening to the dialling tone.

'Touchy,' he said, replacing the receiver.

He picked up the direct phone to Pappenheim, but got no reply. Half an hour later, it rang.

'Are you free?' Pappenheim enquired.

'Tried to reach you earlier.'

'I am back, as all can see.'

'Come on up.'

'Your wish is my command.'

'I got a call from your Silesian,' Müller began as Pappenheim entered.

Pappenheim picked up one of the non-standard-issue chairs and placed it in such a way that he could face Müller, as well as being able to look out on the city.

'Still *my* Silesian, is he?' he said as he sat down.

'Your Silesian. It must have been. Given the arrogance, and his question.'

'Which was?'

'"Where did you get my picture?" Quote. Unquote.'

Pappenheim stared at him. 'That was quick. How long ago?'

'Half an hour.'

'That was *very* quick. I'd only just left Luigi's. We should officially put him on the payroll. He gets results faster than some special investigators I know.'

Pappenheim explained in detail what he had done at the Death Strip.

'Someone obviously did look at the printout,' Müller said in dry comment when Pappenheim had finished.

'Perhaps that someone is one of his Russian musclemen, taking a coffee break.'

'Or someone else – not Russian – who works for him, or is part of whatever he represents.'

'Or that.'

'So what do you think will be his next move?'

Pappenheim glanced at the Monet. 'That magpie worries me.'

'Why?'

'One magpie is supposed to be bad news . . .'

'And?'

'The Silesian reminds me of that magpie. His next move will be to ask . . .'

'Demand.'

'I stand corrected . . . to demand a meeting. He'll be burning his brain cells trying to work out how we got that picture.'

'He'd blow each one if he *really* knew,' Müller said. He reached into a drawer. 'If he does demand his meeting, we'll present him with something extra.' He placed the printout of the seal on the desk.

'That,' Pappenheim said, 'will definitely pop his circuits.' He got to his feet, stretched, and went over to the window. 'Well? Did you call her?' he added, offhandedly casual.

'Whom are we talking about?'

Pappenheim did not turn round. 'So you did. Thought you would.' He made a little sound of amused satisfaction.

Four

V on Mappus led them along the frozen watercourse. Above its steep sides, the snowstorm continued to abate.

Hubertus and Grootemans were at the rear of the small, loosely extended column and ahead of them were Nagel and Moos. Moos slackened his pace slightly so that he could speak to Hubertus.

'Did you really work for a gangster?' he asked in a low, conspiratorial voice.

'You don't believe me?'

'Well . . . I don't know what to think.'

'You'll be even more shocked when I tell you that my boss was a Jew.'

Moos was indeed horrified. 'A *Jew*?' he whispered, as if afraid von Mappus would hear. Beneath his makeshift hood, his eyes were wide. He kept glancing worriedly ahead towards von Mappus and Holbeck. 'A *gangster* Jew?'

'He was a good boss. He paid well.'

'They always have money,' Moos said, confirming the well-drilled prejudice.

'I had a good partner too,' Hubertus went on. 'We worked very well together. He saved my life once.'

'Another Jew?'

'No. That one was a black.'

Moos was even more horrified. 'A *nigger*?'

'You would not have used that word in his presence and lived one second longer. Someone made that mistake. Shot him dead almost before the word was out of his mouth. Very, very good with a gun. Together, we put many people to sleep.'

'The French had n— black soldiers in the last war. They

put them in the Fatherland as occupation troops. Savages. Barbarians. Uncivilized. So the Party says.'

Hubertus made a grunting sound of derision. 'And *we* are civilized? Recognize yourself, Johann. The world is not the way you have been taught to believe.'

'So you like Jews and n— blacks.'

'I don't like them . . . I don't hate them. I respect those I worked with. My boss and my partner never called me Heini . . . which many others did. *They* were all white, and not a Jew among them.'

'Grootemans,' Moos said in a manner that sounded almost like a plea. 'You're an Afrikaner. You know what the Africans are like. You agree with the Party and the Führer . . . or you would not be here.'

Grootemans made no comment.

'What you have seen since the time you've been in this hell-on-earth, Johann,' Hubertus said, 'should make you think a little.'

'I still believe . . .'

'The lieutenant is looking back,' Grootemans warned suddenly, in a sharp whisper.

Hubertus and Moos immediately ended their conversation.

Von Mappus had stopped, and was waiting for everyone to catch up.

'Five minutes,' he said. 'Then we move on.' He glanced at Holbeck. 'No village as yet, *Scharführer*. I don't believe there *is* one. It's a *Bolshevik* trick. They sent the girl to confuse us, and to pinpoint our position. I am not mad enough to believe a child simply wanders out here in this wilderness, all by herself. A *well-fed, well-clothed* child at that. We should get out of this trap of a ravine and head in another direction, before they find us.'

'Yes, sir,' Holbeck said.

Von Mappus fixed him with a look of deep suspicion. '*Yes*, sir? You're *agreeing* with me?'

The other four looked on with sharp interest.

'I've been considering that very possibility for some time, sir.'

If anything, von Mappus became even more suspicious.

73

'I have learned in the short time since taking command, *Scharführer*, that in the unlikely event of your agreeing to anything I say, I should immediately be on my guard. What are you up to?'

'Absolutely nothing, sir. I await your orders.'

For long seconds, von Mappus stared at Holbeck.

'Five minutes are up,' he said to the others, eyes still on Holbeck. 'Let's move!'

He turned and set off, again in the lead, making no attempt to leave the bed of the stream.

'Nice try, Sarge,' Hubertus said under his breath.

'What was that?' Grootemans whispered, as they trailed behind.

'The sergeant is trying to take us away from the village. He wants to save it.'

'You really believe there is one?'

'You saw the major. You saw the little girl. What do you think they were? Apparitions?'

'Perhaps. We could have imagined it . . .'

'*All* of us? Mass hallucination . . . as our sergeant the teacher would say?'

'Perhaps,' Grootemans said. 'Perhaps we're already dead. We're starving, we're cold, and we've got a madman leading us to nowhere . . .'

'Are you talking about the Führer? Or Himmler's darling up ahead? Anyway, ghosts don't bleed, and they don't wriggle like little snakes when you dangle them.'

Grootemans said nothing further.

Müller picked up the phone at the first ring.

'You've got something for me, Pappi?'

'Sorry to kill the spark of hope, but nothing as yet from Rügen.'

'Damn . . .'

'But the goth has found something interesting on the computer.'

'She's still in there?'

'Still there and doing excellent work. I think you should take a look at what she's found.'

'On my way. You?'

'Wouldn't miss it.'

Hedi Meyer swivelled her chair round as Müller and Pappenheim entered.

'This is true dedication, Miss Meyer,' Müller began as he approached.

'I've been enjoying myself,' she said. 'As I said before, sir . . . this is a great machine. Gigs of hard-disk space, and gigs of memory. And I've optimized both . . . so it's even better now. If it had feet and could run, it would burn the ground. Wish I had one like that at home.' She added in a wistful voice as she studied them. 'How computer literate are you, sirs?'

'I press a key,' Müller said, 'and it works. That's the sum of my knowledge.'

'And mine,' Pappenheim added.

She smiled. 'I think it's a lot more than that, but I'll let you humour me. I was doing my tweaking,' she went on, 'when one of my programs found something that shouldn't be there.'

'Which was?' Müller enquired.

She turned back to the machine, and tapped the enter key. 'This.' A page full of strings of code, bright red, and within a yellow border, blinked into view. 'I put it within that border,' she explained. 'It's quarantined.'

'A virus?' Müller asked.

She shook her head. 'Something much more subtle, well hidden, activating only when it's been called.'

'If not a virus,' Pappenheim said, 'what is it? And how did it get here?'

'The minidisc brought it,' she told them, answering the last question.

Müller stared at her. '*The* minidisc from which you copied that information to the CD?'

'Yes, sir.'

Müller glanced at Pappenheim, then said to Hedi Meyer, 'Are you quite certain?'

'Positive. It came from the minidisc. It's now on the CD, and it migrated to the computer when we first ran the disc.

It would have remained hidden when activated, and worked invisibly. If I hadn't run my search program, we would never have found it.'

Müller looked alarmed, thinking of all the highly sensitive data on the machine.

Knowing exactly what he was thinking, she said, 'I've isolated it. It's as if it's in a room of solid steel, with no exit. The machine is clean.' She gave him another quick smile. 'I'll stake my neck on it.'

'Then the two of us may well go down together. So what is it?'

'A beacon.'

'A *what*?' Müller and Pappenheim said together.

'What's that in illiterate-speak?' Müller added.

'Whenever this machine goes on the net, this thing on the screen sends a signal to whoever is waiting out there. That person can then use the signal to zap straight back to the source, and break into the system . . .'

'And then empty it.'

'If that's what he, or she, wants. Although whoever it is would not succeed. I've put my own firewall into the system. It's a fortress.'

'The tone of your voice is saying something else,' Müller said. 'You don't believe that's what this person is after.'

'At the moment . . . no, sir. The code we're looking at does not have that capability. Right now, it's just a basic carrier pigeon. No more. It does not have a mutation command, either.'

'But it could be given one when activated.'

'Easily. I could do that myself.'

'Resist the temptation.'

'Yes, sir,' she said with a straight face. 'But to put your mind at rest, I honestly feel this is intended to be just a simple beacon.'

'Why would someone who has no intention of raiding our files place a ghost beacon in the system?'

'To send us more information?' she suggested. Both men looked at her for long moments, as she continued, 'It's like the service you get with some email programs that lets you know when people with whom you frequently communicate are online, so that you can chat with them . . .'

'Or like the junk mail that finds its way to your mailbox.'

'In a way. But it's much more sophisticated, is one-way only, and target specific; but essentially . . . yes, it's the same kind of thing. Shall I kill it?' she added to Müller. 'One press of delete and it's snuffed for good.'

'Definitely no remnants hiding away in the system?'

'Definitely. All of it is in that yellow box. It can't get out unless I release it.'

'Can you modify it while it's in there?' Müller was peering thoughtfully at the screen.

'No problem.' She looked at him, a query in her eyes as she waited for him to continue.

'Can you modify it in such a way that it will only continue to obey a command to receive information, reject any executable order . . . ?'

'I'm following your thought. Can I say something?'

'Go ahead.'

'I can do that easily; and I can also make it commit suicide if it receives a command to either raid the system, or try to infect it in any way. I can ensure it has a single function that cannot be altered: to operate solely as a receiving station, in isolation. It will be in a world all by itself, and we can milk it at any time we like, if it does receive any information.'

Müller looked at her in wonder. 'Miss Meyer, you could make yourself a fortune on the open market.'

'I know,' she said with unnerving certainty. 'One other thing . . . my intuition tells me that whoever put this in there expected us to manipulate it.'

'Intuition,' Müller repeated.

'Intuition. It is not a simple code,' she went on, 'but it's not a very difficult one, either.'

Pappenheim stared at the screen. 'You could have fooled me.'

'Oh, it's not really that difficult,' she said as she turned again to the computer.

Pappenheim briefly raised an eyebrow at Müller.

'Whoever it is,' she went on, 'left some clues . . . almost like a test . . . This person has respect for you, sir.'

'Should I be flattered?'

'You should. The level of the programming shows it. He, or she, assumes you'll know what to do.'

'Not if I'd been the one trying to unravel it.'

'Perhaps. But this person expects you to have someone . . .'

'Like you.'

'Like me,' Hedi Meyer said. It was not a boast. 'Well, sir? Do I do it? Or do I kill it?'

'Don't kill it,' Müller said. 'At least, not yet.' He glanced at one of the floor-to-ceiling cabinets next to the computer station. 'In there is a disk-to-disk back-up storage system. Back up all data and files, and store them there. Then wipe them off the hard disk. Leave only what is necessary to ensure that the machine continues to run as normal. Then turn the beacon loose.'

Hedi Meyer nodded. 'Yes, sir.'

Müller went over to the cabinet and tapped at its keypad. The lower double doors hissed open. Inside was a gleaming black storage unit, with vertical rows of disk trays.

'This one has plenty of storage,' he continued, turning back to her. 'Much more than you're likely to need. When you're finished, just push the doors shut. Like the door to this room, the cabinet will lock itself.'

'Yes, sir,' she repeated, staring at the gleaming storage unit. 'It looks like an alien monster.'

'If that's what they look like,' Pappenheim said, straight-faced.

In the corridor on the way back to their offices, Pappenheim said, 'What's that on the back of your neck?'

Instinctively, Müller passed a hand along his neck. 'What do you mean? Where?'

'The sudden chill of its exposure. I can see it now. The Great White pops into the room – assuming he finds the time to do so – to look up some sensitive material. He turns on the computer. Oh dear. No files. Nothing. I wonder what he would do. *Müller!*' Pappenheim bellowed suddenly.

Doors along the corridor flew open. Expectant faces looked out. When they saw Pappenheim and Müller, they grinned sheepishly.

Pappenheim paused to look about him as Müller kept on walking, trying to hide a smile.

'Just seeing if you were all awake,' Pappenheim said to them. 'You all look as if you're expecting some excitement. Go back to bed.'

He hurried to catch up with Müller as the doors began to close.

'Thanks, Pappi,' Müller said.

'Don't mention it. Of course, it may never happen. The GW would never go there himself. He's so, so busy, you see.' Pappenheim paused. 'Do you believe that beacon is from Grogan?'

Müller nodded. 'If he intends to maintain contact, it's as safe a way as any . . .'

'Assuming someone else hasn't doctored the disc, so as to keep tabs on *him.*'

'There is that possibility.'

'Now that would be most interesting.' Pappenheim came to a halt. 'Oh. What do you know? It's my office. I've found it.'

Müller moved on, smiling to himself. 'Anything on Rügen comes in . . .'

'You'll be the second to know.'

Von Mappus had called another halt. They had come to another bend.

This time, it curved so sharply to the right, there was no immediate view beyond it, even up close. They stayed low, all pressing themselves tightly against the steep sides of the ravine.

Snow was still falling, but much lighter now.

Von Mappus looked at Holbeck. 'Check it out, *Scharführer*,' he ordered in a sharp whisper.

Without even a word of acknowledgement, Holbeck moved forward to cautiously work his way towards the bend. This time, no one volunteered to accompany him. They well knew what the response from von Mappus would be.

Holbeck paused, listening for a few seconds, then with a perceptible intake of breath slowly moved round the corner, and out of sight of the little group.

A long straight greeted his eyes. There was no one in sight.

He carefully studied the ground within his immediate proximity, and into the middle distance. The lightly falling snow had done so in sufficient quantity to obliterate the girl's tracks.

Holbeck moved slowly on, weapon ready, carefully scanning the terrain about him. The only sounds were those of the still abating snowstorm, his own muted breathing, and the soft crunch of his footsteps.

He had covered about a hundred metres, when something a short distance away to his left made him come to an abrupt halt.

The snow had not yet fully covered the tracks that went from the bed of the stream, in a series of hairpins up the slope.

He lowered himself to one knee and waited, unmoving, for long moments, straining his ears to listen. But nothing untoward intruded.

Even more cautiously now, he moved forward until he reached where the tracks began. The depressions were being rapidly filled by the snow, but their definition was still sufficiently clear.

He looked up the slope and, after a moment, began to follow the trail. At the rim, he lay flat and slowly peered over. Even here the tracks, joined by others, were still clearly discernible.

'*Horses?*' he whispered to himself, astonished. 'Jesus.'

He crawled the rest of the way until he was lying flat near the point where the footprints merged with those of the hooves.

'Was that bastard right, after all?' he asked himself. 'Did a patrol pick her up?'

Holbeck looked about him, scanning as best he could, in all directions. Despite the greatly decreased violence of the snowstorm, the lateness of the day meant that visibility was no better than when they had first entered the bed of the stream. Soon, the real darkness would enshroud everything.

'We should stop for the night,' he muttered, 'whatever that idiot thinks. We could blunder into a patrol if we move on.'

He began to inch his way back down the slope.

Von Mappus was looking irritable.

'Where's that sergeant got to?' he demanded of no one in particular.

'The *Scharführer*, sir?' Hubertus remarked with subtle emphasis. 'He'll be back. Don't you worry.'

Von Mappus glared at him. 'Are you being funny?'

'Nothing to be funny about out here, sir.'

Nagel, who had surreptitiously manoeuvred himself so that he could peer round the bend, suddenly whispered, 'He's coming! He's alright!' He grinned at them all.

Hubertus shot a quick glance at von Mappus. For the briefest slice of time, the lieutenant's expression betrayed disappointment. Then it vanished.

Nagel inched his way back as Holbeck returned.

'Well?' von Mappus snapped at him.

Holbeck ignored the ill-mannered greeting. 'I suggest we remain here for the night, sir, and set up firing positions . . .'

'*You* suggest?'

'I'm doing my job as a sergeant, sir,' Holbeck responded patiently, and with the correct amount of deference. 'Giving the officer in command the benefit of my counsel. It is up to the officer to accept, or to refuse it.'

Von Mappus sensed a trap where there was none, and took avoiding action. 'Why do you think we should remain here?'

'I saw some tracks. Too many to have been the girl's alone. There were also horses.'

Low gasps came from the others, while von Mappus stared at him.

'*Horses?*' von Mappus snapped. 'So I was right! That little *Bolshevik* was a decoy!'

'Not necessarily, sir.'

Von Mappus's eyes were dark sockets in his face. 'Are you insane, *Scharführer*? *Not* necessarily?'

81

'There were just two horses, sir.'

'Two horses are two too many, *Scharführer!*'

Holbeck continued to remain calm. 'The riders could have been two of our own people . . .'

Von Mappus bared his teeth. 'I thought we'd eaten all our horses. Those were *Bolsheviks* on those horses, *Scharführer*. They picked up the girl, now that she's pinpointed us. Subhuman barbarians! Using a child to distract us while they set up their ambush.'

Holbeck remembered the White Rose leaflet. 'One person's subhuman is another's—'

'Don't feed me any of your intellectual nonsense, teacher!' von Mappus snarled in contempt. 'I have no patience with such mind rot! It was not my idea that she was set free!' He glared at the others. 'Get ready to move!'

'I would advise against it, sir,' Holbeck insisted. 'It will be dark very soon. If you are right, we could blunder into a patrol . . . or the ambush. We lose nothing by being cautious. We've got this far. We stand a good chance of making it to one of our units.'

They all waited for the explosion as von Mappus fixed Holbeck with his baleful stare, lips tight, breath coming rapidly. This lasted for tense seconds, while von Mappus fought with himself and the logic of Holbeck's suggestion.

'And what is your . . . "suggestion", *Scharführer*?' von Mappus finally demanded.

The others allowed themselves quiet sighs of relief.

'We rig snow shelters, making them as unobtrusive as possible. Nagel and Moos set up the machine gun beyond the bend, but not too far from it, in case they need to withdraw quickly. The ravine is completely straight for several hundred metres, giving an excellent field of fire. Anyone coming that way will be in a funnel. Hubertus and Grootemans will cover the rear. You and I, sir, take the apex of the bend, one to each side. We will each be able to see both the forward fire team, and the rear. There are natural ledges on either side of the apex, allowing some cover, while still giving us a clear field of fire up the opposite sides, should we require it.'

More long seconds followed as von Mappus, clearly reluctant to take Holbeck's advice, debated within himself. He glanced up at the darkening sky, then at the men.

'You heard the *Scharführer*,' he said with ill grace. 'Get to it.'

As they began to move, Holbeck said, 'Just a minute. Nagel and Moos,' he continued when they had paused, 'how many signal flares have you got?'

'I've got three,' Nagel replied.

'And I, two,' Moos added.

'You shouldn't need more,' Holbeck told them. 'If you see or hear the Ivans, fire a flare – not into the air, but directly *at* them. While they're trying to avoid it, they won't be firing at you. You'll have light, and plenty of time to stop them. Don't let them get close, if you possibly can. Remember, they like to use knives.'

Nagel grinned, and patted his machine gun. 'I'll give them a hot welcome.'

'See that you do. One man catches some sleep, while the other keeps watch. When you feel drowsy, *don't* try to stay awake, or you will both be in dreamland when Ivan comes knocking. Instead, you wake the other man as soon as you begin to feel you're going to nod off . . . and he does the same when it's his turn. That way, you can alternate and, if we're lucky, no Ivans will disturb us tonight. The sound of gunfire will travel. It would be better if we had a quiet time of it. Now off you go. Make your snowhole a good one, and do so as quietly as possible. One other thing . . . have something to eat. But be sparing. Don't wipe out your stocks.'

They nodded, and set off.

Holbeck turned to Hubertus and Grootemans. 'How many flares?'

'Enough,' Hubertus replied.

'Alright. Same procedure, but you two take up positions on either side of the ravine.'

'Okay, Sarge . . . er *Scharführer*.'

'Alright.'

As they went to take up positions, Holbeck turned to von Mappus. 'Was that satisfactory, sir?'

Von Mappus stared unblinkingly at Holbeck, then nodded. 'You won't need to wake me, *Scharführer*. I won't fall asleep.' Without another word, he went off to prepare his position at the apex of the bend.

'Yes, sir,' Holbeck muttered to himself.

No one would remember afterwards exactly when it happened.

Sometime during the night, the snowstorm died completely. The sky became clear. The starlight was so bright, it reflected off the snow to give more than enough illumination, which enabled them to see each other perfectly. At the forward position, Nagel and Moos had a well-defined field of fire that stretched far ahead, before gradually becoming opaque with distance.

Moos was on watch, while Nagel dozed. They had constructed their snowhole so well, and had camouflaged themselves and their weapons so effectively, their position was detectable only when seen at close quarters.

Moos chewed on a scrap of cold meat he had taken off a dead soldier. Under normal circumstances, he would have spat it out in disgust. Under current conditions, it tasted like the best meal in a five-star restaurant. It was probably rat meat, he thought.

Then he paused, and softly touched Nagel on the shoulder. Nagel came awake in an instant.

'I heard something!' Moos whispered.

Nagel did not waste time querying what Moos had said. If Moos said he heard something, then that something was out there.

'Should I warn the others?'

Nagel gave the gun a gentle pat. 'My Lili will give them all the warning they'll need, when she starts to take bites out of Ivans.' He checked the gun swiftly, but unnecessarily, ensuring it was ready for action.

Ever since he had first experienced the Russian winter, Nagel had taken a harsh lesson to heart: the cold metal of the MG34 and bare hands made for an extremely painful experience that could kill. Many gunners had died with their hands frozen to their weapons because they could not properly operate them with mittens. Nagel had solved his own problem by binding his hands – fingers individually and mummy-like – with strips of cloth. To protect them when the gun was not in use, he shoved them into mittens that were slightly too large, courtesy of a dead Russian soldier.

'That gun has never jammed on you yet,' Moos now whispered, staring into the distance, looking for the first signs of movement.

'That's because I look after it. Remember what Hube said about what happened to him in America . . .'

'*Something!*' Moos hissed. 'Movement!'

'I don't see anything yet, but I'm ready. Got the flare?'

'Got it.'

Like a surgeon making ready for an operation, Nagel slowly removed his mittens. 'OK. Let them get close enough.' Seconds went by, then he added, 'You're a bat, Johann. You've got that new thing they call radar. Ah . . . wait . . . I can hear something . . . I think.'

A fluttering whisper on the night came very faintly to them, then died abruptly.

'Those were voices!' Moos said in a whisper so low, it was a breath.

Nagel was not so certain. 'I . . .'

'*Look!*'

On the edge of the far darkness, a shape had appeared; vague and indistinct, but definitely human.

'Alright, Johann . . . let's get ready to welcome some Ivans.'

Nagel and Moos waited as first two, then four, then eight figures, recognizable now as Russian soldiers, came towards them at an easy pace. They did not look like people carrying out an attack. In fact, they seemed to be strolling along the ravine.

'A trick?' Moos whispered.

'They could be on their way to visit their babushkas, for all I care. They're walking into Lili's mouth and she's going to feed on them. They're in the wrong place, at the wrong time. Get ready. Won't be long now.'

'They still haven't spotted us!' Moos was amazed, and thankful.

The Russians were almost relaxed; not talking now, but not seeming to expect trouble, either. They were now well under 400 metres away. For a gun with a maximum effective reach of 2,000 metres, a muzzle velocity of 755 metres per second, and a firing rate of between 800 and 900 rounds per minute, this was slaughter range.

Nagel made a final check that the gun's bipod was steady. 'Close enough,' he grunted. 'Fire the flare.'

Moos did not hesitate. The flare popped away, a fierce burst of light that shot towards the approaching soldiers in a shallow arc.

Their sudden yells of alarm coincided with their desperate attempts to find cover. It was far too late. Pinned in the glare like butterflies on display, they were easy targets for Nagel's terrible and merciless gun.

The MG34 chewed the night with its hellish stutter. Nagel was a machine-gunner of frightening skill; and he proved it. The tracers darted across the starlit snowscape, seeking out each Russian soldier and disappearing into his body, then tearing at him. The carnage was as savage as it was swift. Within mere seconds, it seemed, eight bodies were lying in grotesque postures of death.

'And I didn't even have to change barrels,' Nagel said. 'This was just breakfast for Lili.'

At the other positions, no one moved. They listened to Nagel's gun, and scanned their own fields of fire to see if more enemy soldiers would come at them.

Von Mappus looked across at Holbeck. 'And what was that, *Scharführer*?' he hissed with vitriolic sarcasm in the sudden quiet brought on by the abrupt end of the firing. 'Ghosts? No Ivans out here?'

'Did you notice anything else, sir?'

'What are you talking about?'

'No answering fire.'

'Of course not! Nagel was too quick for them!'

'I don't think it was an attack.'

'Are you mad? You don't think—'

A sudden screaming interrupted them. One of the Russian soldiers was not yet dead. His screaming was an obscenity that scarred the night in the unearthly beauty of the starlit snowscape. It was thin and piteous, yet seemed able to reach far into the distance.

'What is he saying?' von Mappus demanded.

'He's crying for his mother.'

Von Mappus was quite unmoved. '*She* won't help him. Not feeling sorry for that barbarian, are you, *Scharführer*?' he goaded. 'You are Waffen SS, not a nursemaid. People get killed in war.'

'Yes, sir,' Holbeck said, thinking of the thousands of German bodies already littering the Stalingrad landscape, and, remembering the caustic words in the White Rose leaflet, added, 'and all for the hubris of a subhuman.'

'Stalin has only got himself to blame,' von Mappus said, completely misunderstanding.

The screaming continued.

'Someone should put that man out of his misery,' Holbeck said.

'*No* one leaves his position! It's a trap. You should know that. It's one of the oldest tricks in the book.'

'That's usually when they try to make us believe it's one of our own men, sir.'

'I said . . . *no one leaves his post*! Let the savage scream himself to death!'

The mortally wounded soldier kept on screaming.

Holbeck tried again. 'The steepness of the ravine may have cut down the noise of the firing, which was just a short burst. But that screaming could bring any Ivans that may be around . . .'

'I said *no*, *Scharführer*! Don't make me repeat it again. If more Bolsheviks come, they'll receive the same medicine!'

After what seemed like hours of screaming the Russian soldier, mercifully and finally, died.

Nothing further disturbed the rest of the night; but neither von Mappus nor Holbeck fell asleep.

In the morning, Holbeck watched neutrally as von Mappus

took a small tin out a pocket in his battle smock, opened it, removed a glove to rub a finger against what was inside. Von Mappus then rubbed the finger against his chin in a spreading motion. He fastidiously wiped the finger with the end of his scarf and put the glove back on. He then carefully closed the tin, replaced it, took his cut-throat razor out of another pocket, opened it with near ceremony, and began to shave his barely existent growth of facial hair.

Wanting to smile in derision, Holbeck decided to turn his attention elsewhere.

'I'm going to check on Nagel and Moos, sir,' he said to von Mappus.

The *Obersturmführer* nodded.

Don't cut your throat, Holbeck thought, hoping the hand would slip.

'Quiet night in the end,' he said to Nagel and Moos when he got to them. 'After your little party. How many?'

'There are eight Ivans lying out there,' Nagel replied. 'I wanted to go out and put that screamer out of his misery.'

'So did I, but our lord and master refused.'

'Where do you think they came from, Sarge?' Moos asked. 'Part of a bigger unit that's out there?'

Holbeck shook his head. 'I don't think so. That screaming would have brought them running. Cover me. I'm going to have a look.'

'Don't get shot.'

'That's a good one, Nagel,' Holbeck said as he went past them, weapon ready for use.

He made his way along the bed of the stream, every so often checking out the tops of the inclines. It felt good to know that Nagel would respond with devastating fire, should any of the enemy put in an appearance. In the event, he reached the sprawled bodies without incident.

They were not pretty to look at. Nagel's Lili had chewed into them, leaving them as frozen, grotesque puppets. Holbeck found the one he thought had been the screamer. Little more than a boy, his hands were clasped about his middle. He had been desperately trying to contain what had been left of his stomach.

Despite all he had witnessed and experienced in this hell on earth, Holbeck felt a surge of pity for the dead boy.

'This is what we have been reduced to,' he muttered.

The soldiers, all in winter camouflage, had been lightly armed. Not even a sub-machine gun among them. Rifles, a few grenades, and two with binoculars, the straps loosely about their necks. The ones with the binoculars – one of whom wore the sleeve stars of a political commissar – wore pistols. That was all. The rifles were still on each body, attached by their slings. None wore helmets. Instead, each wore the all-ranks *ushanka* – the winter fur cap – with the low-visibility, olive drab star.

One of the bodies was face-down in the snow. Holbeck stared at the gun that lay across its back. A scope was mounted upon it. Mosin–Nagant. *Sniper weapon.*

Gut instinct made him check the others, including those pinned beneath the other bodies. *There were six in all, each one a be-scoped Mosin–Nagant.*

Then he noticed that one of the soldiers looked much older than the others. Save for the commissar, there were no other indications of rank on any of the bodies. An instructor, perhaps? Of *trainee* snipers? And had they been so far out of the battle area because they were on a field exercise? If so, their instructor had been careless.

Holbeck began to search the bodies for documentation that might yield some clue to their identity. They were unique in that there was none; not a single item that would identify either themselves, or their unit. Even their rifles had no markings.

A secret unit? As he began to search the bodies for food, Holbeck wondered what von Mappus would make of this.

The Russians had been travelling lightly, but even the most basic of rations for eight well-fed men would be a banquet for six on the edge of starvation.

He gathered all he could find, and hurried back.

'Food,' he said to Nagel and Moos when he reached their position. He gave them some. 'Better than anything we've got at the moment.'

They eagerly took the food.

Moos stared at it wonderingly. 'This is good bread! Not stale. Is that an *apple* you've got there, Sarge? An *apple*! Where would they get apples from?'

'Who knows?' Holbeck replied. 'One of them was a political commissar. *He* had the apple. Maybe he knew people in high places.'

'A commissar!' Nagel said. 'The lieutenant will wish *he* had killed him.' Nagel said this with great satisfaction, then added a plea. 'Tell him what I killed, Sarge.'

'I will,' Holbeck promised. 'You two deserve the apple.' He tossed it at them.

Nagel caught it with a swift right hand. 'Thanks, teacher.'

Holbeck gave a tired smile. 'If only.'

When he got back to his position, Holbeck found that von Mappus had finished shaving.

Von Mappus stared at the food. 'Where did you get that?'

'The Ivans, sir. There are eight dead ones out there. They take from us. We take from them. I gave some to Nagel and Moos.'

Von Mappus curled his lip. '*Bolshevik* food.'

'We won't get German supplies out here, sir,' Holbeck said with a neutral correctness that hid his true thoughts. 'And even if we could, from past experience, those aircraft that did make it would either drop them behind Ivan's lines, or out in the open where the enemy would practise his shooting skills on our men, fighting each other to get at the drops. And if our men survived that, they'd be lucky to find any food in those packages.'

Von Mappus stared coldly at Holbeck. 'Are you criticizing the Führer's ability to conduct this war, *Scharführer*?'

'No, sir. I am only talking about what I have seen with my own eyes.'

Von Mappus thought about that for a second, then said, 'Let us see your dead Bolsheviks.' He immediately moved away, without waiting for Holbeck to follow.

Holbeck hurried to the rear position where Hubertus and Grootemans waited. 'Food from the Ivans,' he said to them. 'They have no more use for it.'

Hubertus looked up. 'I'll take a food parcel even from the devil himself,' he said with a hard grin. 'Better than trying to dig up a potato from frozen ground. So what happened last night, Sarge?'

'Eight Ivans who chose the wrong place to go for a stroll. Nagel and Moos got them. I'll tell you about it later. Don't eat all of the food. My share is in there. I've got to go with the lieutenant.'

'Poor you . . .'

'*Scharführer!*'

'The master calls,' Holbeck said, and hurried back.

He caught up with von Mappus, who was just passing the forward position.

'I don't like to be kept waiting, *Scharführer!*' von Mappus began.

'Sorry, sir,' Holbeck apologized.

Nagel and Moos looked straight ahead as von Mappus and Holbeck walked past at a brisk pace.

When they reached the bodies, von Mappus stared at the rifles. 'Why didn't you tell me they were snipers?'

'I was in the process of giving you my report, sir,' Holbeck reminded him.

Von Mappus snapped his head round. 'You are very clever with your words, *Scharführer*, but one day . . .'

He stopped, and returned his attention to the bodies. He began to slowly prod at each one with a boot.

'This one's a commissar!' he exclaimed with excitement. 'Why didn't you . . .' He paused again, remembering. 'Yes, yes . . . you were in the middle of your report.' He began to vent his frustration on the body of the commissar, kicking at it in a frenzy of hate, almost punctuating each blow with every word. '*Dirty . . . plague boil . . . of humanity . . . Jew . . . Bolshevik . . . commissar!*' Then for good measure, face savagely demonic, he drew his pistol and shot the body six times.

'He's already dead, sir,' Holbeck said. 'And the sound of the firing might bring . . .'

Von Mappus whirled on him, pistol swinging to a new target. '*Holbeck!*' he snarled. '*You're trying me!*'

91

Holbeck looked down at the pistol, unmoved. 'You're going to shoot me . . . again . . . sir?'

Von Mappus glared at him, then, in a sudden thought, turned to look back at where Nagel and Moos were positioned. The MG34 seemed to be unmistakeably pointing in his direction.

Lips pulled back in a grimace that was reminiscent of a wolf at bay, he stood there for long moments, before returning the pistol to its holster with undisguised reluctance. Then the grimace vanished, as if it had never been.

'Snipers,' he said, still looking at the machine gun. 'Going ahead of the larger force. They're out there, just as I said before.'

'I think not, sir.'

'You think *not*?' von Mappus retorted, voice tight with the effort of suppressing his feelings. He continued to stare at the machine gun.

'I believe they were trainees, sir,' Holbeck insisted. 'They were travelling with far too little equipment to be an assault group. My guess is that they were on a field exercise. There are six rifles . . . five for the trainees, one for the older one to your left, the instructor. The commissar, and the eighth man, have just pistols and binoculars. I believe these two were observers, to assess the performance of the trainees.'

'Except for the commissar, they have no badges of rank.' Von Mappus still did not turn to look at Holbeck.

'No identification of any kind, either. I've searched each one. I'm very surprised the commissar wore his sleeve stars, especially considering the Führer's order to execute them all . . .'

'What do you expect of a Bolshevik Jew commissar?' von Mappus said with contempt. 'He wanted to show his non-existent superiority over the others.'

'I don't think so, sir . . .'

'You don't *think*. Do you ever think, *Scharführer*?' Von Mappus continued to be seemingly mesmerized by Nagel's MG34.

'All the time, sir.'

'Then let's hear what you *think* these dead barbarians were up to.'

'On a training exercise, as I've just said, sir. They were completely surprised to find us waiting. I believe they must have come into the area by some form of transport – horses, or a tracked vehicle – which they have left some kilometres away. We would have heard them otherwise – the horses, or the vehicle – especially now that the snowstorm is gone. They then did a cross-crountry, perhaps stopping to shoot en route, or to carry out tracking exercises. Their lack of identification could mean they were being trained for a special mission . . .'

'Well *I'll* tell you what *I* think, *Scharführer*,' von Mappus rudely interrupted. 'You are right. These were the members of a special unit, but *not* trainees. They had been ordered to infiltrate far behind our lines on a very special mission . . . the assassination of senior commanders. The fact that they have no identification speaks for itself. In case of death, or capture, their unit would be unknown. And we already know that these barbarians fight like gangsters, to the death.' He stared at the bodies. 'And we got them all!'

Holbeck made no comment as von Mappus took credit for the action.

'They may indeed have some form of transport hidden somewhere,' von Mappus continued, 'but their base, or headquarters unit, must be in the area. And we shall find and destroy it!' An obsessed gleam had come into his eyes.

He is seeing Iron Crosses, Holbeck thought.

'The rifles, sir,' he said aloud.

'What about them?'

'There are six. One for each of us. They would give us a long reach . . . if we find their headquarters unit.' Holbeck did not believe it, but felt it prudent to humour von Mappus. 'We are all good shots,' he went on, generously including the lieutenant, 'and Moos is close to being a sniper himself. The rifle is just under three point five kilos. It won't be a problem to carry. Once the ammunition is gone we can dispose of them . . .'

'No! As I've said before, *no* one under my command will in

93

future use Bolshevik equipment. We will destroy these rifles here . . .'

'May I ask how we do this quietly, sir?'

Von Mappus glared at the sergeant. 'We put all the rifles beneath the bodies, *Scharführer,* on a bed of their own grenades, with the pins removed. The bodies will be arranged so that the safety levers remain in place. Any Bolshevik who comes along and moves the bodies . . .' He paused. 'I don't think you need further details.'

Holbeck had a horror vision of the little girl returning and prying at the bodies in curiosity.

'What if the girl returns, sir, and curiosity gets the better of her?'

Von Mappus stared at him as if at a madman. *'We are at war, Scharführer!* And you, are Waffen SS! If the little Bolshevik returns and plays with the bodies, then that is her bad luck! And when we're finshed here, we will go after that unit she has undoubtedly warned. Now follow my orders!'

They arranged the booby trap, then set off along the ravine. They had been travelling for about five minutes, when a series of explosions echoed behind them.

'One of the bodies must have moved,' Hubertus said loudly.

Von Mappus gritted his teeth, but did not turn round.

Five

B erlin. Pappenheim looked at the recent pile of mail on his desk. He placed a cigarette between his lips, and took his time lighting up. He blew a smoke ring at the ceiling, squinted at the small mound of documents and reports, and in particular at the small package on top of the lot. It was addressed to Müller. There was no stamp on it.

'Hmm,' he said.

The package was about 12 by 18 centimetres, and just under 1.5 centimetres thick.

'Hmm,' he said again, continuing to study it and puffing at the cigarette; a sure sign of agitation. 'Are you a bomb . . . in more ways than one? You should have gone through the scanner, but I'm willing to bet you joined the pile *after* Frau Krottke had already put the others through.'

He unlocked a drawer in his desk, slid it open, picked up the package gingerly and just as carefully put it in, slid the drawer shut as if expecting the package to blow, then locked it once more.

'I'll attend to you later.' He began to check out the remainder. 'Paperwork, paperwork. The policeman's cross.' The phone rang, and he snatched at it with relief. 'Pappenheim.'

'Ah . . . Pappi . . .'

'Norbert!' Pappenheim exclaimed, recognizing the voice of Norbert Roth, the police *Kommissar* he knew on Rügen. 'News for me?'

'Nothing, I'm afraid. I don't know where you got your information from, but we have absolutely no indication of anything wrong up here; at least, not what you asked about.'

'And something I didn't ask about?'

'Well . . . we're heavily snowed under, and some fool – not from the island – was driving on summer tyres. Hit a tree.'

'Dead?'

'He's saying hello to his Maker.'

'How old?'

'Thirties.'

Pappenheim felt acute disappointment. 'Not my man.'

'Sorry, Pappi. Do you want us to keep at it?'

'Please. Something has definitely happened. But I can't tell you more, because I don't know any more myself. I can't even tell you where to look.'

'In that case, we've got a big white haystack to search for this particular needle. Right now, Rügen is a giant snowflake, nine hundred and twenty-five square kilometres big.'

'You might have some help coming.'

'Who?'

'My immediate boss.'

'The noble *Hauptkommissar* himself. We are honoured.'

'Don't let him hear you call him noble.'

They both laughed.

'And leave him be,' Pappenheim continued. 'He has his ways.'

'I get the message. We'll keep out of his hair.'

'Don't use the word hair, either.'

They laughed again.

'Anything strange comes up, Norbert . . .'

'I'll be on the phone as if my wife asked me to go shopping with her.'

'That slow?'

'That fast while I'm getting away.'

They laughed again, and hung up.

'Shit,' Pappenheim said.

Rügen was indeed like a giant snowflake, as Norbert Roth had unflatteringly described it. But he was being unfair. The island, under its covering of snow, was quite beautiful.

Even the house of death, keeping its gruesome secret from Roth, looked good enough to eat. The heavy snowfall had almost completely covered it so that it looked for all the world as if coated with a generous helping of icing. It was not the only one to look like that; but it was the only one which, when viewed from the direction of the approach drive, was spookily reminiscent of Monet's painting. There was no magpie, and no rickety gate; and the house was not at all like the one behind the hedge. Yet, the feeling was there.

In the open conservatory, the old man was now quite dead. Beneath the razor, still gripped in the dead hand, a pool of blood had collected. The snow had breached through the opened panel of the French windows, and had formed a low bank just at the entrance. The garden beyond was an expanse of virgin white.

The dead eyes of the old man seemed to reflect the whiteness outside, continuing to stare into a great distance.

'I feel as if my eyes are reflecting all this whiteness,' Johann Moos said.

Nagel glanced at him. 'What was that?'

Moos repeated his remark.

'I wouldn't worry about it,' Nagel said.

'Could be because it's so bright today.' Moos glanced anxiously up at the sky. 'Nice flying weather for the Ivans.'

'Ach. We're too far away from anything they want to hit.'

'How far do you think we've come since the captain died and the lieutenant took over?'

'If you count our cross-country in the snowstorm before we got to this ravine, I would guess we're about a hundred kilometres from where we started.'

Holbeck, who had been trailing von Mappus for some time, now moved back along the line and caught Nagel's reply.

'That was good reckoning, Walter,' he said with approval. 'The Romans could march up to twenty-five miles a day in full kit, and still have the energy to build a fortified camp by nightfall. That's over forty-one kilometres. Several centuries later, we have not improved on that so much. But allowing for this lovely landscape and our condition, a hundred kilometres is not so bad. We've probably done a little more than that.'

97

'But what about that kid? We haven't seen any village. Where could she have come from?'

'We could easily have missed it in the snowstorm.'

'But she said this ravine leads to it.'

'If we're going in the right direction.'

'So you think the lieutenant's right, and we're being led into a trap?'

Holbeck shook his head. 'I don't think so. Don't forget the ravine is the bed of a stream. Water does not continually flow in a straight line, but takes the course that suits it. There are many bends in this ravine, so a straight line across them will be a much shorter distance. If point A to point B in any section is twenty kilometres, the straight line could be just five, or less. It depends on the number, and size, of the bends within the section. The village, if it exists, could be quite close by now.'

'Anyone can tell you were a teacher, teacher,' Nagel said with one of his grins. 'Thank you, teacher, for the lesson.'

A sudden shout from von Mappus interrupted the banter and sent them all scurrying forward. Von Mappus had vanished beyond yet another bend and, weapons ready, they hurried after him.

And stopped, staring at what had caused him to shout.

Six poles were planted, some distance apart from each other, along a section of incline that was less steep. Upon each pole was tied a body in Waffen-SS uniform, without winter camouflage. The top of each pole matched the height of the summit of the incline. Two of the bodies had no heads. The others still had their helmets on, but at strange angles.

Holbeck studied the gruesome calvary without expression. 'The Waffen SS are trophies to be hunted,' he said, voice neutral. 'Our deeds go before us. We hunted them, now they hunt us.'

Von Mappus rounded upon him. 'Is that all you've got to say?'

'It's the truth.' Holbeck began to make his way up the incline.

Von Mappus turned to the others. 'This outrage will not go unpunished! The Bolsheviks must be made to pay!'

'We've done a lot worse,' Hubertus said, following Holbeck's progress with curious eyes.

Von Mappus looked as if he could not believe what he had just heard. 'Do you feel *nothing* for your comrades?'

'I think the sergeant . . . er . . . *Scharführer*'s found something, sir.'

Thwarted in his outrage, von Mappus instinctively turned to look.

Holbeck had positioned himself so that he was level with the shoulders of one of the bodies. Now he was peering closely at it.

'What is he *doing*?' von Mappus asked.

He was not expecting an answer, and received none.

Holbeck went to each of the bodies, which he scrutinized in a similar manner, then began to rapidly make his way back down.

'They were already dead when they were put up there,' he said to von Mappus. 'But they didn't walk here. Frozen. They couldn't have had winter clothing. They belonged to Major Gaegl's unit.'

'What were you looking at?'

'Bullet holes.'

'But you just said . . .'

'They weren't *killed* by those bullets, sir,' Holbeck said. There was no emotion in his voice. 'The cold did that. They were put up there as targets. For snipers, I believe. They are positioned in such a way that from a long distance, they would look like soldiers in snow holes, or trenches. Bullets have also punched through the helmets. What's inside is not pretty,' he continued. 'It was target practice . . . probably by the unit that ran into us. I can't be certain. There may well be another training team prowling around, or even out there getting ready for another round of practice shots. That's why I hurried down. We should get out of here.'

'And *leave* them like that?'

'They are *dead*, sir,' Holbeck responded flatly. 'The Ivans didn't kill them. Their own Führer did that.'

Von Mappus looked as if his eyes would pop. 'This is *sedition*! He is *our* Führer. *Your* Führer!'

'Yes, sir.' Holbeck began to walk away.

'*Stop!* I *order* you!'

Holbeck kept walking.

Von Mappus began to reach for his pistol.

'We need him,' Hubertus said quickly. 'Sir.'

Von Mappus turned round. The others were not looking at him with friendly eyes. He stared at them, and they stared right back; unwaveringly.

He jabbed a pointing arm at the bodies on the incline. 'Remember this when next you see a Bolshevik . . . of *any* kind! Remember it!'

He turned, and began to follow Holbeck, feet crunching the hard-packed snow in his anger.

'One day,' Nagel said as they stood for a while watching the lieutenant move away, 'we're going to have to shoot him.'

'Perhaps the Ivans will get him first,' Hubertus said in a heartfelt wish. 'Perhaps it will be one of those snipers the sarge says could be out there.'

They began to follow.

Some time later, Holbeck had again moved back to speak with Nagel. Moos was over to one side, frequently scanning the tops of the inclines with some anxiety.

'Keep an eye on Johann,' Holbeck said to Nagel in a low voice.

'What's wrong?'

'Ever since those bodies on the poles, he's withdrawn into himself. I've seen this happen before. It's not good.'

'What do you mean?'

'When the condition becomes acute, the person loses control; then two things can happen. He either loses the will to keep on fighting . . .'

'Or?'

'Or he turns into an out-of-control killer.'

'Oh come on, Sarge! Our *Johann*? He's . . .'

'Young, scared, indoctrinated and proud to be a Waffen-SS "Aryan", and shouldn't be here in the first place. None of us should be here.'

'Johann is not someone from one of those *Feldjäger* units that go hunting civilians.'

100

'But many of these units *are* Waffen SS. The Ivans are not going to make any distinction. To them, Waffen SS is Waffen SS, and Johann is well aware of that. Remember his remark about the Ivans tying Waffen-SS soldiers to the muzzles of tank guns? What we saw back there will resurrect the image in his mind. He is also worried about those Mosin–Nagants and their two-, maybe three-kilometre range in the right conditions. Just keep an eye on him. I don't trust von Mappus not to use what we saw back there for his own ends.'

Nagel nodded slowly. 'Alright, Sarge.'

But in one of the ironies of life that sometimes causes what one least desires to fall into one's lap, Holbeck spotted on that day something he wished he hadn't. Had he not paused to chat about Moos with Nagel, he might have missed it completely.

Striding ahead, von Mappus had walked obliviously by; as had Moos. There was the high probability that they would all have missed it; but Holbeck, turning his head after speaking with Nagel and getting ready to return to his position trailing the lieutenant, paused slightly as he spotted the narrow track that led to the left, off the ravine.

It was a snowed-in, dried-out watercourse that in normal spring weather either fed itself into the stream or was a run-off. It curved off at so acute an angle that it was virtually hidden from normal view. Instinct and hope made Holbeck continue to move past the intermittent tributary. It was unfortunate that at that very moment, von Mappus chose to turn round to check where his sergeant had got to.

He spotted the opening, and halted in his tracks. 'What is that?'

'What, sir?'

'*Behind* you, *Scharführer*! Are you blind?'

Reluctantly, Holbeck turned to look, certain in his mind that this was the way to the village.

Müller was studying the printout of the blue seal when the secure phone rang.

He picked it up immediately. 'Müller . . .'

'A meeting,' the arrogant voice said.

Müller said nothing.

'Are you still there?' the voice demanded.

'I'm waiting.'

'I don't like your tone.'

'And I hate yours. Now what?'

'At twenty hundred hours. Tonight.'

Müller remained silent.

'*Did you hear me?*' The voice was frustrated now, clearly annoyed that Müller was not jumping to its command.

'You're shouting. This is a clear, up-to-the-minute, high-tech telephone. There really is no need to shout.'

'You obviously prize yourself as a wit, Herr Graf. Don't try it on me.'

'I'm a busy man. I can't chat all day on the telephone to people I don't know. The clock is ticking to the time I'll hang up.'

Müller could almost hear teeth being gritted. 'The place where your lapdog was today . . .'

'I would not call him that in his presence. You will most definitely not enjoy his reaction.'

'*Twenty hundred hours!*' the voice barked. 'Be there!'

The line went dead.

Müller replaced the receiver, and looked across at Monet's magpie. 'What do you think?' he said to it. 'Should I go?'

Pappenheim had taken the package out of the drawer and was tentatively feeling it, when the direct phone to Müller warbled at him. His sense of guilt was such he almost dropped it. As he grabbed at it, the cigarette between his lips nearly slipped out. He put the package down, secured the cigarette, and picked up the phone, seemingly all at the same time.

'I'm here.' He sounded harassed.

'Are you alright, Pappi?'

'I'm fine. Why?'

'You sound strange.'

'Ah. I nearly dropped my cigarette.' He was able to cover the guilt he felt by sounding appropriately rueful.

'I won't say anything about smoking.'

'Don't. So? What's up?'

'Just got a call from your Silesian.'

'My Silesian.'

'The same. We've got a date. Tonight.'

'Aha!' Pappenheim drew on the cigarette, then extinguished it. 'Another fast move. Where?'

'Luigi's.'

'Am I invited?'

'He called you a lapdog.'

'Then I can't refuse such an invitation.'

'Didn't think you would.'

'How did he sound? My Silesian?'

'As if he expected me to click my heels and bark: *Jawohl, Herr General!* Or whatever rank he used to have in his good old days.'

'Good for some, but not for most of the country back then.'

'Quite. I won't ask about Rügen,' Müller added.

'That's one way of putting it.'

'Something must have happened,' Müller insisted. 'Or we would not have the Silesian to amuse us.'

'I got a call from Norbert Roth,' Pappenheim said. '*Kommissar* on Rügen. None of the seventy-six thousand inhabitants seem to be our man. He also made a point of saying they were snowed under, so getting around to check will take forever. He did report one death.'

'Ah!'

'Don't get excited. Traffic accident, not from the island, and wrong age. Thirties. Someone on summer tyres.'

'This really makes my day.'

'I only tell it like it is.' Pappenheim glanced at the package as he said that, then decided to take the plunge. 'There is something else, though,' he continued, praying the package was not from the mysterious writer of notes. But he had an idea. 'A package addressed to you was in my pile of stuff. Just your name. No stamp. I was about to bring it over. Shall I open it?'

'As long as it's not a letter bomb.'

'Already checked. No wires I can feel.'

'Are you sure you want to do this?'

103

'If you hear a bang, you'll know.'

'Alright,' Müller said after a short pause. 'Go ahead.'

'Here I go.'

With relief, Pappenheim placed the receiver in the crook of his neck and began to open the package, taking great care, while Müller remained on the phone. He had already decided that, should there be a note, he would not tell Müller about it.

He slowly opened up the wrapping, and again felt relief. There was no note; but what the wrapping revealed made him stare.

'Well, well,' he uttered softly.

'This century, Pappi.'

Pappenheim put the receiver back to his ear. 'A book.'

'A *book*?'

'Not a printed book. A diary. Old, slightly bloodstained, with a cut through it. A knife thrust, I would say. Possibly a bayonet. Vintage . . . Second World War . . . Just a minute. Let me get some gloves.'

Pappenheim put the phone down, opened another drawer and took out a pair of thin cotton gloves from the small stock he kept there. He put them on, then put the phone back in the crook of his neck.

'OK,' he continued, and began thumbing through the diary. 'Oh my God . . .'

'Don't keep it all to yourself.'

'The name of von Mappus appears several times . . .'

'Why are you still in your office?'

'I'm on my way.'

Müller was already on his feet when Pappenheim entered in a rush, the diary, still in its wrapper, held before him like a sacred offering. He placed it, with the kind of caution normally reserved for the handling of a newborn baby, on Müller's desk.

Müller looked at it as he would a rare creature, suddenly discovered. 'Von Mappus?'

'He may well have died by bayonet,' Pappenheim said, 'but perhaps not in this instance. The diary is not his.'

Müller gave Pappenheim a quick, sideways glance. He too got out a pair of gloves and, after quickly drawing them on, gently picked up the diary. He was careful to touch it in a way that prevented the incision – just off centre – from extending further. The thrust of the knife, or bayonet, had been so powerful, it had gone right through both covers. A rim of long-dried blood coloured the edges of both the entry and exit gash. He opened the cover, and studied the writing on the first page.

'"My name is Maximillian Holbeck,"' he read. '"I am not proud of myself. Once, I was a teacher, dedicated to the enlightenment of young minds. Now, I am a killer; a *Scharführer* in the Waffen SS. Enlightenment is gone, and in its place, the long shadow of a monstrous horror without end."'

That was all there was on the first page. Müller stopped reading, and quickly thumbed through the little book, pausing randomly to read a passage aloud.

'"We came as conquerors, some units arrogantly believing it would be a short fight; so they came in summer uniforms. The Russian winter has taught them a harsh lesson many will not live long enough to learn. They make perfect targets against the snow, for the snipers."'

'"Wolle, our captain, died today. The last good officer in what is left of our battalion is gone. Captain Wolfgang Dietrich left a wife and kids. There are just the six of us now, if you count von Mappus."'

Müller paused to look sharply at Pappenheim. 'That does not sound like a good recommendation from an experienced sergeant, about a man who's supposed to be a hero.'

'One man's hero,' Pappenheim said, 'can be another's monster.'

'True, but the tone of that line sounds more like an NCO not rating the officer much.'

Müller returned to his reading of the excerpts. 'My God, Pappi. Listen to this. "*Obersturmführer* von Mappus shot Major Gaegl in the back today, in front of us all. For some time now, I have been disturbed by the way the captain had died. I have had the uneasy feeling that von Mappus killed him during the Stalin organ barrage. Wolle and I had our heads down, so I saw nothing. I have no proof of this, but von Mappus was suddenly there when the barrage lifted, though he was nowhere in sight before. Again, I can prove nothing, but it is a feeling that won't go away. After what happened to Major Gaegl, this feeling is even stronger."'

Müller again looked up at Pappenheim, who was looking grim. 'Are you getting the picture?'

'A very ugly one.'

'We should both read this from cover to cover, Pappi, then put it with the disc from Grogan, where it will be safe. One last excerpt for now.'

Müller thumbed a few more pages, then stopped again. '"If only I had not spotted the run-off. It led to the village that was not on any map: on none of ours that I have seen, and on none that I know of, of those captured from the enemy. A haven of peace that seemed far, far from the war. To me, one of the worst tragedies in this terrible human tragedy is the change in Johann Moos. The youngest of us, he is much like the kids I used to teach. Despite being indoctrinated like so many into believing the monstrous lies, he was still an innocent abroad whom I had hoped would perhaps return home with some of his humanity intact, if he survived. Up to this moment, he had done nothing beyond fighting as a brave soldier. But a change came over him since he saw those bodies on the poles. Now I have watched him shooting those poor defenceless people and enoying it, all the time egged on by that murdering Silesian, von Mappus. May God forgive me. I led them here."'

Müller stopped reading, took a deep breath, then slowly let it out. He closed the diary with something approaching reverence.

'Are you having the same thoughts as I?'

'That our Silesian *is* the General von Mappus who's supposed to have died, laden with Iron Crosses, way back there at Stalingrad? Oh yes.'

'So who's the person on Rügen?'

'Ah. Now you've got me.' Pappenheim looked at the diary, then back at Müller. 'And whom do we have to thank for this little gem? Grogan?'

106

'If one considers the phone call, it would seem likely.'

'On the other hand . . . ?'

'On the other hand, it could have come from your intelligence contact with the blue-folder boys.'

But Pappenheim, thinking not about his contacts but about the note writer, was shaking his head. 'It would not have been addressed to you.'

Müller nodded. 'Which, for the moment, leaves us with Grogan as the most likely . . .'

'Or someone connected with him.'

'Or that.'

Pappenheim turned to look at Monet's magpie. 'One brings luck, after all.'

'For now.'

'Pessimist,' Pappenheim said.

About an hour later, Pappenheim received a call in his office. It was from Norbert Roth, on Rügen.

'Norbert! You've got news?'

'Not about your mysterious general, I'm afraid.'

Not so mysterious anymore, Pappenheim thought. 'Pity,' he said with convincing disappointment. 'But?'

'Something very strange. Doesn't seem connected with your case at all, but knowing how you like puzzles . . .'

'Norbert . . .'

Roth gave a short laugh. 'I know how you Berlin big shots like to show you're clever . . .'

'You're sailing close to the wind, Norbert.'

'I can take it.'

Pappenheim relaxed in his chair and grinned at the phone. 'Alright. Let's have the puzzle.'

'That accident I told you about . . .'

Pappenheim quickly sat upright. 'What about it?'

'The car was registered in Schwerin, but the number plate was on the wrong car. The owner of the plate, a petty criminal doing a nice line of business illegally selling cars to the eastern countries, never reported that it had been stolen . . .'

'What a surprise. When was it stolen?'

'Six months ago.'

'It gets better.'

'It gets a lot better. The driver has no documents.'

'*None?*'

'Not even a credit card. No cash, either. Does that make any sense to you?'

'False plates, false car, false driver. Nice. It makes *some* sense, although I'm not sure what kind. Norbert, send me a picture of this phantom driver as fast as you can, will you, please?'

'I thought you might get excited. OK. I'll have it done. Should we keep looking for that general?'

'Oh yes. It's even more important now.'

'I think I'll need a dog sled.'

'That was a good joke, Norbert. And Norbert . . .'

'Yes?'

'Thanks. I owe you one.'

'I'll frame those words in gold.'

'Don't push it.'

They laughed, and hung up together.

Müller had come to the end of Holbeck's diary.

'My God,' he remarked softly, looking up from the small book. His expression was one of shock, and revulsion.

The diary was still open at the last page. The index finger of his right hand moved along it, almost of its own volition; then suddenly, it stopped. The page felt thicker than it should.

Müller looked down, frowning, checking the thickness of the page between finger and thumb. He turned the page over. Something was stuck to it – a sheet of paper folded to fit – the dried blood the gruesome adhesive. Careful not to rip the paper, he began to work at freeing it.

'So that's where he put you,' he muttered. 'My God,' he repeated as at last it came free, and he opened it up. 'It really is one.'

It was the leaflet of the White Rose.

Then the direct phone to Pappenheim rang.

Müller picked it up. 'Yes, Pappi.'

'I've just heard from Rügen,' Pappenheim said, then went on to tell him about what Roth had reported.

'Related, do you think?' Müller asked when Pappenheim had finished.

'The driver could have been just an unlucky car thief . . .'

'But?'

'I'm keeping an open mind. Can't seem to stop those alarm bells from ringing.'

'Neither can I. More so, now that I've read Holbeck's diary right through. It's a chronicle of horror, about man's descent into barbarity. It is also dynamite. I'll say nothing further about it until you've read it yourself. And be careful when you get to the end. There's a leaflet between the last page and the back cover.'

'A *leaflet*?'

'Not just *a* leaflet. This one's an original White Rose.'

'*The* White Rose of the Scholls, Probst, and the others?'

'The very same.'

'A Waffen-SS soldier with such a leaflet? Was he suicidal?'

'It will all become clear when you have read the diary; and it will make your hair stand on end. He also had a camera. A Minox . . . with which he took the kind of pictures some people would not like to see made public, even today. Imagine how those of his time would have reacted.'

'I take it back. He was not suicidal. He had a death wish.'

'Which he may well have fulfilled, if the blood on the diary is his.'

'And someone may have that camera . . .'

'Assuming it's not lying where his bones are . . . wherever they may be.'

'We wouldn't know where to begin looking.'

'We certainly would not. But from what he's written down, the camera is an integral part of his chronicling.'

'You're not suggesting we go to Stalingrad?'

'Stalingrad has already come to us. All we may have to do is wait. I'll bring the diary over on my way out.'

'Where to?'

'I'm expecting Miss Bloomfield, as well you know, Pappi . . .'

'Me?' Pappenheim was innocence itself.

'You. It's a bit early for the airport, but I've a few things I want to prepare. I plan to go up to Rügen tomorrow.'

'It's Alaska up there. Your Porsche won't make it.'

'My Porsche will,' Müller said.

'You sound smug. Why are you smug?'

'Am I?'

'Alright. You win.'

'Wise,' Müller said.

Holbeck followed von Mappus along the narrow run-off, wishing he had gone on past the opening, without pausing to look. Like the main ravine, its sides were steep, but the course it described was much more meandering. The few straight sections were short. In heightened tension, the six of them made their way with great caution, weapons ready, moving in swift, silent rushes, scrupulously checking each bend before carrying on.

There was no talking. Holbeck motioned them on with hand signals. Even von Mappus seemed to wait for the sergeant to direct him, as if he had finally come to realize that the soldiers were a close-knit team that had survived fierce combat, over a long period.

But Holbeck was not fooled. He still did not trust von Mappus.

They made their way in this manner for two kilometres. It took time, but progress was secure. They encountered no enemy.

'I can't believe they're not out there,' Moos whispered to Nagel as they paused near a bend. 'They must be hiding, waiting for us to enter their trap.'

'The sergeant doesn't believe there is any trap. In a choice between him and the lieutenant, I believe him.'

'What about our people on those poles? You saw what the Ivans did.'

'They were already frozen to death when they found them, Johann.'

'Even so. To do that to them . . .'

'We do it to them, they do it to us. And they'll do it a lot worse before this is over.'

Moos said nothing further for some moments.

Nagel glanced at him, conscious of Holbeck's words of warning.

'Don't lose control, Johann,' Nagel advised. 'That's not a smart thing to do in combat. We've all come through so far because we've fought well together with the captain, and now Sergeant Holbeck, to lead us. We're the last of the originals from our unit. That didn't happen by accident. So stay in control. OK?'

'OK,' Moos said, after another long pause.

Nagel gave him a second, anxious glance, but said no more as they moved on, to continue along the narrow confines of the bed of the run-off.

Slightly ahead of them and once more trailing von Mappus, Holbeck struggled with his growing sense of unease. His gut told him something was about to go terribly wrong, and there would be nothing he would be able to do about it. He felt an enervating powerlessness in the face of this unrelenting inevitability.

Half an hour later, a straight opened up before them. It was the longest they had come across since entering the run-off. Its far end curved gently to the left.

'That bend up ahead will take us back the way we came,' Moos said to Nagel.

Nagel shook his head. 'You just think it will. It's all the corners we've turned. You've lost your sense of direction.'

'It's all the same whiteness,' Moos complained, looking intense.

'Relax, Johann. It's OK.'

Moos fell silent once more.

At that moment, Holbeck glanced back and caught an anxious look from Nagel. Holbeck glanced at Moos, then made a surreptitious sign to Nagel, indicating that he should continue to keep an eye on the young soldier.

Nagel responded with the slightest of nods.

They walked along the straight, turning continually to check their immediate surroundings, maintaining a constant

alertness as they progressed. They reached the bend, negotiated it safely, and discovered they had come upon another
long straight. This time, the end of the straight was also the
end of the run-off. It merged into a less steep incline that
rose all the way to higher ground.

Von Mappus called a halt.

'We're finally going to leave this rabbit warren of a trap,'
he said to them.

'I'd say it's kept us safe, sir,' Holbeck countered.

Von Mappus turned eyes full of poison upon the sergeant.
'You would. When we get closer to the far end,' he continued,
shifting his attention to the others, 'two men will move ahead
to check. That will be Moos, and Nagel.' He again looked at
Holbeck. 'Does that meet with your approval, *Scharführer*?'
The sarcasm was undisguised.

'If I may suggest, sir . . .'

'Rejected.' Von Mappus looked upwards, checking the
almost precipitous sides of the run-off. '*You* remain with the
rest of us, *Scharführer.*'

'Yes, sir,' Holbeck acknowledged tightly.

'Let's move on.'

Nagel and Moos went forward to take the lead and,
followed by the others, continued towards the end of the
run-off.

It was after half an hour of cautious progress that Moos
spotted a fleeting movement on high ground.

'I've seen something!' he said in a sharp whisper to Nagel
as he paused and briefly raised a hand to warn the others.

'Where?'

'Up top, to my left.'

Nagel looked. 'I don't see anything.'

'Of course you wouldn't! He's gone, now that he's spotted us.'

Von Mappus hurried forward. 'What's wrong?'

'I just saw something up to the left, sir,' Moos replied.

'Are you sure?'

'Positive,' Moos responded, no doubt in his mind whatsoever.

'Very well. You two move up to check. As you can see,

we're not far from the exit incline. Anything that moves and does not wear a German uniform, shoot it. Don't wait for further orders. You've just got them. Remember what we saw on those poles.'

'Yes, sir,' Moos and Nagel said together.

Nagel glanced back at Holbeck.

'Don't look to the *Scharführer*!' von Mappus snarled. 'He is not in command! I just gave you an order, soldier!'

'Sir,' Nagel said, and motioned to Moos. 'Come on, Johann.'

As they moved on, von Mappus turned to Holbeck with eyes of vitriol, but said nothing.

It took another fifteen minutes for Nagel and Moos, now a little further ahead of the other four, to make it to the exit incline. They began to crawl their way up to the top. Tiny avalanches spilled downwards in their wake.

Von Mappus, Holbeck, Hubertus and Grootemans reached the base of the incline, and waited.

Moos made it first, and shrunk himself against the snow. He swiftly, but at the same time as unobtrusively as possible, made a furrow for his rifle so that he could lie in wait, without being spotted. Nagel crawled abreast of him but stayed just below the summit, keeping the snout of the machine gun out of sight.

Tense minutes passed.

Then all watched with heightened alertness as Moos suddenly went very still.

A shot barked into the day as Moos fired.

Von Mappus glared at Holbeck. 'No trap, *Scharführer*? The Bolsheviks are up there, waiting for us to show ourselves!'

'I don't agree, sir.'

'You don't agree, you don't agree!' Von Mappus was furious, but he bit back what he was about to say and turned to Hubertus and Grootemans. 'Take up defensive positions on the incline. Move!' he ordered, as they appeared to hesitate, clearly waiting for Holbeck's reaction.

'Do it,' Holbeck said to them.

As they set off, von Mappus raged at him. 'I don't need you to confirm my orders, *Scharführer!*'

'No, sir.'

'I make you a solemn promise, *Scharführer* Holbeck, you will not get away with any of this! If it's the last thing I do, I will see to it that you are court-martialled and shot!'

'Yes, sir.'

'Now take up your post where the hell you like!'

'Yes, sir.'

Another shot rang out as Moos fired again. There was no returning fire. It was exactly one o'clock in the afternoon.

And Hell had come to the village.

It was exactly 13.00, Pappenheim read, *when Hell, in the shape of the six of us, came to the defenceless village. The first shot from Johann Moos did not kill, as expected, an Ivan waiting in ambush, but dropped a child. His second shot killed another child. Both had been hiding. He had spotted their movements, and had fired. No one will ever know what was on his mind at that instant. Perhaps the bodies on the poles, and the insanity of von Mappus seeing snipers where there were none, had sent him over the edge. I have no other explanation. But far worse was to come . . .*

The phone rang.

Pappenheim slowly closed the diary, and picked up the receiver. He had been so gripped by what Holbeck had chronicled, he had not smoked since he had begun reading. He now lit up, as the phone rang a second time.

'Pappenheim.'

It was the goth. 'Sir,' Hedi Meyer began, 'I need to go back into the room, if that's alright . . .' Her voice faded uncertainly.

'That's quite alright,' he assured her. 'When?'

'Would now be OK?'

'Now would be fine. I need some air, anyway. Give me five minutes.'

'Thank you, sir.'

As they hung up he drew on the cigarette, and stared at the diary. 'And all this was supposedly done in my name,' he

114

said in a voice that unashamedly displayed a sense of horror, 'before I was even born. Thank you, you bastards, for giving me this legacy. But thank you, Sergeant Holbeck, for having the courage to record it from inside the heart of the darkness.' He locked the diary away in the drawer, and stood up. 'I'll come back to you later; but right now, I do need some air.'

He found Hedi Meyer waiting by the door of the documents room. As usual, she had her long bag with her.

'What's the panic, *Meisterin* Meyer?' he asked with a smile.

'No panic, sir,' she replied, quite serious.

'That was a joke.'

'Oh.'

'That bad?'

'I've heard better.'

'Ouch.' Pappenheim tapped the keypad, and they entered.

'I've asked someone I trust,' Hedi Meyer said, 'to send me a virus . . .'

'*What?*' Pappenheim exclaimed as the door swung itself shut behind them.

'Don't worry, sir,' she told him as she took her seat at the computer. 'My program will kill it. But I want to test all the security systems I've built in. I don't want to find out I've made a mistake when a *real* attack comes . . . if it does.'

'Er . . . fine. Do you need me to remain here?'

'No, sir. I know my way out.' She did not look round as the computer powered up.

'Er . . . fine,' he repeated. 'I'll just . . . let myself out.'

Already calling up her programs, she nodded, all focus on the machine.

Pappenheim let himself out. 'Computer kids,' he said to himself as he walked back to his office.

In the documents room, Hedi Meyer removed from her copious bag some items and lengths of connecting cables that would have startled Pappenheim. Two of the items she placed on either side of the keyboard and began to connect them up to the computer. When finished, she returned to her seat, and clipped another item – a lightweight headset with a

115

tiny boom mike attached – on to her head. It was a very special headset, with motion sensors. She called it the spider.

The items on either side of the keyboard looked like the actual throttle and stick from an F-16 jet fighter. They were not, but the similarity was such that they might as well have been.

She inserted a program disk, and calibrated the peripherals. Another disk – of a highly realistic simulation game of a USAF fighter – went into the machine, and she installed the program. Various set-up screens came on when installation was complete. She had obviously been playing it for some time previously, for she had a logbook screen with many combat flying hours on it. Her combat score was high, and she had attained the rank of lieutenant-colonel in the game. Satisfied with her set-up she exited the game, then went online and made contact with the person she had told Pappenheim about.

'OK,' she said. 'Send it.'

'Are you sure you want this?' the female voice asked. 'It could be risky. This one's a nasty, nasty.'

'The nastier the better. Go ahead.'

'It's your funeral. On its way.'

On the screen, the image of a wriggling bug with a humanoid face appeared, gripped in an armoured glove.

'Aaaaarrrggh!!' it screamed.

A splash of red appeared, then vanished. ATTACK ELIMINATED came on screen, in bright green letters.

'A success!' Hedi Meyer said into the mike.

'How about another one? I have one here that will rip your hard disk to shreds and you won't even see it happening. Next time you try to power up, the computer will be as dead as a dodo, and *everything* gone.'

'Send it.'

'Your bosses will kill you if this goes wrong.'

'Send it.'

'OK,' the voice said, then repeated, 'Your funeral. Don't say I didn't warn you.'

Another wriggling bug, again gripped in the glove, appeared. The result was the same as before.

'Got it!' she said into the mike.

'That was my very best,' the other person said ruefully. 'Whatever you've done, it's hot. Fancy a trip up bandit country?'

'Why not?'

'Fighter sweep?'

'Fighter sweep.'

'Who leads?'

'I do,' Hedi Meyer said.

'You have the lead.'

She started the simulation and soon a very realistic 3-D cockpit was on the screen, flying across a 3-D landscape of a photographic quality that looked so real it fooled the mind.

Then she heard on her headphones, 'Two, in position.'

She turned her head and the view shifted to the right. There, in the virtual world, keeping perfect station, was a lifelike F-16 bobbing as if actually in the air, control surfaces working.

'Nice to see you,' she said. 'Let's go hunting.'

They had been flying for about fifteen minutes without any trade, when on the left multi-function display, a brief message appeared. CONTACT.

Then it winked out.

'Did you just see some large writing on the radar?' she asked.

'No. Nothing.' The reponse was puzzled. 'What do you mean?'

'Look . . . let's exit. I'll be in touch.'

'But . . .'

'I wouldn't do this unless it was serious. Quit now!'

'Quitting.'

The second F-16 vanished.

Hedi Meyer went offline and quickly exited the program. She ran a full diagnostic of the entire system, did a comprehensive virus check, but found nothing amiss.

'This,' she said to herself, 'is very strange.' She decided to call Pappenheim. 'Sir, I think you'll want to see this.'

Pappenheim, continuing his reading of Holbeck's diary, said, 'Five minutes, and I'll be with you.'

He was as good as his word.

'So what's the p—' he began as he entered, then stopped when he saw the joystick. 'Miss Meyer,' he said, looking sideways at her. 'Tell me you're not playing a computer game on the taxpayer's very expensive machine, and in police time.' He stared at the headset. 'And what's that thing on your head?'

'My spider. There's a very good reason for all this, sir,' she went on, swivelling the chair to look round at him.

'I'm all ears.'

'I am doing a field test . . .'

'A field test.'

'Yes, sir. I contacted someone I trust, to help me do a virus and invasion check.'

'And who is he? This person you trust to hit this particular, highly sensitive machine?'

'*She*, sir. We worked together on some projects when I was at university. She is brilliant with computers . . . but not as good as I am, of course.'

'Of course. Well . . . *Meisterin* Meyer? What did you call me here to see?'

She turned back to the machine, and loaded the flight simulator.

Pappenheim stared at the screen. 'I can almost believe it's real.'

'This is only the beginning.'

He watched, impressed despite himself, as she ran through the pre-take-off checks and took off on full afterburner, climbing steeply.

'You can actually fly that thing? It looks very complicated.'

'You get used to it. It's very faithful to the real thing. I've been flying it regularly on my computer at home, which is not as powerful as this, of course. Although it's very smooth on mine, this is fantastic!'

'I'm glad you approve.'

'Look what happens when I turn my head.'

She looked in several directions to demonstrate. The in- and out-of-cockpit views corresponded to the movements.

'Very useful in a turning fight,' she explained. 'And every switch and button you see works. Most of the time, though, I do the essentials on the throttle and stick.'

'I . . . see . . .'

'I got my friend to hit us with a very nasty virus someone had sent her,' Hedi Meyer said. 'She quarantines viruses, then modifies them.'

'Nice pastime. Can *you* do that?'

'Of course,' Hedi Meyer replied, making it sound like child's play. It was not a boast. 'I'm going to dial her up now. We often fly together, but we don't join any online gaming. This is our private battlefield. She'll be along soon. I'll put on the speakers so you can hear her as well. She's my wingman today. Flying like this is very educational.'

'Educational.'

'Yes, sir. You can play with the code to make your aircraft skins look seriously realistic.'

'I . . . see . . . I think.'

'We're going to fly the same course as before . . .'

'Then what happens?'

'That's what I want you to see, sir . . . if it happens again. Keep an eye on the radar . . . the left MFD . . . there.' She briefly placed the mouse cursor on the radar display, which was in track-while-scan mode.

'Two, in position,' Pappenheim heard.

'She's here,' Hedi Meyer said. 'I'll turn my head slightly to the right, and you'll see her. She can see me too, of course. Well . . . the jet, not me exactly. She can't hear us when I deactivate the mike.'

Pappenheim stared at the very real-looking aircraft that was keeping close station. The landscape below, the clouds, the sky, were all rendered so perfectly it was hard to believe he was looking at a virtual world.

'This is . . . remarkable. Quite amazing.'

'We've taken it a long way from the original. A lot of people out there have done wonders; but I like what we've done best of all, because we've tailored it to our own preferences . . . which might not work for everybody.'

'What was that all about?' came the voice of the wingman.

'Something weird's happening,' Hedi Meyer replied, activating the mike with a key press. 'I just want to check again. If I say quit, just do it. OK?'

'OK,' came the uncertain acknowledgement. 'You say "quit", I'm out of here.'

'OK. We're covering the same route.'

'Got it.'

They flew for five minutes, but nothing happened. Ten. No bandit trade, but nothing else, either.

Then at exactly fifteen minutes, CONTACT appeared on the radar, then blinked out.

'Quit!' Hedi Meyer called.

The second F-16 vanished.

She exited the program, and began to run another diagnostic and virus check. Then she turned to Pappenheim as the programs did their stuff. 'Did you see it, sir?'

'I did. Is that not part of your game?'

She shook her head. 'Not any part. Someone else is in our virtual airspace.'

The blisteringly quick programs did their check. As before, nothing was wrong.

'We're clean,' she said, turning round, 'except . . .'

'Except for the beacon we left in.'

'Yes, sir. Whoever it is, is using that as a pathway. My firewall is stopping everything else . . . so he, or she, can't get to us without it. Killing the beacon would make us a hundred per cent proof. I can do that easily, as you know.'

'I know. But the boss wants it left in, so it stays in. We'll have to see who wants to make contact, and why.'

'Should we try now?'

Pappenheim shook his head. 'Wait till he gets back.'

'What amazes me,' Hedi Meyer went on, 'is that this person could actually access our battlefield. Normally, you can't do that unless you've got the same simulation, and exactly the same version. That would have to include our own enhancements.'

'Perhaps the person's a simulation fan,' Pappenheim suggested, 'who has got them all.'

She gave him a stern look. 'Not *our* enhancements.'

'Perhaps he's some poor soul who just wants to join your squadron of two.'

'That was a joke, was it, sir?'

'That bad?'

'Not good.'

'I must be slipping. I think I'll get back to my office. Need me for anything else?'

She shook her head.

'Very well. Don't let anyone catch you flying that thing.'

'I'm leaving too. I'm finished here, for now. But can I leave the program in? And all the gear? I want it set up for when the *Hauptkommissar* gets back.'

'That will be fine,' Pappenheim said with a straight face.

He waited until she had shut down the computer, then they left together and went their separate ways in the corridor.

'Computers,' he said to himself as she turned a corner. 'The aliens are already among us.'

He carried on to his office, took his seat, and unlocked the drawer with the diary; then he put the gloves back on.

'And,' he continued, taking out the bloodstained chronicle once more, 'the aliens must have been at Stalingrad too.'

He opened the small book at the page he had been reading when Hedi Meyer's call had come.

There were only women and children in the village, he read, *with the exception of just one man. He had one leg. The other had been amputated above the knee. He walked on crutches. Von Mappus, certain that the man had been wounded in combat, saw this as a sign that we had found a secret Ivan supply dump . . .*

Six

Long minutes had passed without any returning fire. They remained in the positions they had taken after Moos had fired.

Holbeck looked across at von Mappus, a few metres away.

The lieutenant looked coldly back at him. 'What?'

'Something is wrong, sir,' Holbeck said, keeping his voice low. 'No return fire. I should check.'

Von Mappus continued to stare at the sergeant.

'If you want to get your head blown off by a Bolshevik sniper,' von Mappus said at last, 'don't let me stop you. Go ahead. It's the only thing that will save you from a court-martial.'

'Thank you, sir,' Holbeck said, and began to inch his way up the slope.

His route took him close to Nagel.

'Watch yourself, Sarge,' Nagel whispered.

'Just watch my back,' Holbeck whispered in return.

Nagel understood that this meant both von Mappus, and any enemy that might be out there.

'I will,' Nagel promised.

Holbeck took his time, crawling towards the summit, keeping as low as possible. When he reached the top, the ground stretched out before him in a wide, flat sweep. Five hundred metres straight ahead was a thick screen of conifers, standing like sentinels in the snowbound landscape. He was not certain, but through them he thought he could see the vague outline of a building.

The village?

He reached for his binoculars in a hip pouch, and focussed

on the area. It was definitely a building. He had to get closer.

He put the binoculars away and began a crouching, zig-zagging run, mindful that at any moment a bullet could rip through his body. But nothing happened. He went on, using any undulations in the snow as cover. It took him a while, but he reached the nearest tree without incident.

Then he heard a soft noise. He froze, ears straining to identify it. He was startled when he realized what it was.

A child whimpering; and quite close.

Cautiously, he moved closer, until he could see behind the tree directly after the one where he had taken cover. The bright red on the snow told him what had happened. But he did not expect to see the little girl; nor the blood seeping through the fur of one of her rough but sturdy winter boots.

Moos had shot a child.

She stared at him through pain-filled eyes. 'Why did you shoot me?' she asked him in German.

'I did not shoot you.' He put down his weapon. 'Let me have a look. I must tend to it, then get you home. I thought I saw a building. Is it in your village?'

She nodded, then fearfully watched as his hands moved towards her wounded left leg. 'Don't hurt me!'

'I'm trying to help.'

'Help Nikolai first. He's my friend. He's not moving.'

Oh God, Holbeck thought. 'Where is he?'

'He was running over . . . there.' She pointed. 'Then I heard him fall. He didn't get up again.'

'Alright. I will go and look for him but first I must stop the bleeding. Can you move your toes?'

'Yes.'

'Well that's good. Perhaps you were lucky and it's just a graze. Thank God he missed.'

'He didn't miss! He hit me!'

'Believe me . . . for the person who shot you, that was a miss. He thought you were a soldier.'

'I told you before. There are no soldiers here.'

'I know, I know. Do you feel any wetness inside the boot?'

'No.'

'That's good too. Perhaps it is better to leave it if you're not far from home . . .'

'My horse is not far.'

'Your . . .' Holbeck stared at her. 'Your *horse*?'

'Yes.'

'We saw horse tracks. Two of them.'

'That was my brother's horse. Andrei. He came to find me.'

'So much for the ambush, Herr von Mappus,' Holbeck said under his breath.

'What?'

'I'm just mumbling.' Holbeck picked up his gun. 'I'll carry you to your horse.'

'But Nikolai!'

'Show me where he is.'

Holbeck picked her up gently. She winced, but did not cry out. He carried her to where she said her friend had fallen. They found him behind another tree. This time, Moos had been accurate. The boy, about the same age as the girl, was quite dead.

Holbeck briefly shut his eyes. Now we are child killers.

'We can't help him for now,' he said to her. 'Let's find your horse.'

They found the pony not long after, quietly waiting within the woodland.

'Where's his horse?'

'He doesn't have one. The two of us rode mine.'

'What were you doing out here, anyway?'

'We always come out here to play,' she replied, looking at him as if he had asked a foolish question.

And why not, he thought. This is her land.

Holbeck put her on the animal. 'Can you make it home?'

'Yes.'

'Alright. Go on. I'll bring in your friend.'

She looked at him gravely, nodded, then rode off.

Holbeck returned to the dead boy, and picked him up. He began walking back to where the others waited.

It was Moos who spotted him coming out of the trees.

'The Sarge . . . the *Scharführer*'s coming back! He's OK. But . . .'

'But what?' von Mappus demanded as Moos paused uncertainly.

'He's . . . he's carrying something!'

'Perhaps you shot a wolf, Johann,' Nagel teased. 'Johann and the wolf . . .'

But Moos was looking strange. 'I . . . think it's a person.'

'He's *carrying* an Ivan?' Nagel was astonished.

'N-no. I . . . I think . . .'

'You think?' von Mappus snapped. 'Think what?' He began to make his way up the slope; then he stopped as he reached flat ground, got to his feet and stared at Holbeck.

'I . . . think it's a child,' Moos got out at last. He looked sick.

'I can see that!' von Mappus said.

He stood there glaring as Holbeck came up, to stop before him.

'What are you doing, *Scharführer*?'

'This is a child, sir.'

'I am not blind. Why are you carrying that little *Bolshevik*?'

'This is what Moos shot, sir.'

'So? He shot twice.'

'Yes, sir. He hit another child. Luckily, it appears it was just a graze.'

'And where's that one?'

'I put her on her horse, sir. She's gone back home.'

Von Mappus peered at Holbeck. 'Has the snow finally got to you, *Scharführer*? *Are you mad?* The Bolsheviks *use* children against us. There are partisans everywhere. Stalin has decreed that every city, every town, every village, every settlement, turn its hand against us *and you let her go*? Was this the same little Bolshevik who came to spy on us before?'

'She was not spying, sir,' Holbeck said patiently.

'So, it was!' von Mappus snarled.

By now, the others had come up.

Von Mappus rounded upon them. 'Get back to your positions! You make perfect targets!' He did not seem to be bothered by the fact that he, too, was a perfect target.

'There are no Ivan soldiers out there, sir,' Holbeck said.

'I have your absolute word on that, have I?' Von Mappus sneered, then he looked down at the dead boy with palpable contempt. 'And what are you going to do with *that*?'

'Take him to his people.'

Von Mappus looked as if he were listening to someone demented. 'What are you, *Scharführer*? Waffen SS? Or a sister of mercy?'

Without warning, he hauled the dead boy from Holbeck, and dropped the body to the ground. Despite the snow, it fell with a sickening thump. He then pulled out his pistol, and shot the body twice.

'Now he's quite dead.' He stared challengingly at Holbeck.

Holbeck slowly lowered himself, and picked up the body. Leaking blood stained his combat smock. Without another word, he began walking in the direction of the village.

The others had not dispersed as von Mappus had ordered and, in an attempt to calm the lieutenant's bloodlust, Hubertus spoke up quickly.

'Look at it this way, sir,' he began. 'If the Ivans are out there, the *Scharführer* will make good bait. Then we can get them. We should follow, sir . . . using the trees as cover.'

Hubertus glanced quickly at Moos, Nagel, and Grootemans, signalling with his eyes that he was trying to protect Holbeck. He was relieved to see that they understood.

Long moments passed while von Mappus stood there, staring at the receding Waffen-SS sergeant. Then he jabbed the pistol back into its holster.

'Very well,' he said at last without looking round at them. 'Follow me.'

I entered the village with the dead boy in my arms, Pappenheim read aloud, gripped by Holbeck's documentation. *The girl, Galina, as I now know her to be, had told the villagers about what had happened. I was not sure of the reception I would receive from them, but she must have said something positive about me because although they stared at the boy in my arms,*

126

no one attacked me, the enemy, with an axe, pitchfork, any other implement, as Stalin had decreed to all citizens. Then I heard a terrible scream. The dead boy's mother was running towards me.

Pappenheim stopped to light a cigarette. He took a deep drag, and stared at the ceiling as he blew smoke towards it.

'You poor bastard,' he said of Holbeck. 'Serving the devil, and trying to hang on to your humanity.'

The phone rang.

'No, no, no!' Pappenheim said. 'Not now!'

He let it ring. It continued, unabated.

'Oh, alright,' he said with a sigh. 'You win.' He picked it up. 'Pappenheim.'

'I have something for you. Don't know if it will help . . .'

'Norbert!' Pappenheim greeted him brightly. 'Any news is a help.'

'Our accident victim had a steel tooth . . .'

'You're suggesting he could be Russian?'

'Well . . . I know he was young, not like the old comrades who would have those; but the Soviet era is not so far in the past. Who knows? I thought it might be of use.'

'It is, Norbert. It gives us a dimension . . . but not one I'm certain we're going to like. But thanks. It *is* a help.'

'And a picture is on the way.'

'At this rate, I'm going to owe you too much.'

Norbert Roth laughed. 'You'll soon find a way of making me owe you again.'

'How well you know me,' Pappenheim said as they hung up. He looked at the diary. 'Hear that, Sergeant Holbeck? *Russian.* We're getting a picture. Now if only we could find your camera.'

He was about to continue reading, when a knock sounded on his door. He gave another sigh and quickly locked the diary away.

'In!'

Berger entered, carrying a photograph. 'You've got strange friends, Chief.'

She placed the print before him, glanced at the cotton gloves he wore, but made no comment.

'Don't be rude to your superiors, or you'll find yourself in St Pauli.'

'Promises, promises,' she said, hurrying out before he could say anything.

'Hmm,' he said to the closed door. He picked up the photograph, and studied the face of the man who had died in the accident. 'Another one Hedi Meyer would hate to meet on a dark night. If you *are* Russian,' he went on softly, 'I wonder if the Silesian is one bodyguard down at the moment.'

On Rügen, the snow, which had stopped for just over an hour, was again falling. At first, it fell lightly, fluttering down in a lazy, drifting motion to the picture-perfect whiteness on the ground. Within half an hour, the fall had become an intense curtain that quickly laid a fresh, deepening layer. Visibility had become severely restricted.

Into this, and dressed as before, came the young man who had watched the old man dying. He returned to the house via the same route he had taken on leaving, vaulted the gate, and walked unhurriedly back to the open conservatory. His footprints were covered almost immediately by the snowfall.

He stepped over the small mound of snow at the door, and fastidiously wiped his feet on a small Persian rug just beyond; then he went up to the body.

'I'm back, as you see,' he said to it conversationally, drawing back his hood, 'to look for what I couldn't find on my first visit. And talking of finding . . . no one has found *you* as yet. Good for me, not so good for you. Not that it really matters, in your case.'

He walked about the room, glancing idly around.

'I have an idea where you may have hidden it,' he continued. 'I've checked every possible hiding place already; and then, I remembered. What was the favourite hiding place for these items during the days of the DDR? I'll answer that, if you don't mind. The specially made, *hollow* handles of everyday tools: wrenches, hammers and the like.'

He turned, addressing the body directly. 'With my background, I should have remembered, of course. But since the world turned its back on the Cold War, people like us have become a little . . . rusty, if you get my meaning. So, my dead friend, in which tool have you hidden it? Have a look around, shall I? Thank you.'

He again searched the conservatory minutely, but without success. He left the room, and proceeded to carry out the search in every other room, working his way up from the ground floor. He took his time, doing so with unhurried precision.

But it was all still in vain.

He did not lose his temper, nor grow impatient. It was clear by the calmness of his manner that he did not feel in imminent danger of being discovered.

He entered the main bedroom and stared at the iron bed, with its four posts topped by brass spheres.

'No,' he said to himself. 'Not inside the bedpost. On the other hand, hiding in plain sight is one of the best ways . . .' His voice faded as he went up to the first of the posts.

He grabbed at the sphere, and tried to unscrew it. It did not move. The other three were equally immovable.

'Not there then.' He did not sound disappointed. 'To be honest, I did not really expect it.'

He was about to turn his attention elsewhere, when he paused. He returned to the bed, and inspected the base of each sphere closely. Each was an integral part of its post, the brass colour burnished upon it. Three of the posts showed no sign of being removable. The fourth was different: two countersunk screws, so tiny they would be easily overlooked in all but the most detailed of inspections, were mounted opposite each other.

'Aah, *Herr General*. Smart. *Very* smart.' He fished into an inside pocket. 'But, as you can see . . . I came prepared.'

He withdrew two items from the pocket: a pencil torch, and a small case that was slightly bigger, but flatter than a packet of cigarettes. He opened the case. In it was a set of watchmaker's screwdrivers. He selected one, and tried it on the closest screw. It fitted perfectly.

'Now let's see if I am right.'

After some turning pressure, the screw began to move. As it came out, it proved to be longer than expected. The tip was also a surprise. Instead of the normal point, it was blunt and hollow, and threaded internally. The second screw moved more easily, and was almost the same length.

He put the screws together and gave them a counter twist. They locked into each other.

'I have to say, *Herr General*, that was very neat. It locked the top so solidly, no one would imagine it was false. Except for me, of course. Now to see what you've hidden in there . . .'

The brass top came away smoothly, to reveal the dark hollow. He shone the torch into the cavity. Something nestled deep down.

'And there you are,' he breathed. 'But how to get you out? No time to waste trying to fish you out, so I'm afraid it's brute force . . . of a kind.'

He quickly removed the bedclothes and the mattress, then tipped the frame over. As the hollow post rose then began to cant downwards, the small package slid out. Protected by its wrapping, it dropped with a soft thud to the carpet.

'After sixty years, Waffen-SS *Scharführer* Holbeck's camera, I believe,' he said with reverence.

He first returned the bed to its upright position, ensuring the legs fitted the carpet indentations exactly. He remade the bed, taking great care that it looked just as it had before. Then he replaced the brass top, screwing and locking it exactly as previously. He put his tools away. Only then did he pick up the package.

Carefully, as if with a precious relic, he opened up the wrapping.

'Oh yes,' he said, staring at the dull silver rectangle in his hand.

It was indeed Holbeck's Minox Riga.

As carefully as he had unwrapped it, he secured it again, put it into a zipped, inner pocket of his all-weather, and hurried back to the conservatory. He took out a small digital camera and took many shots of the body from various angles.

'Proof of your one-way trip to hell,' he said to the dead old man as he put the camera away. 'I am judge and executioner.' He drew on his hood, glancing outside. 'Snow's still falling heavily.' He paused to give the body a look that was devoid of all expression.

He went out, leaving the door open, and made his way across the garden. He again vaulted the gate, and disappeared from view.

The falling snow once more obliterated his footprints.

He walked a long way – for about an hour – going through a woodland of snow-coated trees. When deep within them he stopped, and quickly got some tightly rolled material out of one of the many pockets of his all-weather. He snapped the stud of the retaining strap and the material sprang open into a lightweight pair of waterproof over-trousers, with elasticated bottoms. He slipped them on over the white, combat-type trousers he already wore. Now, it appeared that he was wearing light grey. Another tightly rolled package turned out to be a pair of thin, calf-length shoe covers of black plastic with elasticated tops, and grip soles. When he put them on over the white boots, they gave the impression he was wearing a type of black wellingtons. Finally, he unzipped the outer layer of his all-weather, removed and reversed it, then zipped it back together. It was now dark blue.

He continued through the woodland, eventually ending on a beach that led him to a seaside town which, in summer, was a popular resort. There were a few people along the seafront, hardy souls who, like him, seemed to be out for a walk. Heads down against the falling snow, they barely glanced at him.

He walked on, until he came to his seafront hotel. He entered, shaking the snow off him, and drawing back his hood before entering the lobby. The receptionist at the desk smiled at him in greeting.

'Did you get some good pictures, sir?'

'I got perfect ones,' he replied.

'Rügen is beautiful in the winter.'

'It certainly is. Now I need a hot shower.' He paused. 'Oh, and could I please have an order of food and drink sent up?'

'Of course, sir.'

He gave her the order and went up to his room. When he

entered, a dark-haired woman, slightly younger than he, came up to him. People in the hotel believed them to be a couple from Berlin.

'How did it go?'

'Perfectly.'

Her eyes lit up. 'You *found* the camera?'

He grinned and showed her the package.

'At last,' she said, looking at it with the same kind of reverence he had displayed when he had first opened it. 'Are you going to call him?' she added.

'Not from here. I'll use the mobile.'

'Will you give it to him?'

'It's not his, is it? I'm grateful to him for putting me on the right track . . .'

'He's not going to be pleased.'

They were not speaking German to each other.

'I don't trust him. It has taken us a long time, Galina. Now that we've got this far, I want to make sure we're ready for him, if he decides to betray us.'

'And we need to find the diary,' she said.

'When we do,' Zima Andreivitch Rachko said, 'that's the time he *will* try to betray us. I'm certain of it.'

Holbeck was standing with his legs slightly apart, the dead boy held across his body almost as an offering, as the woman who had screamed came up to him.

She stopped directly before him, perfectly still, eyes searching the boy in his arms for signs of life. She seemed too young to have a child of that age. Despite the rigours of living in such a place, there were no ravages upon her features. Her tragic eyes now looked at Holbeck.

'I'm sorry,' he said in his halting Russian. 'It was a mistake.'

A single unpaved road, vanishing into an empty distance in both directions, bisected the village. A track branched off it, feeding itself into the sloping decline which led to the run-off. This was the secondary road. Excess snow had been cleared off the main road, and what remained was a hard-packed surface.

The rough houses of solid wood were widely and haphazardly dispersed, each with its own snow-covered field. Some had outhouses. A couple had barns. There were twelve family houses in all.

Over to his right, Holbeck heard the snort of a horse. The woman kept on staring at him.

People had come out of their homes to look, and they stood in a silent group, a respectful distance from the distraught mother. Their faces all carried the healthy pallor of the boy's mother. For some reason, despite being almost surrounded by people who were supposed to be the enemy, he did not feel threatened.

Then the woman gently took the child from him and turned away, never speaking. She was swallowed by the crowd, who now walked back with her. They trailed her in continuing silence until eventually they all disappeared into a single house.

Holbeck remained standing there, wondering what would happen next. I'm a perfect target, he thought, if anyone wants to take a shot.

He was almost resigned to it, but kept his weapon lowered.

He looked about him. No one came out of any of the houses. For a second time, he heard an animal snort. He remained where he was. After what seemed like an eternity, and after he had turned to check where the rest of his comrades had got to, he heard a strange noise that gradually increased as it drew nearer.

It was a measured, double pock, impacting with the regularity of a metronome upon the frozen surface.

Holbeck looked round. A man on one leg and crutches was approaching, coming from the direction of the house the boy's mother and her village friends had entered.

Holbeck remained where he was, weapon still lowered, and waited.

Just as with the boy's mother, the one-legged man stopped before him; and like her, despite his disability, the man's face bore the same air of healthiness.

'You must be Galina's benefactor, Sergeant,' the man

began in only mildly accented German. 'She talked about you.'

'And your German is very good,' Holbeck said. 'I can see why she speaks it so well.'

'I am her father,' the man said. 'I was in Germany before things got bad,' he went on, then gave a sad, deprecating smile. 'I was a student in a big city. Coming from this tiny village, anything bigger than a small town was a big city to me. But it was big enough.'

'Berlin?'

'Oh no. But not far from there. Potsdam. I wanted to be a teacher.'

Holbeck stared at him. 'Wanted?'

'I did not finish. I came back when things began to look ugly in the early thirties. I wanted to teach in this village, and in others, about the outside world. Many generations have lived here in my village. But dreams die . . .'

'Too often, when taken over by events.'

The man gave Holbeck a searching look before continuing, 'I returned to the family farm; but I am also the village teacher.' He gave another deprecating smile. 'I think it is because I have been away from here.' A further, searching look probed at Holbeck. 'From what Galina said, it seems strange that you are with the Waffen SS. She told us how you saved her. Twice now.'

'It was nothing.'

'I think not. She said you argued with your officer, and lied to him about the village.'

'I did not want us to come here.'

'But now, you are here . . .'

'And we have brought the first death.'

The man said nothing for some moments. 'What were you, Sergeant,' he went on, 'before the Waffen SS?'

Holbeck took his time before replying, 'I was a teacher.'

The man nodded slowly, as if he had already guessed. 'It would explain many things.'

'As you have yourself just said . . . dreams die . . .'

The man nodded once more, was again silent for some

moments before saying, 'I am Andrei Rachko.' He propped himself on his crutches, and held out a hand.

Holbeck shook it. 'Maximillian Holbeck.'

'For this moment in time,' Rachko said, 'we share a profession as teachers.'

'For this moment,' Holbeck said. He indicated the crutches with his gun. 'Combat?'

The man looked sheepish. 'Nothing so dramatic. My horse was pulling a log uphill. The bindings snapped and the log rolled back. I was in the way. It crushed the leg.'

'I'm sorry.'

'Don't be. It was my own fault. Well, Sergeant . . . we have food . . .'

Holbeck could not believe it. 'You have shaken my hand; and now you would give us food, despite what has happened?'

'Why not? I am the only man here among women and children, and not much of a threat at that. We are far from the war, and there is nothing of strategic value here. We will of course mourn our lost child. An unknown talent has been taken from us. It could have been much, much worse. We are not Stalinists and so far the war has passed us by. We would like that to continue, even though all the other men have gone to fight . . .'

'We saw eight of them . . .'

'If you mean the people without insignia . . . they were not from here. They are deserting soldiers.'

'They had sniper rifles . . .'

'Which they stole to use against their own commanders. Some are less than willing to die for the political commissars.'

'There was a commissar with them.'

'Not his uniform.'

'How do you know this?'

'They spent a day here. We gave them food. They talked freely. Everything was stolen.'

They might indeed have talked freely, Holbeck thought; but he was certain, whoever those soldiers had been, they had lied to the village teacher–farmer.

'They are dead,' he said with deliberation, looking at the man closely. 'They ran unexpectedly into us.' He said nothing about the German bodies that had been used for target practice.

But there was no overt reaction to the news.

'So do fortunes change,' the man said.

'Would you have gone to fight, if not for the leg?'

'Yes. As I've said, I am not a Stalinist . . . but my country has been invaded; however, with this leg . . . or the lack of it . . . my duty now is to ensure the survival of the village, in the madness of the outside world. This village has no strategic or tactical value. So we hope both sides will leave us alone. And now, Sergeant, will you accept some food? You must need it.'

'We do, but I believe it best that we, too, pass you by. We have already done enough damage. My lieutenant does not see things as I do.'

The lieutenant in question was within the woodland, and now close to the village. From his vantage point, he could see Holbeck and the one-legged man very clearly. He had seen the handshake.

'He shakes hands with a dirty Bolshevik!' von Mappus fumed. 'The man has not only lost his senses, he is fraternizing with the enemy! I am entitled to shoot him down like a dog!'

Hubertus, who was close by, said, 'If there are soldiers hiding in the village, sir, now would not be a good time to start shooting.'

Von Mappus thought about it for a second. 'You're right. We'll use grenades. You, Hubertus . . . take your grenades, and throw them into the house where all those people went.' He turned round to Nagel and Moos. 'You two, set up the machine gun so that when those who survive come running out, you can finish them off . . . as well as anyone else who comes your way. Keep moving position to enable you to engage the soldiers who will come running. Grootemans, you go with Hubertus . . .'

They all stared at him.

136

'Sir,' Hubertus began, 'the *Scharführer* may be negotiating some food for us. The dead boy . . .'

'Don't you pick up Holbeck's bad habits, Hubertus!' von Mappus snarled. 'At every opportunity, he has opposed me! He argued against interrogating the girl, who was sent to spy on us. He *let* her go again when he could have made her our prisoner! He kept insisting there were no enemy soldiers around, but we had a clash with eight of them. We come upon a village, obviously a secret supply dump, and what does he do? *He shakes hands with a Bolshevik!* They send a man with one leg to fool him, and he takes the bait! Holbeck is not fit to be a *Scharführer*! He is not fit to be a member of the Waffen SS! It is obvious he no longer wishes to serve the Führer . . . if he ever did. He has let down his comrades, and that includes you! Now . . . am I looking at four members of the Waffen SS, or *traitors*?'

Indoctrinated discipline overcame deep misgivings. The situation was completely outside their experience and with Holbeck not there to instil some reason, the bullying of von Mappus won them over. They did not really believe Holbeck had betrayed them; but they were in enemy country and, out there, was the enemy's people.

Sensing he was winning, von Mappus pressed home his advantage. 'These are *well fed* Bolsheviks. We are in the heart of enemy territory, with no immediate help available. Remember the bodies on the poles. Those men did not get there by themselves. And as for this supply dump . . . where better to hide it than in a village in the middle of nowhere? By destroying it, and everything here, we will deal a severe blow to the enemy. The Führer himself will decorate us! But to achieve this we must maintain total surprise. Any objections?'

There were none.

The multiple explosions of the grenades took Holbeck and Rachko completely by surprise.

Holbeck whirled towards the sound. 'What the . . .'

Rachko swung awkwardly round on his crutches.

Then came the screams, followed by a terrible chattering sound Holbeck knew only too well.

'*Nagel!*' he shouted in horror. '*No!*'

Eyes wide, Rachko yelled. '*What is this? What is happening?*'

'The insane lieutenant. This is his doing ! Find some cover! I'll . . .'

'You'll what, *Scharführer?*' the cold voice said from behind him. 'Insane, am I? At last, I've got you!' Von Mappus came round to face the two men, while the merciless chatter of the machine gun continued. 'Consorting with the enemy.'

Von Mappus was pointing his machine pistol, covering them both.

'You are insane!' Holbeck shouted at him, not caring anymore. '*This is a harmless village! There are no soldiers here, you moron! Just women, children, and this man with one leg!*'

Von Mappus was so enraged, Holbeck expected to feel the slam of the entire magazine emptying into him. But for some reason von Mappus chose not to fire.

A fierce grin appeared. 'Hear that sound, Holbeck? It's the sound of Bolsheviks dying. Now drop your weapons! *Drop them!*' And when Holbeck did not, von Mappus continued, 'I'll start with your Bolshevik friend . . .'

Holbeck was in no doubt that von Mappus would do it. He slowly put down his MP40, then removed his pistol from its holster and put that down too.

'That was wise,' von Mappus said, looking smug as Holbeck straightened. 'Now step back! *Back!*'

Holbeck reluctantly did so.

'Don't try to run,' von Mappus warned. 'You would never make it.'

Holbeck's eyes did not waver. 'I would never run from a creature like you.'

'Continue to dig your own grave,' von Mappus again sneered.

All the while, Nagel's gun continued its hellish chatter.

A distraught Rachko launched himself at von Mappus. '*You madman!*' he screamed in terrified outrage. 'You're killing my village! What have these people ever done to you? We were offering you food!'

'*Take your filthy Bolshevik, subhuman hands off me!*' von Mappus yelled, lips pulled back in the snarl of an enraged dog. 'As for the food, we'll take it anyway, when we're finished here!'

He gave Rachko a shove that was so hard, the man toppled off his crutches and fell heavily to the ground. The crutches went skidding across the hard-packed snow. Von Mappus viciously kicked the nearest one further away.

As Rachko struggled to retrieve them, Holbeck began to move forward, intending to reach down to give him a helping hand.

'I would not advise it, Holbeck,' von Mappus said. 'You'd still never make it.' Holbeck stopped. He looked at Rachko helplessly.

But despite his appalling situation, Rachko displayed a powerful, though foolhardy courage. He looked up at von Mappus with unrestrained fury.

'You animal!' he shouted. 'You and your kind desecrate the land of Goethe Schiller and Beethoven! You are a *barbarian!*'

He spat with such surprising force, the ball of saliva surged upwards with seemingly inspired accuracy. It exploded directly upon the bridge of the Waffen-SS lieutenant's nose, sending rivulets of spit in all directions across his face.

Von Mappus gave a bellow of murderous rage. '*You wretched disease!*'

Before Holbeck quite realized what was happening, von Mappus had reached into a pocket of his combat smock. He pulled out the cut-throat razor, opened it swiftly, and in a sweeping downward stroke, drew it across Rachko's throat. The wound was deep, and blood welled out of it, spilling down the neck and on to the snow.

With seemingly the same ease and speed of movement, von Mappus then made a vertical incision from the base of the neck to the chin. He straightened, razor in one hand, machine pistol ready for use in the other.

He held the razor, tip down. The specks of blood upon it

appeared to be frozen there. Abruptly, he dropped the razor to the ground, next to the dying man.

'You won't spit anymore,' he said, staring coldly down as Rachko vainly tried to stop the blood. 'I'll never again use that razor on my face, now that you have contaminated it with your blood, Bolshevik.'

There was a sudden crack that sounded very different from those made by the weapons of the soldiers. Something hummed past von Mappus, ripping through the right sleeve of his smock.

He darted a savage glare at Holbeck as he ran for cover. *'No Bolshevik soldiers? I'll be back for you!'*

'And I'll be waiting, you murdering bastard!' Holbeck yelled as he hurried to Rachko.

The man who had dreamed of teaching was violently shaking as he tried to speak. A grotesque, bubbling sound came out of the obscene wound in his throat, and a bloodied hand darted fitfully to grip Holbeck's. The eyes were still full of consciousness. They blinked with each burst of machine-gun fire.

The firing, the screams and the explosions continued as the light in the eyes began to fade.

Holbeck could hear von Mappus, shouting and urging the others on, telling them there were soldiers firing from the other houses.

'That's how we turn ordinary people into criminals,' he said to Rachko.

As if he had been waiting to hear this, the light faded completely out of Rachko's eyes. The dream of teaching had finally died.

Holbeck rose to his feet. Leaving his weapons on the ground, he took out his Minox and began to photograph the terrible things that were happening. Three houses were now ablaze, and a fourth was pouring dark smoke. Somewhere, horses were whinnying.

Holbeck went from vantage point to vantage point, photographing as fast as he could. Though he had not as yet spotted von Mappus, he worked the camera in a frenzy, as if he could feel time running out.

He got pictures of Hubertus, Grootemans, Nagel, and Moos. The young soldier's face was flushed with killing. Moos looked directly at him, without recognition. Holbeck photographed bodies of the villagers, piled as they had died, untidily upon each other.

Then he saw von Mappus come out of a house, pursuing two young boys. Von Mappus stopped, and deliberately fired a long burst from his machine pistol. The boys dropped as if felled by stones. They did not move again. Von Mappus calmly reloaded.

Holbeck got it all in his Minox.

Some malevolent instinct made von Mappus turn at that moment. Both men stared at each other for stretched moments within which all sounds seemed to fade. Then Holbeck took the picture.

This seemed to shock von Mappus out of his stasis. He swung the machine pistol round; but Holbeck had already dived for cover, even as the stream of bullets chattered out of the gun.

He made his way to one of the far houses that for the moment appeared to be untouched. He entered. A family photograph on a wall displayed a younger face of the one-legged man.

He was in Andrei Rachko's home.

He recognized the girl, Galina, and thought he had seen the wife's face among the crowd that had gathered earlier. He assumed the boy next to Galina was Andrei junior.

A swift check proved the house to be totally empty. Though simple, it was a surprisingly comfortable home. Holbeck found a cramped room with no door, which seemed to have served as a kind of study. It was filled with books in Russian, German, and English. Their varying states of wear showed they had been gathered over a great number of years. A small table and a single chair barely fitted into the crowded room. Both, like the rest of the furniture throughout the house, seemed home-made.

Holbeck took off his pack and returned the camera to its hiding place. He then took out his diary and placed it on the makeshift desk. He sat down. Next to an ink bottle at one corner was a fountain pen that had been well looked after. He picked it up, and began to write feverishly.

It was appropriate, he felt, to record what had happened with Rachko's pen.

As he wrote, he could hear the muted sounds of firing and, every so often, the thud of grenade explosions. He kept on writing.

He was not sure for how long he had been pouring out his thoughts and feelings into the diary, when he sensed a presence behind him. He whirled in his seat, expecting von Mappus.

It was the boy, Andrei. Tears on his cheeks, Andrei had a weapon, a hunting rifle that seemed too heavy for him to carry, and it was pointed at Holbeck. Man and boy stared at each other, neither saying a word.

Then Andrei lowered the rifle.

Holbeck slowly let out his breath. 'Do you speak German too?'

The boy nodded.

'And was that you who fired at the lieutenant?'

Again the nod.

'Why did you miss?'

The boy's eyes widened slightly, as if he had not expected such a reaction. 'I . . . am not yet good with . . . this gun,' he said hesitantly. 'I have a smaller one, but this is . . . was . . . my father's.'

'It is yours now. I tried to help him . . .'

'I saw. I saw it all. That is why I have not tried to shoot you . . . and because of what you did for Galina.'

'Andrei . . .' Holbeck began. 'It is Andrei?'

Andrei nodded.

'Andrei . . . you must get away from here. Take your sister and hide where they will not find you . . .'

'I shot one,' the boy said in a rush.

Holbeck paused. 'Which one?'

'The young soldier . . .'

Holbeck closed his eyes briefly. Moos. All through the hell of Stalingrad to die in a remote village that should have been left alone.

'He shot my mother!' Andrei cried, as if afraid that Holbeck would become angry with him.

'I would have done the same,' Holbeck said.

Again, the boy looked surprised. 'You are not like the others . . .'

'Oh yes. I am. I am as condemned.'

'But Galina likes you . . .'

'She likes what I used to be.' Holbeck picked up the diary, and held it out. 'Here. Take this, I have written many things down. It isn't finished, but I don't think I'll be writing in it anymore, after today. Keep it safe. One day, people will know what happened here, and in other places.'

Andrei stared at the diary, but made no move to take it.

Holbeck kept his hand outstretched.

At last, the boy reached out, and slowly took it.

'Remember what I said,' Holbeck told him. 'Keep it safe! Now go before the others get here.'

The boy hesitated. 'And you?'

'It comes to us all,' Holbeck said.

The boy looked confused.

'One day,' Holbeck told him gently, 'you'll understand.' Then suddenly remembering, Holbeck began to reach into his pack for the Minox. 'One other thing . . .'

But it was too late. There was shouting in German, close by.

'Go!' Holbeck ordered. 'Now!'

The boy ran from the room. Holbeck hoped he would get away in time.

The sergeant got to his feet and slowly put on his pack. He looked about Rachko's cramped little study.

'Many dreams are dying, Andrei,' he said quietly.

Running footsteps sounded, too light to be those of soldiers. Andrei returning?

It was Galina. She stared at Holbeck. Her face was smoke-streaked and marked by dried tears.

'My mother,' she said. 'My father. Where's Andrei?'

'He was here. I told him to take you and find somewhere to hide, until this is all over. He'll be looking for you. You should go quickly. Those people out there will be here soon.'

143

The wise old eyes looked up at him. 'Your people.' There was sadness, as well as accusation.

'My people . . . and not *my* people.'

She seemed to understand.

'Now please,' Holbeck said. 'Go from here . . .'

Heavy footsteps sounded loudly within the house.

Galina stared uncertainly at Holbeck then, too late, decided to run.

Von Mappus barred her way. 'Well, well, well! What have we here? Holbeck and his little Bolshevik spy.' The machine pistol was aimed at Holbeck.

A demonic expression distorted the lieutenant's face. His eyes blazed with a feral gleam that belonged more to a predator high on bloodlust than to a human being. There were blood spatters on his combat smock, evidence that he had done much of his killing at very close range.

Galina shrank back towards Holbeck.

'He's of no use to you now, little spy!' von Mappus snarled at her. 'One of my soldiers is dead! Killed by your Bolshevik . . .'

'We have no soldiers!' she shouted with the courage of the very young.

Von Mappus gave an evil, disbelieving smile. 'Do you see?' he said to Holbeck. 'Even *now*, she continues to deny it These creatures are impossible!'

Holbeck put himself between the child and von Mappus. 'You are mad,' he said quite calmly. 'There are no soldiers here. No secret supply dump – which, by now, even a mad butcher like you must have realized. You have killed these people for *nothing*, von Mappus. And you know it!'

Von Mappus said nothing for a few moments then suddenly the machine pistol was barking.

'*I have had enough of you, Holbeck!*' he shrieked. '*Enough, enough, enough!*'

He fired until the entire magazine was empty. Then he stood there, breathing heavily.

Holbeck had died almost instantly, falling upon Galina. But even then, he had not protected her. Hit from such close range, many of the bullets had gone through him to hit her. By the time he had fallen upon her, she was already dead.

Von Mappus reached down to roughly move Holbeck's body. He stared at the dead child. Her face was unnervingly peaceful.

A twitch darted across the lieutenant's face as he turned from her to rummage into Holbeck's pack.

'Where is your damned camera, Holbeck? *Where is it? Where is it?*'

He searched frantically, emptying the pack's contents in demented rage. At last, he found it.

'*Yes!*' It was a howl of triumph.

He put the camera into his smock and straightened.

'You were smart, Holbeck,' he said to the dead sergeant. 'But not smart enough. Enjoy the fire.'

He turned away and left the house. Outside, he found Nagel waiting. Multiple palls of smoke rose from the fires of the burning village.

'Have you found the *Scharführer*, sir?' Nagel asked. 'I heard firing.'

Von Mappus shook his head. 'I'm afraid the Bolsheviks have got him. There was one hiding in there. This is the last house. Burn it. Remember, they shot Moos.'

'I'll remember,' Nagel said, and began to rake the building with his machine gun.

Then he stopped, took a couple of grenades, and threw them into the house. The explosions lit a bright fire inside.

Von Mappus clapped him on the shoulder as they turned away. 'We have paid them back for Moos.'

When they eventually left, restocked on food, every house was burning; and every villager dead.

Save one.

Andrei returned to the smoking ruins of his village. He went to his father's body, still lying where it had fallen. He saw the razor, and picked it up. He did not wipe the blood off it.

Then he made a vow.

145

Seven

A curse on those in Berlin who brought us this war. I may survive what is happening here today, Pappenheim read, *or I may not. It all depends on . . .*

Pappenheim stopped to light a cigarette.

'You clearly did not survive the day, Sergeant Holbeck,' he said, blowing smoke towards the ceiling. 'So who cut short your chronicling? Did von Mappus succeed in killing you? Or did Russian troops arrive? Did they put the bayonet, or knife, through this? We've got your diary . . . but who's got your camera?'

He opened up the White Rose leaflet, read it through twice, then folded it back in place.

'If only there had been more of you,' he said.

A knock sounded, and Müller entered.

'You're back,' Pappenheim said.

'You know how it is. Can't keep away.' Müller glanced at the diary. 'Read it?'

'In its entirety,' Pappenheim replied. 'Gruesomely chastening. A testimony to human cruelty and stupidity.' He put the diary away, removed the gloves and put them into the drawer with it.

'No lessons have been learned . . . as we both know. Any news?'

'Some interesting, some baffling.'

'I'll take the baffling first,' Müller said.

Pappenheim leaned back in his chair. 'Are you ready for this?'

'Try me.'

'The goth was checking out the machine . . . by playing a computer game. She even has a throttle and joystick which

146

look as if they came directly from a jet fighter, hooked up to it.'

Müller was staring at him. 'She *what*?'

'Bear with me, O Great Chief. It will all soon become clear. But I think you should see for yourself. And as for the interesting news, we have a picture of the man who died in that accident on Rügen. He has a steel tooth.'

'*Russian?*'

'Norbert Roth seems to think so; and on reflection, so do I.' Pappenheim showed Müller the photo printout of the dead man.

'Even in death,' Müller commented, 'he looks a hard case. A dead Russian without any means of identification,' he continued, 'on Rügen, in winter. A general who's supposed to be on Rügen, but who also supposedly died at Stalingrad, in winter. A Silesian who – unasked – brings us 'evidence' of the general's demise, except that he was just a lieutenant-colonel at the time. Same Silesian appears in a clandestine video, wearing the ring of a grey organization we have yet to identify. Same Silesian gives the distinct impression that he and the Waffen SS were more than just good friends. The Silesian then requests—'

'Demands . . .'

'Demands. Of course. Must not forget that. Silesian *demands* a meeting, within less than an hour of his photograph being seen in Luigi's. *We* have the strong suspicion that the Silesian is von Mappus, though no proof.'

'Which makes him a mass murderer running free . . .'

'If he *is* von Mappus. And there's still that person to whom something is supposed to have happened on Rügen . . .'

'Von Mappus . . .'

'Who can't have died at Stalingrad, be the Silesian, *and* also have something happen to him on Rügen.'

'We do have a problem,' Pappenheim said, blowing six smoke rings.

Müller glanced at them as they wafted upwards. '*Six* smoke rings?'

'"Six little romeos", Major Gaegl said,' Pappenheim remarked. 'All there in the diary.'

'You're coming to the same tentative conclusions that I have, that von Mappus did survive the war, and may have been responsible for the genesis of the Romeo Six operation which gave us that headache last August.'

'Which is still giving us a headache. Tentacles everywhere.'

'Tentacles everywhere,' Müller agreed. 'We also do know that after the war, many Waffen SS melted as if by magic into the DDR forces at all levels.'

'We do indeed,' Pappenheim confirmed.

'A dead Russian, on Rügen, in winter,' Müller said again. 'An undead general, from the winter of Stalingrad. Winter, and the general . . .'

'Who can't be dead, because we think he's the Silesian . . . perhaps identified as such in Holbeck's dynamite little book . . .'

'How's your Russian, Pappi?'

'Like my German. Terrible.'

'Do you know what the name Rachko stands for?'

'I give up.'

'It means "judge".'

'I am judge and executioner,' Pappenheim remarked softly. 'Rachko's son, Andrei, may have seen his father having his throat cut by von Mappus. If you're thinking vengeance . . . we have another problem. The village was wiped out.'

'We don't know that the son was also killed. He could have survived the massacre.'

'He'd be younger than the Silesian, but not by much. Perhaps by ten, maybe eleven years. No spring chicken.'

'What about a younger generation?'

'A *grandson*? You're clutching, Jens.'

'I'll clutch at anything, if it gets me nearer to untangling this. Grogan knew exactly what he was doing when he made that call.'

'Then perhaps you should see the goth's computer game.'

'Is this a joke?'

'No joke. I've got to be more careful with jokes. The goth shot one down.'

'Brave woman.'

148

'She'll make someone a good wife one day.'

'Uh-oh. She must have hit home.'

Pappenheim stretched his lips across his teeth. 'I'm smiling. See?' He picked up a phone and pressed an extension button. 'Miss Meyer, could you please join us at the documents room? Yes.' He glanced at Müller. 'He's back. She's happy you're back,' he added, as he replaced the receiver.

'Don't say it,' Müller warned.

'I wouldn't dream.'

'All preparations made?' Pappenheim said as they made their way to the documents strongroom. 'Ready for Rügen?'

'What's really behind that question, Pappi?'

Pappenheim's blue eyes were at their most innocent. 'Such calumny!'

'I know you, Pappi. The answer is I've heard nothing as yet from Miss Bloomfield. But she'll be here.'

'Checked with the airlines, have we?'

'She'll be here,' Müller repeated.

'As you've mentioned it,' Pappenheim continued shamelessly, 'when are you going to the airport? We've got our meeting with the Silesian . . .'

'If she's here by then, we take her.'

Pappenheim shot Müller a glance. 'Is that wise?'

'I have an idea about that man. I want to rattle his chains.'

'With Miss *Bloomfield*?'

'Wait and see, Pappi. Wait and see.'

They found the goth waiting, with her usual bag of electronic tricks.

'Miss Meyer,' Müller greeted.

She smiled at him while Pappenheim punched in the door code. 'Sir.'

Pappenheim kept a straight face as they stood by for her to enter.

'New equipment?' Müller said to her, staring at the joystick and throttle.

Hedi Meyer took her seat at the computer and powered it up. 'All in a good cause, sir.'

149

'It had better be,' he said, thinking of Kaltendorf's reaction.

He glanced at Pappenheim, who seemed unusually mesmerized by the computer screen.

Hedi Meyer loaded the simulation and put on the spider. Müller stared briefly at the contraption on her head, but said nothing.

'I'll have the speakers on, so you can hear everything,' she told them.

The game's main screen came on. She made her selections, including online connection. When she got to the cockpit, Müller was astonished by its fidelity.

'Very realistic,' he said.

'It gets even better.'

She did her pre-flight checks, got clearance and taxied to the designated runway. She took off, and turned on to the same course as before.

'I'll climb to the same altitude,' she explained, 'and wait for my wingman.'

Müller again glanced at Pappenheim, on whose lips the tiniest of smiles had appeared. 'Your *wingman*?'

'Two, in position,' he heard a female voice say.

'She's here,' the goth said. 'Look. There she is.'

'It's an all-female squadron,' Pappenheim murmured to Müller.

'Don't be such a chauvinist, sir,' Hedi Meyer scolded.

'I'm suitably chastened,' he responded.

Hedi Meyer shifted the coolie hat switch on the joystick to the right. Müller stared at the very lifelike image of the F-16.

'Remarkable,' he said.

'What *is* going on?' the voice on the speakers asked. 'Are we going to hit some bandits, or what?'

'Bear with me,' Hedi Meyer replied. 'I'm trying to isolate a bug. Just like the last time, if I say quit, just do it.'

'OK,' came the uncertain acknowledgement.

As before, no hostile aircraft were encountered in the first minutes.

Hedi Meyer looked briefly back at Müller. 'We're coming up to the position, sir. Keep your eye on that.' She moved the cursor to indicate. 'That's the radar display. Now let's see . . . *there*, sir!'

At precisely the same time into flight as before, the single word CONTACT appeared.

'Quit!' she called to the wingman.

'I'm gone!' came the response.

Again as before, the second aircraft vanished.

'Shall I stay on?' Hedi Meyer asked Müller with some urgency.

His interest fully engaged, Müller said, 'Stay. See what comes next. Can you still get out if it's an attack?'

'No problem.'

'Then let's wait and see.'

The wait was not long. A new message had appeared: AWACS PICTURE.

'I didn't ask for an AWACS picture,' she said to the machine. To Müller and Pappenheim, she went on, 'AWACS is . . .'

'I think . . . we know what it is,' Müller said.

'Of course, sir. I only . . .'

Hedi Meyer stopped as the entire radar display blanked out, and something else took its place. All three stared at the twenty-six horizontal bars, arranged in pairs, in a vertical group. No two bars were of the same length, which ranged from the very long, to the extremely short. Each bar had an unbroken border at the top, beneath which were tabs of different colours, seemingly placed in haphazard order.

'A DNA profile!' the three of them exclaimed together.

At the top of the group of DNA strands, were two letters: VM.

Müller and Pappenheim glanced at each other, then Müller said to the goth, 'Can you save that?'

She nodded. 'I'll save it as a screen shot, then expand it for a printout.'

'Do it,' he said.

'Done.'

151

As if whoever had sent the profile knew what had happened, the radar screen again went blank, and another profile appeared. This one differed significantly from the first, and the letters at the top were VG.

'Save that too,' Müller said quickly.

'Done.'

The radar screen blanked out again and the normal display returned. Then a message appeared: COMPLETE.

When that too had vanished, they waited to see if anything else would come on. Nothing did.

'I think that was it, Miss Meyer,' Müller said. 'Now can we have the printouts?'

'No problem, sir. But I'd like to do a full system check, just to make sure nothing nasty came for the ride.'

'Alright.'

'Shall I kill the beacon?'

'No. Leave it in. You never know what other bounties we may receive.'

'Yes, sir.'

She ran the system check and, as before, there were no nasty surprises. She then printed out the profiles.

'Thank you,' Müller said as he picked them up from the tray. 'Miss Meyer, you are a genius.'

She beamed at him.

'Fly some more, if you want to,' he continued. 'But not too long, or Herman Spyros will start thinking we've kidnapped you. Let yourself out when you're done. As usual, make certain everything is secure when you do.'

'Yes, sir.'

'My office,' Müller said to Pappenheim.

'Your office.'

'And, on the way, we stop by yours to pick up a few things.'

'Alright, Pappi,' Müller began when they were back. 'Let's look at the big picture, as certain people like to say.'

'Not us . . . because we don't carry the exalted rank of *Polizeidirektor* . . .'

'Probationary. Let's not forget that.'

152

For response, Pappenheim gave one of his lip-stretching grins, as Müller began to put the items they had brought on the pristine surface of his desk.

Müller stood back to study his handiwork. Centrepiece was the picture of the Silesian, flanked by the DNA profiles. Below that was Holbeck's bloodstained diary. Beneath the diary was the photo of the unknown man who had died in the accident on Rügen. Next to the DNA profile identified as VM, he had placed the file with the details of the death at Stalingrad of von Mappus. Crowning the lot above the Silesian's head was the mysterious seal.

'Very pretty,' Pappenheim commented.

'Glad you like it. Now that we have read Holbeck's diary,' Müller continued, 'we can fill in some pieces. Look at the man from the accident. Supposedly Russian. He looks like a thug, even in death. Somehow, I can't believe he was the grandson – assuming there *is* a grandson – of the teacher who would rather feed his enemy than shoot him.'

'Something which cost him the ultimate,' Pappenheim remarked with grim irony, 'or we wouldn't be looking at this. But I agree. This . . . person looks more like a hit man, or bodyguard . . . probably one of the Silesian's.'

Müller nodded. 'I've considered that. But then I run up against a problem. Why would the Silesian have von Mappus – supposedly already dead these long years – killed on Rügen?'

'Especially if *he* is von Mappus.'

'Quite. Which leads us to the DNA profiles from our unknown benefactor.'

'Grogan?'

'Until we know to the contrary, it must be.' Müller tapped at the left-hand profile. 'VM has to mean von Mappus. But who would go to such lengths? Who would search for and *find* the remains among the hundreds of thousands of Stalingrad dead, to extract a sample of DNA?'

'Someone who knew where to look? Easier if he were *not* dead. People get sick, even fit murderers. They go to doctors, hospitals . . . Getting a sample under those conditions would be child's play.'

Müller again nodded, and tapped the right-hand sample. 'This is radically different. At first, when I saw VG, I thought he had changed his name.'

'According to Holbeck,' Pappenheim said, 'von Mappus made a big deal of being a 'von' by default, and showed contempt for the title. Funny how people who despise titles do their best to hang on to them . . .'

'Don't look at me,' Müller said with dry humour. 'I was dropped into mine at birth. Blame my grandfather.'

'Touchy.'

'In fact,' Müller continued firmly, 'I'm certain your Silesian—'

'You keep calling him *my* Silesian.'

'You found him.'

'He found *me* . . .'

'Alright, *our* Silesian. Better?'

'Much.'

'I'm certain,' Müller went on, 'that he has changed his name from whatever it used to be, when the war ended.'

'A common habit during the rat run in those nice times.'

'And, as we agreed earlier, he would have merged seamlessly into the DDR.'

'Another common habit when no one cared to look for blood-group tattoos and the like.'

'Exactly. If . . . as my itches tell me . . . he found his natural home in what later became the state police, he could well be the man – or one of the shadowy men – behind the special romeos we had to deal with last August. Which takes us neatly to this.' Müller now tapped at the printout of the seal. 'The seal Grogan put on the envelope he used to send me the minidisc. Is he one of them? Or has he in some way come by a seal, and wanted to point me in the right direction?'

'People who belong to organizations like that don't willingly give themselves away . . .'

'Which means he was laying a trail for us to follow. I'd still like to know his motives . . .'

'That makes two of us,' Pappenheim said.

'We leave the seal,' Müller went on, 'and come to this.' He pointed to Holbeck's diary. 'A chronicling of stupidity, brutality, and all that is disgusting about mankind, from a man living in a horror that was all around him. I'm amazed that Holbeck, caught in his own private hell, retained enough of his senses to put all this down. But thank God he was able to. He had a very strong mind.

'The diary ends in the village, as it is being destroyed. He is in Rachko's house, writing down the last words he is ever going to, with Rachko's own pen. We know someone interrupted him, because the last sentence is unfinished.'

'The question is . . .' Pappenheim began.

'Who,' Müller finished. 'And how did this diary safely get from Rachko's house to us, sixty years later? And what of the razor which – according to Holbeck – von Mappus left lying on the snowy ground after using it on Rachko? Is it still lying out there? And where did the Minox get to?'

'Now you've got me.'

Müller returned his attention to the DNA profiles. 'Look at the profile for VM . . . let's assume it *is* von Mappus. If we take just the top strand, the sequence of the first section of code is: cytosine-adenine-adenine-thymidine-thymidine-guanine-guanine-adenine – CAATTGGA. The same section of code on the VG profile is radically different . . . TTGGGACC. Two very different animals . . .'

'Neither of which could be our Silesian.'

'Perhaps we can get a sample from him.'

'Oh-ho. We are treading on dangerous ground. Taking samples without the owner's permission. The constitutional boys would have a field day with that one. Because I'm certain he's not going to give it, even if you ask nicely . . . and . . . he'll have a regiment of very expensive lawyers who could drive even you to poverty. We are not talking about sneaky fingerprint-lifting from a glass he's used. This comes under personal invasion, constitutional rights, you name it. Even an unpleasant piece of humanity like that will scream about his rights . . . which he does have, in our priceless democracy.'

'Heavy with the irony, Pappi. I do get the point . . . but sometimes, even the humble glass trick can work in a situation like this. When people drink, they leave saliva residues. We all do.' Müller paused. 'Moos died in the village. Holbeck must have died there too. I wonder what happened to the others? Did von Mappus kill them? We know he killed the major, and probably even the captain. Perhaps the others all died there . . .'

The phone rang. He reached across to pick it up. 'Müller.'

'Sir,' came Lene Berger's voice. 'Is the *Oberkommissar* with you? I just tried his office . . .'

'He's here.' Müller handed Pappenheim the phone. 'Berger.'

'Yes, Lene?' Pappenheim said.

'You're popular today, Chief. Something just came for you.'

'Who from?'

'A man who didn't speak much. He was able to get into the building without any trouble. I saw him on the way to your office. I stopped him and asked what he wanted. He just said 'Pappenheim'. I went ahead to warn you, but saw you weren't there. He gave me the stuff and just walked away without saying anything else.'

'What was he like?'

'Tall. Very short hair. Tanned. Real sun, not sun studio. Neat suit, but questionable . . .'

'It's a blue folder, with a black border.'

Berger was surprised. 'How did you know?'

'I know the type you described. Could you bring it over please?'

'On my way.'

Pappenheim glanced at the printout of the seal as he put the phone down. 'Blue folder, black border,' he repeated. 'Blue seal . . . nah. Too easy.'

'All the same,' Müller said, 'hang on to that thought.'

Pappenheim gave him a long stare. 'You're serious.'

'I'm suspicious,' Müller corrected. 'True, they have thrown snippets our way. True, you have your contact in there. However, I don't think they're doing this because they like the length of my hair, or your taste in ties . . . or even Kaltendorf's . . .'

'Which is horrible.' Pappenheim said that with feeling.

Berger knocked at that moment.

'Come in!'

'Sirs,' Berger said to them as she entered. She handed Pappenheim the folder, glancing at the display on Müller's desk.

'Thanks, Lene,' Pappenheim said as he took it. 'Real sun tan?' he added.

'Real,' she confirmed. 'He's been to somewhere hot.'

'Hell, probably,' Pappenheim said. He jerked his chin at Müller's desk. 'And you haven't seen that.'

'Seen what, sir?' she said as she went back out.

'Hmm,' he said as the door closed behind her. He opened the untitled folder, as Müller watched with interest. 'Well, well. We have a name for our Silesian.'

'Response to your email?'

Pappenheim nodded. 'Our man's name is . . . don't laugh . . . Helmut von Graff.'

'You're joking.'

Pappenheim looked up from the folder. 'Nope. With two Fs. The VG in the profile?'

'Possibly . . . possibly not. Until we know about Rügen, we keep it open. What else?'

Pappenheim studied the details he had been sent. 'According to this, he is indeed a general. Police,' he went on after a pause. 'A retired DDR police general. Hmm.'

'We're getting somewhere.'

'He's also very rich. No details about how he made so much money. The suggestion is he made it *after* the fall of the Wall. His age is down as seventy-two . . .' Pappenheim snorted. 'He looks younger, but I think he's a lot older. It's in the eyes.'

'Why would the blue-folder boys lie?'

'Why not? If von Graff is a fake identity, why not the rest?' Pappenheim passed the folder over. 'See for yourself. It smells doctored to me.'

'But it's from your contact,' Müller said as he took it. 'Would she lie to you?'

'*She* wouldn't. But we don't know the source of her information. That's where the doctoring could have originated.'

'Or she sent it, knowing you'd be suspicious,' Müller said, studying the contents for some moments.

As with the information on the death of von Mappus, the folder contained just the one sheet. He shut the folder, and handed it back.

'Von Mappus, von Graff.' He turned back to the display on his desk. 'One a dead lieutenant-colonel; the other, a very much alive, retired general of police. But the dead lieutenant-colonel is a *general* in some kind of trouble – possibly dead a second time – on Rügen. A Russian unknown – who looks like the kind of person who would be a hit man, dies in a car accident on Rügen. The rich, retired general has Russian bodyguards. With all that weaponry going spare after the fall of the Wall, no prizes for guessing how he made his money. And then . . .' He looked at Holbeck's diary. '. . . we have Rachko, judge . . . and executioner. Perhaps. Getting clearer?'

'Darker,' Pappenheim said.

The mighty F-15E Strike Eagle swept along the brightly lit runway at Lakenheath, England, in the winter dark, and banked hard in preparation for the landing. Wheels down, vast dorsal airbrake extended, it touched down smoothly, slowed, taxied off the runway to its allocated spot on the ramp, and came to a halt. As its engines spooled down, the huge clam-shell canopy raised itself open, allowing the cold air to flood in.

In the back seat, Carey Bloomfield removed her flight helmet and began to disconnect herself from the aircraft she had sat in for six and a half hours.

'Thanks for the ride,' she called to the pilot up front.

He twisted his head round briefly. 'Anytime, sir, ma'am. You're a pretty good whizzo there in back. You should try for the front seat.'

'Thanks for the compliment,' she said. 'I am back-seat qualified, but no chance. You wouldn't get me up in one of these things.'

The pilot was slightly confused. 'But you've just been up . . .'

'That's the point.'

She rose, and began to climb out of the Eagle, picking up her flight bag as she did so.

The pilot followed, went round to the nose of the big fighter, and patted it.

'Ferrari on steroids,' he said with a grin.

'Someone else said that.'

'I know. It's still a Sierra Hotel description. Dinner in the officers' club?' he suggested hopefully as he signed the aircraft off to the crew chief.

They began walking.

She shook her head. 'Sorry. Another plane to catch.'

He gave a rueful smile. 'Lucky stiff, whoever he is.'

'He doesn't know how lucky.'

'Dumb stiff.'

'Dumb he isn't,' she said, knowing he had no idea whom she meant.

The pilot was looking confused again.

'Quit while you're ahead,' Carey Bloomfield said to him.

Carrying her helmet and flight bag, she walked on to where an executive jet, in civilian markings, was waiting.

The pilot stopped. 'Er . . . yes, sir . . . ma'am.'

But he was talking to himself. He stared after her as he entered the aircrew minibus that had come to pick him up.

Carey Bloomfield went up the steps of the executive jet. The only person aboard was its pilot, in civilian clothes.

'Hi,' he greeted. 'Berlin?'

'Berlin.'

He pressed a button and the steps began to retract. The door shut with a soft hiss.

'Care to sit up front?'

'Why not?' Carey Bloomfield said. 'But first I've got to get out of this flight gear. There should be a bag waiting.'

He pointed to a built-in cabinet where one of the cabin seats would have been. 'In there, and untouched. Press at the doors and they'll spring open.' He gave a fleeting smile. 'I'll be on the flight deck, behind the door. Join me when you're done.'

'Thank you.'

The pilot went to the flight deck and, as promised, shut the door behind him.

She first opened the flight bag and took out a big, holstered automatic pistol, a Beretta 92R. It was her personal favourite weapon. She checked the cabinet and found the bag that had been left there for her. It had a seven-wheel combination lock. She rapidly aligned the code numbers and opened it. A change of clothing, a shoulder bag, plus spare magazines for the gun, were in it.

She changed into civilian clothes, put her gear and helmet in the flight bag, then placed that, too, in the cabinet. She put the gun and the magazines in the shoulder bag, and took it with her when she joined the pilot on the flight deck. She got into the right-hand, co-pilot's seat, but did not touch the controls.

The pilot, an officially moonlighting fighter pilot with wide experience on many aircraft, did a fast taxi, got clearance for take-off, and lifted the executive jet into the air in a manner that would have done justice to a Strike Eagle.

Carey Bloomfield closed her eyes. It was 18.30 CET.

Müller glanced at his watch. It was now 19.30.

'If she's not in the country soon,' he said, 'we'll have to go without her.'

He had checked with all the airlines expecting flights from Washington DC. Her name had not been on any passenger manifest.

'Of course,' he went on, 'she might not be using her real name.'

Pappenheim had been looking out, as usual, on the city. He watched the play of a fluttering snowfall in the brightness of the spread of lights.

'She may not come at all,' he suggested, not turning round.

'She'll be here.'

'So you said before. She may not be as predictable as you think.'

'I know my Miss Bloomfield, Pappi . . .'

'*Your* Miss Bloomfield.'

'Don't read too much into it.'

'*Moi?*'

Müller glanced at his watch a second time. 'It's time we left for our meeting with the arrogant Silesian. Miss Bloomfield will have to wait.'

He rose from behind his desk, and picked up a plain brown envelope. In it were the printouts of the seal, and of the unknown accident victim. The other material had been safely put away in the documents strongroom, in the same cabinet as Grogan's minidisc.

'What baffles me,' Müller continued, 'is von Graff's – as we should now call him – reason for coming to us in the first place. He could not have known we received that call from Grogan. On the other hand . . .'

'His organization may have access to highly sensitive, national institutions.'

'I would bank on *that*. His coming to us with that file on von Mappus was a pre-emptive strike. Let's make it work against him. We've got weapons he certainly does not know about. Alright, Pappi. Let's see why von Graff is so eager to talk to us.'

They were waiting near the lift that would take them to the underground garage when they saw a familiar figure striding towards them.

'Miss Bloomfield!' they said together, taken completely by surprise.

'I've just spent six and a half hours in the back seat of a fighter jet,' she greeted, 'sat through three refuellings, and the pilot asked me for a date. I changed to a bizjet in England. I'm jet-lagged, and here I am. This had better be worth it, Müller.'

'Forthright as ever,' Müller remarked with a smile.

'He said you'd make it,' Pappenheim said, holding out his hand.

'Hi, Pappi,' Carey Bloomfield said, shaking it. She looked at Müller. 'I'm so predictable?'

'I certainly did not expect a jet fighter,' Müller said. 'They're putting one at your disposal these days?'

'I got a ferry ride.'

'I see.'

'Look,' Pappenheim said, 'you two have some catching up to do. Why don't I wait by the car?'

'Good idea, Pappi,' Carey Bloomfield said, still looking at Müller.

'I thought so too,' Pappenheim responded. 'Er . . .' He patted his midriff and looked at Müller. '. . . will we all get in?'

'We will. Don't worry.'

The lift arrived with a *ping*.

'I always liked being a sardine,' Pappenheim said as he entered.

The doors hissed shut.

'Well,' Müller began to Carey Bloomfield.

'I'll give you "well",' she said. '*Months*, Müller . . . and not a word.'

'You didn't make contact either,' he countered. 'And besides . . .' He lowered his voice. '. . . I don't think we should discuss this here, in the corridor.'

Her gaze did not waver, but she lowered her voice too. It was more of a hiss. 'That guy I just told you about? He asked me to dinner. Are we going to eat?'

'It can be arranged. We're going to a restaurant for a meeting.'

'Oh good. Is it one I know?'

'The Death Strip.'

'What do they do there? Shoot you?'

'Hmm . . . as Pappi would say.' He glanced down at a ring she wore, but could not see it clearly. 'How did you get into the building without an escort?' he added.

The lift returned, and they got in.

'Would you believe the first person I saw was Berger? Miss Hawkeyes herself. She let me in.'

'Oh dear. You are feeling good.'

'I've not had much sleep, Müller. Someone woke me up in the middle of the night and, as I said, I'm as jet-lagged as hell. I don't feel in too good a mood right now.'

Müller said nothing as the lift made its way down.

162

They found Pappenheim walking slowly around the car they would be using, a brand new Porsche Cayenne Turbo.

He stopped, looking a bit sheepish, like a child caught out. 'Now I know why you were so smug when I talked about Rügen. At least I won't be a sardine.'

'Now you know,' Müller said, hiding a smile.

Carey Bloomfield stared at the big sports utility. 'Why have one Porsche when you can have two? Going town and country, Müller? The Carrera Turbo for town, and this for country? And in the same seal grey. Nice work.'

Pappenheim looked at them curiously. 'Er . . . I think I'll sit behind. I hate getting caught between warring couples.'

'I'm not warring,' she said. 'I'm just jet-lagged.'

As he climbed into the back, Pappenheim did not look as if he believed it.

They drove out of the garage in silence. A light snow was falling, but did not settle.

'Have you brought your cannon?' Müller asked Carey Bloomfield after some minutes.

'Are we going to shoot somebody?'

'Not if I can help it. But it would be a good precaution.'

'I've brought it.'

More silence followed. In the back, Pappenheim looked from one to the other, the tiniest of smiles on his lips.

'What's on Rügen?' Carey Bloomfield asked.

'A very baffling mystery, sixty years old. You might find it of interest. You might also find much to interest you in the person we're about to meet.' Müller glanced at the thick black coat she wore. 'Warm as that coat looks, you'll need to bring more practical winter wear. Cross-country stuff. It's a snow-field up there. I'm certain I can find you something . . .'

'If there's time to shop before we leave . . .'

'I plan to leave at nine tomorrow morning.'

'Oh.'

'Earlier today, I got some gear I thought you might need. It's in the back. Hope I got the sizes right. You don't have to use it, of course. If you'd prefer . . .'

'If it fits, I'll use it.'

'Fine. Has your hotel been booked?'

'Are you making me an offer?'

'You've only just got in . . . if you have nowhere to stay . . .'

'A hotel's not a problem . . .'

'Fine . . .'

'But I'll take your offer.'

'Fine,' Müller said for a third time. 'And you can stop smiling before your cheeks crack, Pappi,' he added to Pappenheim.

Pappenheim, who had been listening to the exchange with a wide grin of amusement, became suddenly interested in a passing traffic light.

They arrived at The Death Strip exactly one minute late.

Pappenheim led the way in, and headed directly for the corner table he had occupied on his previous visit. Von Graff was sitting by himself, back protected by the corner. At a nearby table were two hard-faced men. The way they had positioned themselves clearly indicated they were von Graff's bodyguards.

Carey Bloomfield glanced about her as they made their way towards von Graff. Soulless eyes raked them, then looked away.

'What's this?' she whispered to Müller. 'The united nations of hardcases?'

'Pappi finds this place a mine of information.'

'Better him than me. We're going to *eat* here?'

'Not if you're too afraid.'

'Watch it, Müller.'

They stopped before von Graff's table. Pappenheim positioned himself so that he had the bodyguards well covered, if they tried anything.

The Silesian looked coldly up at Müller. 'You are late, Herr Graf von Röhnen. I am a busy man. I cannot afford to waste time waiting on others.' He did not stand to greet them, nor did he invite them to sit at his table.

'There's a first time for everything,' Müller said.

Von Graff's dead eyes studied Carey Bloomfield. He switched languages.

'Miss Carey Bloomfield. A singular pleasure.' His English was perfect. 'We may speak English, if you prefer. But I believe your German is quite proficient. We can continue in German, should you wish it.'

Müller, Pappenheim and Carey Bloomfield were astonished.

'Do I know you?' she asked von Graff in German.

'No, Miss Bloomfield. You do not. But I know rather a lot about you. I once knew someone who knew your brother . . . closely.'

Von Graff's malevolently cold eyes appeared to be smiling. Carey Bloomfield felt a chill descend upon her.

'What do you mean?' she asked, voice tight with the tension of a nightmare memory.

'I believe you know precisely what I mean, Miss Bloomfield. You, and the noble *Hauptkommissar*, killed the man who so efficiently and painfully stripped your brother of his skin. I taught him that trick.'

Carey Bloomfield had gone so pale she was ghostly.

Pappenheim watched the bodyguards with the intensity of a hawk about to strike. Müller remained very still.

Von Graff smiled thinly. 'Tell me, *Hauptkommissar* Müller . . .' His eyes switched with feral deliberation from Müller, to Carey Bloomfield, and back again. '. . . have you yet slept with this physically appealing . . . Jewess?'

The backhanded slap, when it came, was so swift and loud it took everyone by surprise: Pappenheim, the bodyguards, von Graff, and Müller. Everyone in the restaurant broke the unwritten rule, and turned to stare. The atmosphere in the entire place was suddenly high with an electric tension, as they all waited to see what would happen next.

For the first time, von Graff's eyes showed emotion. Pain, and rage. His hand was pressed tightly to his right cheek, a slow trickle of blood seeping from beneath its edge.

'Once,' he said to Carey Bloomfield, fighting to control the rage boiling within him, 'you would have been shot for that, an instant later.'

'In the good old days?' she responded in a soft snarl.

'You've just been slapped by an "Untermensch", Herr *General*. Would you like to try now and see how far you'd get?'

Pappenheim looked hard at the bodyguards and shook his head slowly. They looked from him to von Graff, whose eyes glanced away from Carey Bloomfield's long enough to command them to do nothing.

Luigi Bocca arrived anxiously. 'Lady! *Commissarios!* Gentlemen! No trouble, please! This is neutral territory . . .'

'Go back to your kitchen, little man!' von Graff barked savagely.

Bocca retreated without another word.

Müller got out a handkerchief, which he offered to von Graff. 'This is a noble handkerchief. Pure aryan. Don't mind her. She's jet-lagged. And anyway, only her father's Jewish. As you know, it resides in the mother . . .'

The dead eyes looked at Müller. 'Your humour escapes me,' von Graff snapped. He glared at the handkerchief with contempt, then took out one of his own to put on the wound.

'Nasty gash,' Müller remarked as he put his away. 'If you cut yourself shaving tomorrow, it will balance out nicely.'

The barest of sparks showed in the dead eyes, before vanishing as swiftly.

Carey Bloomfield glanced at Müller. 'What are you talking about, Müller?'

Müller's eyes were riveted upon von Graff. 'I just wondered whether *General* von Graff – retired – likes shaving. His cheeks are so smooth . . .'

Von Graff's cheeks were suddenly hollow as his sharp intake of breath showed the extent of his surprise; but again he was swiftly back under control.

'You may think you know something, Müller,' he said in his cold, hard voice, 'but you have no idea of what you're dealing with.'

'Where have I heard that tune before?'

'You should have listened.'

Müller suddenly reached forward and grabbed the hand with the handkerchief that von Graff still pressed to his

166

cheek. He slammed it to the table. Von Graff tried to pull away, but Müller's grip was vice-like.

The bodyguards began to rise to their feet. Pappenheim took a single step forward, pushed his coat slightly back to place his hand on a pistol at his hip. Another gun was in its shoulder holster.

The bodyguards sat down.

Von Graff glared at Müller. 'In my day . . .'

'This is no longer *your* day, von Graff,' Müller cut in. '*Wake up*. It is gone forever! The law I serve and enforce will make certain of it. You called me here for a purpose,' he went on. 'What was it?' He still held on to the hand.

'It is *not* over!' von Graff said in a strangulated hiss. 'The mission was not completed. You believe, my noble, Armani-suited policeman,' he went on contemptuously, 'that you are some kind of knight on a white horse, fighting the world's evils. But you are not as clean as you would like to think you are. Your armour is not shining. You are just another, deluded Galahad. Or a Lancelot. I prefer Lancelot. He, certainly, was not clean. Be warned, Müller, you have just made the biggest mistake of your life.'

Von Graff, glaring, tried to free his wrist from Müller's grip; to no avail.

'And as long as I am alive,' Müller said, 'your kind will *never* again control this country.'

'Be very careful, Herr Graf,' the Silesian spat. 'Do not offer your life so easily. One day, it may come to it.'

'You will be long dead before that day arrives.'

Von Graff, eyes still full of outrage, continued his attempt to free his wrist. But Müller's grip was unrelenting.

'You have more knowledge than I expected,' von Graff said. 'One wonders how you came by it. But remember . . . a little learning can be a dangerous thing.'

'*Is*,' Müller corrected. 'A little learning *is* a dangerous thing.'

'Of course . . . with your *English* education, you would know . . .'

'I've had a German education too . . .'

'And I know exactly what I mean.'

167

'That remains to be seen,' Müller said, unimpressed. He squeezed the wrist harder.

Von Graff could not help slightly relaxing his hold on the handkerchief.

Müller whipped it away. 'Dispose of that, shall I?'

He let go of von Graff, to go over to Pappenheim. 'Watch the shop, will you, Miss Bloomfield?'

'With pleasure.'

She pulled her Beretta out of her bag and pointed it at von Graff as the bodyguards, expecting a chance, began to rise to their feet once more.

'He'd never make it,' she told them, 'and you'd be out of a job.'

They sat down again.

Müller, holding the handkerchief by a corner, dropped it into a small plastic exhibit bag that Pappenheim had taken from a pocket.

Von Graff gave an uncertain frown as he glanced at Müller and Pappenheim, then turned back to Carey Bloomfield.

'You have no idea whatsoever what you're dealing with,' he said to her. 'All three of you.' His lips pulled back in a feral snarl. 'And you, Miss Bloomfield, will die very slowly, regretting it.' The small gash on his cheek no longer leaked blood, but a bright red weal had taken up residence there.

'Amazing,' she said. 'Guys like you, still in a time warp. That beauty spot hurt much? Nice planet we've got,' she went on. 'Shame about some of the people. Life . . . you gotta puke.'

Von Graff just stared at her, the predator surveying its next meal.

Then Müller was back. 'If that's all you got me here for, Herr *General*,' he said, 'I have much to do. So . . .'

'You will remain until I have finished!' von Graff snapped at him.

'No, *General*. You have got this all wrong. You don't give me orders. Your days – and I will say it slowly so that you understand – are . . . *over*. But while you're trying to decide whom you can give orders to, perhaps this will give you some food for thought.'

Müller removed the printout of the seal from the envelope, and placed it face down on the table.

'I think we'll eat somewhere else this evening,' he said to Carey Bloomfield.

'I had the same thought.'

Müller looked at Pappenheim. 'We're finished here.'

Pappenheim nodded. As he moved past the bodyguards, he gave them each a pat on the head. 'Be good, boys,' he said to them in Russian.

They glared at him, but did nothing.

At his table, von Graff slowly turned over the printout. He paled and leapt to his feet when he saw what it was.

His gaze darted to the exit but Müller, Pappenheim and Carey Bloomfield were already gone.

Müller had waited outside, just out of sight, to peer back into the restaurant. From his vantage point, he had seen von Graff leap to his feet. He now smiled to himself as he walked on to join the others by the Cayenne.

'And?' Pappenheim prompted.

'Jumped to his feet,' Müller replied, 'white as a sheet. We hit home. He'll be talking to a few of his pals tonight.'

'Somebody going to let me in on what's going on?' Carey Bloomfield asked them. 'If you can give me permission to blow away a diehard old nightmare, shouldn't I know why?' She was looking at Müller. 'And how did you know he would recognize me?'

'I was as surprised as you were,' Müller said.

'But?'

'Does there have to be a but?'

'With you, Müller? Always.'

'I had a gut feeling,' he told her. 'But the development was very unexpected. I'm sorry for what he said.'

'About sleeping with me? Or about my brother?'

'Both.'

Her first smile since her arrival was a tired one. 'You were really angry back there . . .'

Pappenheim cleared his throat. 'I hate to break up this cosiness, but I think it would be wise for us to get away from

169

here, children. If von Graff is as shaken as you say, Jens, he may decide to send his geniuses after us, just for the hell of it. Somehow, I don't think mere policemen frighten him.'

'He's certainly enraged enough. We'll take your advice, Pappi. Besides, now is not the time for a gun battle. Too many other pieces to be fitted into the puzzle before that happens.'

'Perhaps we should give Miss Bloomfield a little light reading,' Pappenheim suggested as they entered the car.

'What's he mean?' she asked Müller, clipping on her seatbelt. She twisted round briefly. 'What do you mean, Pappi?'

Pappenheim was looking at Müller, waiting.

'It's an idea,' Müller said to Pappenheim. 'That was quite a slap you delivered to von Graff,' he went on to Carey Bloomfield, 'and he deserved it. That ring of yours is a formidable weapon.'

'I've seen you glancing at it, Müller,' she said. 'It's a sorority ring. Sometimes I wear it. Sometimes I don't. That answer your question?'

'Your ring, Miss Bloomfield,' Pappenheim chipped in from the back. 'May we borrow it?' He was leaning forward, cotton gloves on, a snap-seal exhibit bag held open.

She studied the hand with the ring in the interior lighting. The sorority symbol was in raised Greek lettering.

'Ugh!' she said. 'There's blood on it and . . . a strip of skin. Here. You can have it with pleasure.'

'Wait,' Pappenheim said quickly. 'I'll do that.' With his gloved hand, he gently slid the ring off her finger and put it into the bag, which he snapped shut. 'Thank you.'

'As long as I can have it back, Pappi.'

'You have my promise,' Pappenheim assured her. To Müller, he added, 'We didn't need the glass trick, after all.'

'Which would have been difficult, considering he made sure he did not have one on the table. Look,' Müller continued to Carey Bloomfield as he started the Cayenne and the interior lighting switched itself off. 'About the ring . . . I wasn't . . .'

'I need to eat,' she said.

Eight

'*Pizza!*' Carey Bloomfield grumbled. 'Great. I come all the way across the Atlantic for a *pizza*?'

The three of them were walking along the corridor, each carrying a boxed pizza, and heading for the documents room. Pappenheim hung back, allowing Müller and Carey Bloomfield to get ahead of him. He watched them in amusement, their body language for the moment unguarded, saying it all.

When they got to the door, Müller handed Pappenheim his pizza. 'I'll get the coffee while you show Miss Bloomfield in.'

'He makes very good coffee,' Pappenheim said to her as Müller went off. He balanced the pizzas in the crook of an arm as he punched in the entry code. 'After you,' he continued when the solid door had swung open.

The first thing that attracted her gaze was the computer and its appendages.

'You guys play *flying* games in here? Does Kaltendorf know?'

'Ah. Well. It's a long story . . . and no, we're not playing computer games. It's the goth.' Pappenheim placed the pizzas on the large central table. 'You do remember Hedi Meyer?'

'Of course. Your electronics genius.'

'That's the one. She's the game player.'

'In *here*? What's Kaltendorf got to say about that?'

Pappenheim began to open the box that contained his own pizza. 'Second part of the question first. Our esteemed chief does not know and at the moment – thank God – he's on one of his networking trips. As for the gaming, there's a very serious purpose behind it.'

171

'Which you're not going to tell me.'

'For the moment . . . no.' Pappenheim looked at his pizza with relish. 'Ah! Hawaiian with every possible topping. Now that . . . is a pizza!'

'It's . . . well . . . huge,' Carey Bloomfield observed as she opened her box.

He grinned at her. 'I am hugely hungry.'

'I've got Four Seasons . . . let's see if I'm going to kill Müller for getting me pizza from what looked like a hole in the wall, instead of dinner in a fancy restaurant.'

The pizza had already been cut into segments. She took a slice and bit into it.

'Mmm!' she said in pleasant surprise as she chewed. 'Gawd . . . this *is* good!' she added when she'd finished. She picked up another piece. 'If they can make pizza as good as this, they can be a hot-dog stand, for all I care.'

'It's the only place in town from which he'll have a pizza,' Pappenheim informed her. He looked at her with benign interest as she ate.

'Don't you look at me as if you think I'm fat,' she warned.

'You, Miss Bloomfield, are most definitely not fat.'

'Besides,' she went on, as if he had not spoken. 'If he likes skeletons, he should go rattle a closet. I'll not look like I need a UN food parcel for anyone.'

'"He",' Pappenheim began, with dry emphasis, 'does not like the skeletal type of woman. And if you tell him I said that, I'll be forced to shoot you.'

'If I were mad enough to tell him you said that, I'd save you the trouble and shoot myself.'

Pappenheim gave one of his smiles that could have meant anything.

'He has specific choices of places all over the country, he continued, where he likes to eat. There's a coffee-shop restaurant on the Rhine near St Goar . . . you do remember St Goar . . . ?'

'Oh I do,' she replied grimly. 'I nearly got blown up on that boat not far from there, last summer.'

'Well that coffee shop serves one of his favourite cakes. The best, as far as he's concerned. He discovered it during his

172

student days.' He saw that she was looking at him curiously. 'Is something wrong?'

'You were smiling, Pappi, as you told me that little story. If you ever discovered something about Müller you didn't like, what would you do?'

Pappenheim slowly put down his unfinished slice of pizza. His baby-blue eyes gave nothing away as he looked back at her.

'Your reason for saying that, Miss Bloomfield?'

Slightly taken aback, she said, 'Hey, hey, Pappi. Lighten up. I'm not attacking him. It's just something very curious von Graff said back there. That Sir Lancelot thing.'

Pappenheim smoothly picked up his unfinished slice. 'We made von Graff nervous. His type hates being on the defensive. They like to control events, not the other way round. Worse, the people doing it are a couple of *policemen*, whom he sees as being beneath the exalted status he has given himself. He lashed out the only way he could.'

'It's an answer.'

'It is an answer.'

Just then Müller entered with three steaming cups of coffee on a tray.

'Coffee!' they said together, each relieved for very different reasons that the awkward moment had passed.

'I wasn't gone that long,' Müller said, looking from one to the other as he placed the tray on the table. He handed a cup to each. 'Here you are. Müller's best.'

'Now that you're back,' Pappenheim said as he took his cup, 'I think I should go off to arrange a forensic test of the items. Besides, I need a smoke. Haven't had one since we left for Luigi's.' He picked up the box with the remains of his pizza.

Knowing exactly what Pappenheim really meant, Müller said, 'Alright, Pappi. I'll take it from here.'

'Will you be coming back in the morning, before you set off for Rügen?'

Müller shook his head. 'We'll be heading straight out.'

'And if by any unfortunate chance, the GW turns up in your absence?'

'I'm following clues. You don't know where.'

'The Great White Shark? Ah. Well, so many things I don't know.' Pappenheim gave Carey Bloomfield a parting nod. 'Very good to see you again, Miss Bloomfield. Sorry we dragged you out without giving you time to recover from your flight.'

'I'll survive, Pappi. Look after yourself.'

'Always.'

'How do you like your pizza?' Müller asked Carey Bloomfield as Pappenheim went out.

'Perfect. I wouldn't have believed it.'

'Smart restaurants don't always serve the highest quality . . . except perhaps for the prices. That amazing little place is owned not by Italians, but by a Belgian–French couple. He's French – from Arras, and she's from Namur. They came to Berlin just after the Wall came down. I'll have pizza from nowhere else.'

'I know. Pappi said.'

'Pappi thinks my choice of such places a little . . . idiosyncratic.'

'I don't think so,' she said, but did not explain further.

They had nearly finished eating when Pappenheim returned, his expression clearly showing there had been an important development.

'Results already?' Müller asked, the last slice of pizza halfway to his mouth.

'Not from what you're thinking of. I've just got a call from Norbert Roth.' Pappenheim glanced at Carey Bloomfield.

'Go on, Pappi. Miss Bloomfield is going to do a little bedtime reading, so she might as well hear this too.'

'They found a gun.'

Müller put down the pizza. 'Where?'

'Under the car involved in that crash. They had taken it to the police garage. First inspection had been cursory. Stolen car, false plates, so on. Nothing outwardly different from the usual run of petty crime. After we first talked, Norbert himself decided to have a second look; then a third when he discovered our unknown victim could be Russian; then a fourth look out of curiosity. That's when he found it.

'A section of the car seemed to have withstood the impact better than the others. It had been covered with a thick coating of underseal. Scraping at it, he found much newer metal underneath. More scraping revealed that a shallow box section had been welded where there shouldn't have been one. Still more scraping revealed catches. He pressed them, praying it wasn't a bomb. Out dropped one of Evgeniy Fedorovich's beauties in a nice weatherproof case.'

Both Müller and Carey Bloomfield stared at him.

'A *Dragunov*?' they said together.

'*Snayperskaya Vintovka Dragunova.*' Yep. The very same. E. F. Dragunov's long-range killer. But this one's the latest variant. SVDS with a load of accessories,' Pappenheim continued. 'Newish, with lightweight folding stock, be-scoped, and with enough ammunition to take out a regiment at long distance. I exaggerate, but you get the picture. It was actually six fully loaded, ten-round magazines, one already snapped into the rifle.

'*Six* full loads . . .' Carey Bloomfield turned to Müller. '. . . and one of *the* best sniper rifles in the world. These babies can kill at over three and a half kilometres.'

'Three point eight, to be precise,' Pappenhem said. 'Although I know someone who claimed he could score with one shot at *four* kilometres. He was drunk at the time, though.'

Carey Bloomfield's gaze was still on Müller. 'What are you getting me into, Müller?'

'I don't know what *I'm* getting myself into,' he replied.

'Now there's a confidence booster.'

'What has Roth done with it?' Müller asked Pappenheim.

'He's keeping it under cover till you get there,' Pappenheim replied. 'He closed the box and reset the catches so that it looks as if the box was already empty. I got the impression he'd be more than happy to get rid of the thing.'

'I'll grant him his wish tomorrow. A late-version Dragunov,' Müller went on thoughtfully, 'Was our man a roving executioner? And was his next target on Rügen?'

'Like the general who died, and rose again,' Pappenheim suggested. 'And who may have died a second time.

'Or he could have been a courier, and was *delivering* it.

If so, the intended recipient may still be waiting up there. Pappi, tell Roth no one else is to know about that rifle. If he gets into trouble over it later, we'll sort it out at this end with his bosses.'

'And who's going to sort out *our* boss?'

'Don't ask difficult questions. You know they give me a headache.'

'I've got plenty of aspirin,' Pappenheim said as he left.

Carey Bloomfield looked steadily at Müller. He raised an eyebrow at her and waited.

'It's not that I'm worried,' she began. 'But if I'm going to walk into a hornets' nest, I'd at least like to know what type of hornet.'

'Bedtime reading,' he said. 'Then we'll talk.'

He went to the cabinet in which the Grogan minidisc was stored and opened it. He slid out the drawer and removed Holbeck's diary, which, still inside its plastic bag, was now in a plain, protective envelope.

'If you're finished,' he said to her as he shut everything again, 'we'll take the cups and boxes, stop by my office for a few minutes, then it's home.'

Mouth full, she nodded. 'I'm done here.'

In his office, Müller got out a pair of cotton gloves and handed them to her. 'For your bedtime story.'

She glanced curiously at them, then looked from the model of the Hammond organ on his desk, to Monet's magpie, and back again. 'The Mondrian's gone . . .'

'It hasn't gone. It's back home . . .'

'And you've got a baby Hammond on your desk . . . You're sending some conflicting signals here, Müller. Do you play that thing?'

'After a fashion.'

'Which means you play it damned well. I hate guys like you.'

He smiled at her. 'Shall we go?'

Rügen; 21.00 Central European Time.

Zima Rachko double-checked the time on the small travelling clock on his bedside table.

Galina, sitting in a comfortable armchair with her bare feet on the bed, said, 'Do you think the boat will come tomorrow afternoon as he promised?'

'Nothing to do with promising. He wants the camera. Now that I've told him we've got it, he, and the boat, will be there. Without the camera, he would leave us here.'

'Or have us killed.'

'That too. He might still try to double-cross us.'

'I wish we didn't have to deal with him, Zima.'

'We need him, just as he needs us. He helped us to get von Mappus. Now he wants the camera as payment.'

'But *we* want it.'

'He doesn't know that . . . yet.'

'Perhaps he does.'

'Then we'll just have to be very careful. We still need to get the diary, which he says he knows is in Germany.'

'I think he'll want to have that too,' Galina said, full of mistrust.

'I'm certain he does,' Zima Rachko said.

He did not seem unduly worried.

Berlin-Wilmersdorf.

Carey Bloomfield looked up at the classic architecture of the well-lit building, as they waited for the steel door at the entrance to the underground garage to roll itself upwards. A bright red light switched to green as the door locked into place.

Müller drove down the gentle slope of the entry ramp and into the spacious parking area, the main lights coming on as he did so. The door began to lower itself and by the time the Cayenne had parked next to the Carrera Turbo, the entrance was again secure.

Carey Bloomfield looked about her. 'Three-car families?'

There were three sets of triple parking places, including Müller's. Sleek BMWs abounded.

'Each household has three parking bays,' Müller explained. 'One apartment per floor.'

'Just *three* apartments in this big building? This car park

177

is so clean, if I ate off the floor *it* would catch something. How much of your blood do they take to pay for it? And which floor is yours?'

'Er . . . the penthouse.'

She was silent for long moments. 'That figures. So who owns the building?'

'I do. I inherited it from my father, who inherited it from his. It was bombed out during the war, but my grandfather had it rebuilt to its original standard in the fifties. I have my own separate entrance.'

This time, she was silent for even longer. 'Oops,' she said at last. 'That figures too.'

'You don't approve?'

'What's to approve? If my grandfather had left me something like this, I'd dance in the street. I'm just jealous, Müller.'

'I'm not sure I believe that.'

'Believe it,' she said as they climbed out. 'How fast does this thing go, anyway?'

'Two hundred and sixty-six kilometres an hour,' he replied. 'One hundred and sixty-five miles per hour to you.'

'Hey,' she said. 'Why not?' She stood back a little to look at the two Porsches, side by side, the fat twin exhausts of the sportscar complementing the quadruple ports of the Cayenne. 'They look so good together, they should get married.'

Müller gave her a tolerant glance.

A wide, marbled staircase took them upstairs. When they had entered the apartment, Carey Bloomfield stood in the middle of the polished floor of the large colonnaded hall and turned slowly around.

'I take it back,' she said. 'If I ate off *this* floor, it would faint.'

Müller looked at her with some amusement. 'You do have a way of expressing yourself.'

'I'm afraid to see where I'm going to sleep.'

'It's just an ordinary bedroom.'

'There's ordinary, and then . . . there's ordinary.'

'Would you like to have a look around?'

'That, is an offer I can't refuse.'

178

They began the tour, Carey Bloomfield giving her own running commentary.

'High ceilings,' she began. 'I like. This hall would not be out of place in a Roman villa . . . and those paintings . . . Müller, you'd give a thief a heart attack. Living room . . . *sitting* room . . . *dining* room . . . Persian rugs . . . bedroom one, with a bathroom suite. Gawd. This is *huge*. Look at these walls. Müller, this is a palace . . . Bedroom two . . . yeah, with its own bathroom suite. Is it bigger? It's bigger! I get to sleep *here*? The bed's all made. You *expected* me to make it here. Don't know whether to be flattered, or annoyed. This is big enough for a fancy ball . . . Don't you get lost in this place? The kitchen! Oh wow! Stainless-steel temple. I know of two apartments that would fit in here and leave room for an airfield. Do you cook? You can't have a kitchen like this and not cook. You do! God. I hate guys like you. I can't boil water. And what's this room? It's empty. No it's not. *Two* Hammond organs? You really like these things . . .'

'My study,' Müller said, interrupting her flow. 'One is a B3, in my book *the* Hammond of all Hammonds. The other is its electronic brother, the XB3. They each have their own individual sound. I enjoy the difference.'

She prowled slowly around the room, noting everything; checking the neatly shelved books and music scores. She stopped to look at the only two pictures on the walls: portraits of his mother and father.

Müller stood to one side, silently observing her.

'You must miss them,' she remarked quietly.

He made no response for so long she began to believe she had somehow offended him.

At last, he said, 'I frequently wish I had known them better. Many other things take precedence in the mind of a twelve-year-old. Parents are there to feed, clothe, house, and do all the other countless things a child expects as his right. But knowing who these people really are . . . that takes longer. Time ran out.' He gave a sudden, fleeting smile. 'Here endeth the lesson.'

'This is a great room, Müller,' she said. 'I guess this is where you let yourself go?'

'Sometimes. And thank you.'

'For what?'

'For not asking me to play.'

'Hey, I was a kid once. I know that horror. *Come on, Carey, play the violin for Grandma.* I played the violin like a cat can sing. I used to hide whenever the grandparents came to visit.'

They laughed.

'I sympathize,' Müller said. 'A nightcap?' he added.

She shook her head. 'I think I'll catch up on the zizz that you, mister, deprived me of.' She glanced down at the envelope in his hand. 'The bedtime read?'

'The bedtime read.' He handed it to her. 'Don't forget to use the gloves, it's vital evidence. We left the outdoor gear in the Cayenne,' he went on. 'If you would like to try it on for size, I can easily go back down . . .'

'Müller, if the size is right, it will fit. If not . . .' She shrugged.

'In that case, I'll let you catch up on your interrupted sleep.'

She briefly held up the envelope. 'Is what's in there going to give me nightmares?'

'I wish I could say it will be pleasant reading. But you need to read it to understand what's going on. We'll talk in the morning.'

'OK. Müller?'

He waited for her to speak.

'This is a great place. Goodnight.'

'Goodnight.'

He smiled to himself as he watched her go. He loved the slight toe-in of her walk. It gave her body a movement that was an exceptional pleasure to watch.

'Goodnight, Carey,' he added softly after she had gone into her bedroom. 'Now you've entered my real territory for the first time.'

Carey Bloomfield discovered a plain white, luxuriously soft bathrobe hanging in the bathroom suite. Huge white towels were also neatly stacked in an opaque-fronted, marbled shelf unit that had been recessed into a wall. She took a steaming-hot shower, unhurriedly patted herself dry, then, wrapping the robe about her, went back into the bedroom.

She thought about calling Toby Adams, then decided against it.

Using the large pillows as a prop, she sat on the bed, put on the cotton gloves Müller had given her and took Holbeck's diary out of its protecting envelope and bag.

She stared at the blood-ringed gash. 'Jesus,' she said softly; then she opened at the first page and began to read.

She read it right through – including the White Rose leaflet – without once dozing off. When finished, she very carefully replaced the diary, then took off the gloves and put them on top of the envelope. She slid beneath the covers with the bathrobe still on.

'Jesus,' she said again.

She did not turn off the bedside light.

At about the same time, von Graff was in a vast office that overlooked the Spree from several floors up. He was on the phone to someone he had been trying to reach all evening. The wait had exacerbated his anger.

'I want him stopped!' he snarled at the phone. 'I don't know where he gets his information from, but he knows far too much. How he manages this is a question that needs an answer . . . and quickly. Find out, then stop him! I don't care how you do it.'

'And if he won't be stopped?'

'There are other means!'

'You're asking me to kill a police *Hauptkommissar* . . . or have him killed.'

'I am not asking! *I am telling you!* And that Jew with him! You owe us plenty. It is time you showed your gratitude!'

Von Graff slammed the phone down. *'I am surrounded by incompetents!'* he raged.

His two bodyguards stood at a respectful distance and tried not to catch his eye as he touched the small reddish scar that Carey Bloomfield's ring had scythed across his cheek.

'Incompetents!' he snarled a second time.

The bodyguards hoped they were not included.

Berlin-Wilmersdorf, the next morning; 07.00 CET.

Müller, fully dressed, was laying out breakfast on a breakfast bar in the kitchen that looked like the flying bridge of a rakish yacht, without seeming the slightest bit nautical. Beyond the tall window, the city lights cut through the fading gloom of the early winter's morning.

Carey Bloomfield, also fully dressed, entered. 'Morning,' she greeted. 'Mmm, this all smells good.'

'Good morning. Slept well?'

'I shouldn't have, after that bedtime story. That was quite a read, Müller. Gruesome, and sad at the same time. Faustian, even. Holbeck lost his soul. I never would have believed I could ever feel sorry for a Waffen-SS soldier, especially when you consider my own family background. But this guy . . . it's almost as if he deliberately sacrificed himself, to bear witness. I thought so much about that, I didn't think I'd be able to fall asleep, jetlag or no jetlag. But that bed of yours beat me. I slept like a log.'

'Then a good breakfast will set you up for the day.' Like a chef touting his wares, Müller continued, 'Fruit juices, cereal, fruit, omelette, toast, hot bread rolls, bacon can be supplied, if you want it, assorted jams, and fresh coffee . . .'

She studied the spread, trying to decide where to start. 'If I ate all of this, Müller, you'd have to roll me down the stairs. But I'm going to have a damn good try. I could eat a horse.'

'No ceremony here,' he said to her. 'Just help yourself to anything you like.'

'Just try and stop me . . .'

'And,' he went on, 'we're going to have good weather all the way to Rügen. A dry day.'

'What about Rügen itself?' she asked, beginning to make her breakfast choices.

'Still under a heavy blanket of snow; but no fresh fall expected for the next forty-eight hours. If the sun manages to take a look, the day could be quite beautiful up there. Listen.'

He picked up a remote with row upon row of buttons, pointed it at a kitchen unit, and pressed. A blank screen at the top, which she had believed to be a microwave, turned out to be a combined TV/radio.

The radio came on. 'And now, the weather for Rügen. The snow continues to be thick on the ground, but the day will be fine and dry. It will remain so for at least two days. The main access roads to the Rügendamm have been cleared, as is the Rügendamm itself, after snow blockage. Good walking weather along the coastal . . .'

Müller turned it off. 'Along some stretches of the coast, parts of the inshore waters can sometimes freeze hard enough to walk on. The Rügendamm is still the only way to get to the island by wheeled transport . . .'

'That's the bridge. Right?'

'Yes. Traffic, even in winter, can be a pain. In summer, especially when the bridge is raised for water traffic, it can turn into a nightmare. People call it the pre-programmed traffic jam. But we should be fine. We'll arrive between the bridge-raising times.'

'Then you'd better start telling me about what's waiting for us up there on the beautiful island of Rügen.'

As they ate, he gave her a brief rundown of events, commencing with the first call he'd received.

She remained silent for a while after he had finished, reflectively working her way through the breakfast.

'So who is supposed to be on Rügen?' she finally asked. 'Von Mappus can't have died at Stalingrad, be on Rügen today, *and* be von Graff – as you suspect – all at the same time.'

'This is the point at which Pappi would have said . . . *Unless he discovered time travel.*'

'He's managed to do something. What if von Graff really *is* von Graff?'

'Pappi is trawling his network to see if anyone can trace von Graff's military history during the war. My guess is no one will. Whoever he was at the war's end, that identity was not used during the time of the DDR. I believe he became von Graff when many returning soldiers eased themselves into the services of the emerging DDR. It was a time of confusion. The new workers' republic needed experienced people to help it keep order. The Russians were not really interested. Their own soldiers were barely controllable. Many German and Russian soldiers frequently fought each other, or turned to crime . . . both petty and major.

'Despite its loud anti-fascist posturings, the DDR turned a blind eye to the histories of those who signed up. I believe von Graff was one of them. One can say that von Mappus is buried at Stalingrad . . . but metaphorically speaking only. He is alive and well, and still true to the cause. People like that never die in battle. Their followers and underlings do the dying for them. This pattern is etched in history. You've read Holbeck's diary. As a teacher, Holbeck had experience in judging the character of an individual. He drew a very detailed word-picture of von Mappus. The man comes alive off the page, in all his gruesome glory. You saw and heard von Graff last evening. You tell me.'

'I'm heading for cover,' she said. 'It's too close to call. It would be interesting to know what happened to the others in the group. If one of them were still alive, he'd be able to tell.'

'Assuming von Mappus let them live. As you've read, Holbeck had the strongest suspicion that he had killed his own commander, Captain Wolfgang Dietrich. The entire group saw him shoot Major Gaegl in the back. Holbeck witnessed the killings in the burned village. Holbeck is certainly dead, but as yet we have no idea how he died. But my gut instincts tell me von Mappus was responsible. In the terror he brought to the village, it would have been easy to stab or shoot Holbeck, then blame it on enemy action. But his men would not have believed it when the dust settled.'

'So he'd have had to either bribe them somehow . . .'

'Or kill them, or manage to get them killed in combat. That would be more his way. Remember the myth that was circulated. He is supposed to have bravely destroyed a secret Russian supply dump. Without Holbeck's diary, we would never have known the horrible truth of that day.'

184

'That still leaves you with the big question. Who's on Rügen?'

'That, is what we'll try to find out today.'

After the leisurely breakfast, and while Carey Bloomfield was collecting her stuff from her bedroom, Müller put Holbeck's diary in a safe that was hidden behind one of the floor-to-ceiling bookshelves in his study. There was nothing to indicate that there was anything behind that bookshelf, except solid wall.

He collected his own bag for the journey and at precisely 09.00, they left the apartment.

Rügen; 10.00 CET.

Polizeimeister Harald Kreuz drove carefully along the snow-bound lane. Though in civilian clothes and not yet on duty, he carried his personal weapon and radio. All around him was open country, white fields punctured by the skeletal woodlands of winter. He was heading towards a small clutch of houses, a hundred metres or so beyond which was his destination.

He had three hours to spare before going on duty, and he was looking forward to continuing a game of chess that had been running for two weeks. It was part of a tournament, and the score stood at three–one in his opponent's favour. He was desperate to win a second game. The man he was going to play against was someone he had known for many years.

Kreuz, who as a boy had left the DDR with his family, had returned as a man, and had joined the unified police force. Johann Seeberg, his opponent, had always lived in the DDR, but Kreuz had not known of him. They had met accidentally when Kreuz had been walking along the stony beach below Seeberg's house with his wife. He had liked the affable Seeberg from the instant of that first meeting. He had later discovered – when Seeberg had invited the couple to dinner after learning of Kreuz's great love of chess – that Seeberg was a widower who lived alone in a splendid house.

Though clearly rich and able to afford a live-in staff, Seeberg had none. A cleaning woman went there regularly, and a gardener tended the garden once a week during spring, summer and autumn. Seeberg was also fond of gardening, and enjoyed preparing the garden for the rigours of winter.

Seeberg was extremely fit for his age, Kreuz often thought. Though he cooked for himself, he frequently ate out; and, despite having retired, travelled regularly. His big, black Mercedes was a familiar sight. Friendly enough to his neighbours, he nevertheless kept his distance from them. When he had guests – mainly off-islanders – one of his favourite restaurants handled the catering. Kreuz and his wife had eaten many a superb dinner there.

The police sergeant felt very flattered to be on such terms with Seeberg, and was glad that his chess-playing had netted him a companion of this status. Even so, one of his greatest wishes was to win at least one tournament. In the time they had been playing he had won some games, but never a single tournament.

But, even in defeat, Seeberg was always generous. Each time Kreuz had won, he had presented him with a gift. Once, it had been an extremely rare magnum of champagne. On another occasion, it had been a long weekend for himself and his wife in a Berlin hotel of such magnitude, Kreuz could never have afforded it on his policeman's pay without digging into his savings, for a once-only treat. And on yet another, it had been a short cruise across the Baltic, on a yacht belonging to one of Seeberg's friends.

Kreuz did not consider such gifts bribes, and eagerly looked forward to winning. It did occur to him, however, that by donating these gifts, Seeberg also ensured that their chess battles were fierce; a situation in which Seeberg took great pleasure.

'You are far better than many of those I sometimes play, Harald,' Seeberg had once said to him. 'I hand them gifts when they win, of course, but none have ever had as many as you.'

It was a source of pride to Kreuz to know that many of these other opponents were often men as rich as Seeberg himself.

Kreuz had never sought to question, even in his mind, the

source of Seeberg's wealth; though he had noted that, from time to time, Seeberg had been visited by people who looked equally rich and important.

Kreuz drove past the clutch of buildings, and on towards the familiar house. He idly thought that, due to the heavy snowfall, the cleaning woman would not have called for a few days. Seeberg, having no chauffeur, drove his lavishly outfitted car himself.

As he drew closer, Kreuz noticed there were no tyre imprints in the snow; either from the fat winter tyres of the Mercedes, or from the narrow ones of the cleaning woman's little Fiat. He felt relief. Seeberg had not forgotten their meeting, arranged three days previously.

'If he hasn't gone down to the beach for a walk,' he said to himself, 'he's waiting to be checkmated. I'm looking forward to this. I've got him on the run. Wonder what kind of gift he has in mind this time.'

Kreuz was keenly anticipating victory.

When he arrived, he brought his car to a halt at the front of the house; but instead of going up to the main entrance decided instead to go through the garden. He had done so on many occasions, for their games were usually held in Seeberg's favourite room, the winter garden. Seeberg normally left the tall front gate to the garden unlocked when he knew Kreuz would be coming.

Kreuz pushed at the gate, fully expecting it to be open. It did not budge.

He frowned uncertainly, pushed at it again, then shook it, thinking it might have jammed. It still did not move. He checked the lock. Fully home.

'What the hell's going on?' he asked aloud, going up to the main entrance.

He pressed the doorbell and waited. Nothing. He tried again, leaning on it. Perhaps Seeberg was dozing, and had forgotten to unlock the gate. But in all the time he had known him, Kreuz could not remember Seeberg dozing off prior to a game.

Kreuz received no response to his ringing.

At first, he felt annoyance. Was Seeberg trying to avoid

defeat? He immediately discarded the thought. That would be cheating. Again, Seeberg had never once cheated.

The policeman in Kreuz became curious. He went back to the gate, looked up at it to see if he could climb over. But it had been deliberately constructed to prevent just such an attempt.

'I could never understand this,' Kreuz said to himself. 'This gate's here at the front, but it's easy enough to get into the garden . . . from the back . . .' His voice faded as the thought came to him.

He decided to try that way in. It was a ten-minute walk round the property in good weather. In the snow, it would probably take twice as long; but he had no choice.

Leaving his car where it was, he began walking.

It took him a little longer than expected because the snow lay deeper the further he moved from the road. Despite his sturdy ankle boots, it was slow going.

He finally made it to the rear gate. That was locked too, so he began to climb over it, glancing towards the conservatory. As he did so, he paused.

One of the door panels was open, and a barrier of snow had collected.

'What the hell?' he said, puzzled.

He dropped into the garden and hurried to the house. His rush spilled snow inside as he came to a stunned halt. He stared in shock at Seeberg's cold body, and at the strangely patterned throat wound.

'Oh my God!' he exclaimed in horror.

He touched nothing, and spoke urgently into his radio. Then, despite realizing that whoever was responsible should have been long gone, he drew his weapon, and began to search the house.

Müller and Carey Bloomfield had been on the road to Rügen for two hours.

The snow lay thick on either side of the cleared Autobahn. The Cayenne, high off the tarmac, rumbled smoothly on, giving a sense of total security. Rodrigo's *Concierto de Aranjuez* swelled with a soft richness out of the sound system. Carey Bloomfield had slightly reclined her seat and was enjoying the music. Her eyes were closed.

Müller glanced at her.

'I felt that,' she said.

'I thought you were asleep.'

'I've been enjoying the ride, and the music. This car makes you feel insulated.'

'And the other one?'

'Adrenalin rush.'

'Like an F-15?'

'Without the wings.'

They smiled at each other as he turned the music down.

'So tell me,' he began, 'what do you know about Rügen?'

'Professionally? Or personally?'

'Both.'

'Professionally,' Carey Bloomfield said, 'I know a little about it. I've seen files that would fill your kitchen, particularly about Bug, named after Antonius de Buge. My professional interest in Bug, and Rügen in general, comes from its importance during the war, and the Cold War. In World War Two, it was the site of Hitler's many secret units – which was of serious interest to the Allies, not surprisingly; especially with Peenemunde and its ballistic missiles just round the corner. We got ourselves a neat crop of rocket scientists after the war, including SS *Obersturmführer* von Braun. Puny rank, considering his high value. Then there's the Prora complex, a four point five kilometre monstrosity like something out of *Metropolis*, where *Kraft durch Freude* was supposed to make everybody happy: twenty thousand battery chickens – er, holidaymakers – at a time, I guess to produce nice little aryans for the boss. Something that would have gladdened the hearts of joy-makers like von Graff.

'During the time of the workers' paradise, the DDR's NVA took up residence in the colossus. And, talking of Peenemunde, the DDR navy's First Flotilla was HQ'd there, and the Sixth Flotilla was at Dranske, on the island. The islanders could gaze with longing and dream about what was beyond the horizon, but they could never get off; like in Hotel California. Now Prora is a museum. During the war

189

U-286, based at Rügen and commanded by *Oberleutnant* Willi Dietrich, was sunk twice. First time, a collision off Rügen with another U-boat. Half the crew survived. It was raised, refitted, and sent back to sea. It was sunk again, just before the end of the war, by the Brits, in the Barents Sea. No one survived that time. More?'

'My God,' he said. 'You sound like one of your files. Did you really have to check all of that?'

'And plenty more. I also have a special reason. My brother . . .' She paused briefly, remembering. 'My brother went on his first mission to Rügen, a year before the Wall came down. I had an instructor,' she hurried on, 'who used to say . . .' She mimicked a snappy Boston accent. '"Learn from the past. It's never gone. Everything is there."'

'He was right. We are chasing a past, from sixty years ago. And the personal?'

'Apart from my brother's mission?'

Müller nodded.

'Many people in the States,' Carey Bloomfield continued, 'have got roots on the island . . . at least, some I know. At school, I had a friend whose family originally came from there. She used to tell us some tall stories about Rügen myths. She said it was incredibly beautiful, lots of long piers, something she called the herring run where hordes of people fish off the bridge, and the chalk coast was amazing. She got it all from her grandmother, who apparently went on and on about Störtebeker, gentleman pirate, who eventually lost his head, literally. My friend had never been there herself. I guess the family must have visited it by now, with the Wall gone. And here I am, on my way there. Weird. Now you, Müller. Have you ever been?'

He shook his head. 'No.'

She stared at him. 'What? You've got to be kidding me.'

'I'm afraid not. I think my father did. As it was the time of the DDR, it was not a holiday. Aunt Isolde told me. She never did explain why he went there.'

'Don't tell me your father was a spy, Müller.'

'Not as far as I know.'

'Oh come on. He goes to *Rügen* . . . during the DDR times?'

'Don't forget, a branch of my family comes from the eastern part of Germany. He probably wanted to save some property from being wrecked by the people who had taken them over. Many western Germans also travelled on visits to the east; and many who had gone west tried to recover what had been left of their property. Most did not succeed. Aunt Isolde was one of the lucky few to find theirs still standing . . . just . . . after the Wall came down.'

She nodded. 'Her *Schlosshotel* near the Saale; once a family home appropriated by the comrades . . .'

'And where you and I met my late, unlamented cousin, Colonel of Police of the former DDR . . .'

'Torturer and murderer of my brother . . .' Carey Bloomfield said with grim remembrance.

'And whom we both sent to perdition.'

'Strange, isn't it, Müller? How our paths crossed? They began to get together all those years ago when my brother went on his first mission to Rügen, when your cousin was planning, or was involved in the planning of Romeo Six, when the Wall came down and the Colonel of Police was out of a job . . .'

'But still active . . .'

'Still active, and meets up with my brother in the Middle East, where he . . . where he . . .'

'Put it out of your mind.'

She fell silent. 'Yeah,' she said at last. Then, forcing some levity into her voice, she continued, 'Know what, Müller? After this, why don't we . . . ?'

The communication display on the central console pinged, and Pappenheim's number appeared on the screen.

'I'll stop at the next rest place,' Müller said with urgency.

The ping came once more and the number faded.

Carey Bloomfield stared at the screen. 'You've got the same system in there as in the other car?'

'Yes.'

'And the hidden police lights?'

'Not yet.'

She laughed suddenly. 'You're nuts, Müller. You know that?'

He grinned at her. 'If you say so.'

'I'm nuts too. I'm here.'

'Somehow, I don't think either of us is nuts, as you so eloquently put it.'

Nine

O ne kilometre later, Müller pulled into a layby that was well off the Autobahn.' If you'd like to stretch your legs . . .' he said to Carey Bloomfield.

'Are you kidding? I'll stay in here where it's nice and warm, and listen to some music. You go talk to Pappi.'

'As you wish.'

Müller got out and walked a little distance from the Cayenne. He took out his mobile and called Pappenheim. The connection was security-hardened.

'Tell me, Pappi.'

'We've found our victim.'

Müller felt a rush of excitement. 'Where?'

'A big house, slightly isolated, high off a beach, which has a steep path down to it, but not directly from the house. But he was no general . . . just a rich chess player.'

'A *chess player*?'

'I tell it like it is.'

'You said victim . . .'

'As dead as ten doornails,' Pappenheim said, after a swift inhale of his inevitable cigarette.

'Who found him?'

'A *Polizeimeister* named Kreuz, with a taste for chess.' Pappenheim went on to give Müller a quick background brief on Kreuz. 'It's these little unforeseen things,' he continued, 'that make me enjoy police work so much. Who would have expected a chess-playing police sergeant with reason to go to an out-of-the-way house in his off-duty time?'

'Who indeed. Now the big question . . .'

'Thought you'd never ask. Throat cut, shape of a cross. Kreuz found the cross.'

'I had hoped you would not have said that, Pappi.'

Pappenheim drew on his cigarette. 'Close to the edge, that one. I admit it. It was done with the razor,' he added.

'*The* razor?'

'Must be. It was left in the victim's hand. Remember – according to the sergeant – von Mappus threw the razor to the ground, saying it was now contaminated with Bolshevik blood, and he would never use it again. Well, seems he got it back, sixty years on. Nice touch, that. Kreuz thinks it's a ritual killing. Must be all that Viking history they've got on the island . . .'

Müller remained silent.

'Hello? Are we still there?'

'Rachko,' Müller remarked quietly.

'So it looks as if you were right, after all. Revenge down the generations. I must say you don't sound too happy to have hit the nail so squarely on the head.'

'Even after our little light reading, I still hoped we would have found him alive. I wanted that bastard to face the world. Now . . . I've got to find the descendant of the man who was so brutally and needlessly murdered, and arrest him.'

'If he's still around . . . '

'According to a Rügen weather report I heard this morning, the Rügendamm has only just been cleared for traffic, and inshore waters in some areas are frozen enough to walk on. So he may not have left as yet, if going by road. And if by boat, he'll have to walk to it. Risky, if the boat's too far out.'

'Perhaps you'll get him, even though I can sense your reluctance. I share your feelings, Jens . . . but we are the police. We don't let killers go, however much we might sympathize, in this case, with the motive.'

'I know it, Pappi. I know it. Warn Roth to keep this very quiet for the moment. That means no cars, no sirens, no press, and no one up there except Kreuz, until we get there. And, even then, I want us to be left alone for a while.'

'Already done.'

'You know me so well, Pappi, you see into my brain.'

'Flattery. I love flattery. Ready for the other big news?'

'There's more?'

'Oh yes. The goth got herself another AWACS picture . . .'

'Profile?'

'Yep. This time, it was marked AR. No prizes for guessing.'

'Rachko's. But which generation?'

'No other clue in the profile; but someone's obviously been very, very busy. Then a message came on the goth's radar screen. 'Blood not Holbeck'. That's an exact quote. I'm assuming that the red stuff on the diary did not come from our philosophical warrior.'

'It would seem like it . . . assuming the information is correct . . .'

'I'd bet my cigarettes it is.'

'At such a high price, I bow to your instincts. This means someone else had picked up the document – perhaps off his body – and that person was later wounded, or killed.'

'And now, *we've* got it. Still a mystery how, but I'm looking no gift horses in the mouth.'

'Nor I. Any results yet on the handkerchief?'

'*Patience, mon brave.* The equipment these days is magical. Long gone are the times of months, or even days, of waiting. We are talking mere hours. I'm standing on heads. I fully expect to have something back later today; quite possibly while you're still at the scene.'

'That would be excellent.'

'Now that we have a victim, so graphically marked, how do you feel about our Silesian?'

'I still have my doubts.'

'Oh well, since you put it like that . . . here's another little item to gladden your heart . . . or perhaps not. The Silesian is missing.'

'What does "missing" mean exactly?'

'Did a trawl of my network of unsavouries. The underworld web vibrated. "Exactly" means he's gone out of Berlin. Destination so far . . . unknown.'

'Shit!'

'I knew you'd love it. But I won't chuckle. We don't even know whether he *lives* in Berlin.'

'I would say he does. He needs to be at the centre of power.

195

I suppose there's nothing as yet on his war record, if there is any.'

'You suppose correctly. So . . . what now?'

'I'll continue as planned. I don't believe we've seen the last of him. He's not running . . . at least, not yet. *I'd* bet your cigarettes on it.'

'You keep off my daily bread; but I get your point. I'll stay with it.'

'Alright, Pappi. Thanks. I'll get back to you when we've got there.'

'Talking of which . . . how's the passenger?'

'Behaving so well, I don't know whether to be pleased or worried.'

Pappenheim's laugh sounded in Müller's ear as they ended the call.

Müller hurried back to the Cayenne and opened the driver's door. The sounds of Jimmy Smith extemporizing with masterly fluidity on the Hammond in 'Walk on the Wild Side', pounded out at him, to be lowered in volume almost immediately.

'Sorry,' Carey Bloomfield said. 'Got carried away. I've never known anyone with such a wide taste in music, Müller. You can't be pinned down, damn it.'

For answer, Müller put the volume back up. 'Now we can both enjoy the master at work.'

The Cayenne's V8 rumbled powerfully as he started the SUV, pulled out of the layby, and back on to the Autobahn.

The Cayenne lowered itself on its air springs and surged along the Autobahn, while Jimmy Smith sped them on towards Rügen.

When the piece had ended, Carey Bloomfield said, 'Was that good? Or was that good? I can still hear echoes of it in my head.'

'That, Miss Bloomfield, was a Lord of the Hammond. Feel privileged.'

'I do. Are you going to tell me what Pappi had to say?'

'We've found our victim.'

She sat up in her seat. 'Dead?'

'Very. Throat cut, exactly as Rachko's in 1942 . . . with the same razor. It was left in the victim's hand.'

'Jesus. So the son got von Mappus . . .'

'Not the son. *His* son . . . perhaps.'

'Why perhaps?'

'We don't know it is Rachko the Third. At least, not yet.'

She stared ahead at the ribbon of road between the white banks of snow. 'Sixty years. A long revenge.'

'Perhaps you would have done the same. Perhaps I would. Remember how you felt about your brother.'

'I do remember,' she said in a quiet voice. 'If it is Rachko's grandson . . . what will you do?'

'Arrest him . . . if I do find him. As Pappi just said to me, whatever sympathies I might have for his motives, I'm a policeman. I cannot let him go, even if I know I might have done the same to that monster myself. The crime . . . and it is a crime, whatever you or I might feel . . . was committed on German soil . . .'

'Against a German who committed an even worse crime on Rachko's soil . . .'

'Don't misunderstand me. I feel no sympathy for that bastard. He deserved it a thousand times over, and years ago. I would have liked to have dragged him out into the light of day from his lair, to face the world's justice for his own crimes. But Rachko did this *here* . . . Look, if it makes you feel any better, I'm praying that Rachko – if he *is* the perpetrator – is long gone. I, for one, would not weep.'

'But knowing how these things go . . .'

'He's still here. There's a momentum in this. It is as if I am destined to meet him. I feel it.'

Rügen; 12.00 hours CET.

Zima Rachko and his sister, Galina, were sitting in the hotel cafeteria, eating a light lunch. They had already checked out and their bags had been left behind the reception desk until they were ready to leave.

Here, in public, they spoke Berlin-accented German to each

other. Their conversation was lightweight, unremarkable. They gave the classic impression of a couple more interested in each other than in the world about them. They could see who came in and who went out. They sat side by side, backs to a high wall, with a full view of the place. No one was near their table.

Frequently, they talked with their heads close together. Anyone watching would see this as normal behaviour for a couple so intent upon each other. They also had a good view of the beach, which was covered with hard-set snow. Few people were in the cafeteria. Even fewer seemed keen to venture out. Now and then, someone walked past. The beach itself was empty.

There was an indeterminate set to the day: neither grey, nor particularly bright, despite the lack of threatening bad weather. It was as if the day itself were uncertain of what it wanted to do.

Galina again brought her head close to her brother's. 'What if someone finds him before we leave?' she whispered.

'As you can see,' he began in a low voice, 'hardly anyone is around. No one will find him in time. The roads out that way are snow tracks. It's over at last. We'll be fine.'

'But what about the diary?'

'We'll try for it later; but first, we must get away from here. There is nothing to connect us with him, so even when someone does find him, it will be a mystery that won't be solved. Those who know his real identity won't talk. Too much to explain if they did.' Rachko smiled fondly at her. 'Our grandfather has been avenged. And the sergeant, who tried to save our aunt even to the end, can finally have some peace for his soul. You will soon be back with your Nikolai, and you two can get married at last.'

'We both want a son. We have agreed to call him Maximillian Nikolaievitch.'

'After the sergeant.'

'Yes.'

Zima Rachko nodded approvingly. 'That is good.'

The Cayenne arrived at the Rügendamm at 12.30, hours

ahead of the next bridge opening. They had been lucky with the traffic and had made good time. There was no bottleneck waiting across the two-and-a-half kilometre spanning of the Strelasund and, thirty kilometres later, Müller pulled into the car park of Norbert Roth's police building.

Two officers about to get into their car stared at the Cayenne with deep curiosity, then stared even more when Müller got out. Their eyes seemed unable to decide which was more fascinating: his ponytail, or his single earring.

When Carey Bloomfield got out, they stared even more. She smiled brightly at them. They were still trying to decide who these people were, when Müller walked up to them.

'Hello,' he greeted. 'Müller. *Hauptkommissar.*'

They straightened visibly, eyes now confused. 'Sir,' they said together.

'Norbert Roth?'

One of the men pointed to the building.

'Thank you,' Müller said, walking on.

'They're still staring!' Carey Bloomfield whispered as she joined him.

'It's the Cayenne.'

'Yeah. Sure.'

Roth arrived at the entrance just as they did, hand outstretched. 'Saw you arrive. Welcome to our little patch. Norbert Roth.'

He shook hands first with Carey Bloomfield, then with Müller.

Then he glanced out at the two policemen. 'Don't you have work to do?' He shook his head slowly as they got into their car in a hurry. 'Sometimes . . . My office is just along here. Coffee?'

'Yes, please,' Carey Bloomfield said.

Roth gave her a sideways glance. 'Pappi says you are American.'

'Pappi is right.'

'In the days of the DDR we were told that West Berlin was a Hollywood set created by the Americans.' He said this with a smile.

'We can be so inventive at times,' she responded dead-pan. 'We even created space. Those are not real stars up there at all.'

For a moment, he was taken aback; then he grinned. 'Pappi warned me about you.' He glanced at Müller. 'The two of you . . . er, sir.'

'That's Pappi,' Müller said.

Roth was a small man with a quick walk, a kind voice, and pleasant eyes that seemed perfectly happy with his life. A second-generation islander, he seldom left Rügen. His office was larger than expected, and had a fabulous view of a lake whose surface was currently frosted over. Little drifts of snow populated the frost, islands on a sea of white. There was open ground from the shore of the lake to the building.

Among the normal accoutrements of a policeman's office was, unexpectedly, a coffee machine. Fresh coffee was being made. Three empty mugs, a jug of milk and a bowl of sugar were on a tray nearby.

'This is a nice place to work from,' Carey Bloomfield said, peering out.

'The lake is beautiful all year,' Roth said. 'Every season is a special wonder. I love it,' he added unashamedly. 'I love the island.'

'I can see why. Coffee smells good.'

Roth beamed at her. 'While we wait,' he said to Müller, 'I'll get you my find.'

He went to a tall steel cabinet, unlocked it, and took out a long bag. He handed it to Müller as if expecting it to bite.

'May I use your desk?' Müller asked.

'Of course.'

They watched as Müller laid the bag on the desk, then unzipped it. The bag opened out like a book. Within padded compartments were the pristine Dragunov and its accessories.

'Wow!' Carey Bloomfield said. 'This, is a beauty. May I?'

'Be my guest,' Müller said.

Roth looked at her with heightened curiosity as she picked up the gun.

She checked it out with impressive familiarity, then picked up one of the loaded magazines. Standard rounds. She picked up another. Tracer. Then a third.

She stared at the first round, astonished. 'Armour-piercing incendiary! What the hell were they up to with all this stuff?'

'I didn't hear that,' Roth said. 'And I did not see you handle that gun like an expert. I don't even know you are here.'

'Pappi briefed you well,' Müller said to him with the faintest hint of a smile. 'Don't worry, Norbert. The gun comes with us.'

'That's a relief. Believe you me, sir. Ah. Coffee's ready.'

As Roth went to the coffee machine, Carey Bloomfield offered the rifle to Müller, who shook his head. She returned the weapon to its bag, placed the magazine with the armour-piercing rounds in the empty compartment and zipped the bag shut.

'Who wants what?' Roth called.

'With milk and sugar, please,' they said together.

'An off-island woman who is not afraid to take sugar.' Roth sounded impressed.

'Are you calling me fat, Mr Roth?'

Roth was shocked. 'No! I meant . . .' He stopped when he saw she was smiling at him. 'Oh. A little joke.'

'She's like that sometimes,' Müller said. 'Strange, even to people she doesn't know well.'

'Ah. Yes.' Roth was again looking uncertain as he handed out the coffee, took his mug to his desk and sat down.

Müller leaned against a wall near the desk, while Carey Bloomfield stood near a window to look out as she sipped her coffee.

'This is great coffee,' she said to Roth.

He beamed at her again, very pleased. 'Thank you.' He turned to Müller. 'I've done as Pappi asked. No one's been up at the place. Poor old Kreuz is still there, though, keeping his dead friend company.'

'He must be desperate to leave. He won't have much longer to wait. Is he from your team?'

Roth nodded. 'Luckily. Or I'd have had to twist some arms to keep it quiet for now. The accident happened on my patch, as did the killing. The murderer could have based himself in the area. He might still be here. The *Damm* was blocked until a few hours ago. There's been no flight as yet from the airfield at Guettin. If he tries a boat, he'll have to walk on water to get to it . . .'

'He could still be here,' Müller said.

Again, Roth nodded, glancing at the Dragunov bag. 'What kind of people are we dealing with?'

'As Pappi might have hinted, very dangerous ones. I would advise keeping your people away . . .'

'We've got a small special unit, if you need back-up.'

'Thanks, Norbert . . . but I'm hoping we won't need anything like that. I want this as low-key as possible. There are people we do not wish to alert.'

'I understand. But if you do need the help . . .'

'Pappi will be in touch.'

'OK. Have you arranged accommodation?' Roth went on. 'You should stay a few days when you're finished with this. Get to know Rügen.'

'I'm not even sure we can, or should, stay the night. It's a long drive back . . . not really a problem. But the weather could change things. Why do you ask?'

Roth fished into a pocket and brought out some keys. 'Holiday villa. Already warmed up.'

Müller smiled, seeing Pappenheim's hand in it. 'Pappi?'

The corner of Roth's eyes crinkled. 'Yes. Pappi knows this villa well. He used to come up here often with Sylvia, before she . . .'

'I never knew that,' Müller said in some surprise.

'He hasn't been back since. I'm sure it's because he wants to keep the memory of what it was like for them.'

'I think I understand. Knowing how he felt then . . . and how he still feels, I am not surprised.'

Müller took the keys. 'Thanks, Norbert. We'll use it . . . if we stay. Whose is it?'

Roth cleared his throat, slightly embarrassed. 'My wife's. She has a small business with holiday places. That was how we first met Pappi and Sylvia. They came for a holiday. We had no idea then he was a policeman.'

'Then business is business. We must pay her for it.'

'I can't do that. Pappi would kill me. He expressly said—'

'You leave Pappi to me . . .'

But Roth was looking more uncomfortable by the second.

Müller peered at him. 'Something's wrong with the picture.'

'Pappi has already paid,' Roth said, looking as if he wished he had not been forced to confess. 'I think he wants you to go there . . . to enjoy what he used to.'

Müller was touched by Pappenheim's gesture. It would be a slap in the face to refuse.

'Alright, Norbert,' Müller said. 'I accept. Don't tell him I made a fuss . . . or you'll answer to me.'

'The middle of a Pappenheim–Müller sandwich,' Roth said ruefully. 'Not a good place to be; and I'm a policeman.'

Carey Bloomfield looked at him with obvious sympathy, but said nothing as he reached into his desk to bring out two large-scale maps, the first of which he now spread out. It was of the area containing Seeberg's house, and the scale was sufficiently large to give a sizeable depiction of the building and its immediate neighbours.

Müller and Carey Bloomfield went to look.

'This is of the section near Seeberg's house,' Roth continued. He drew a finger along a route. 'The best way to get there quickly. The roads are a little icy with a thin covering of snow, but, in that vehicle of yours, I'm sure it's no problem. Harald Kreuz got there in his car, so it can't be that bad.'

Roth's finger moved to the back of the house and again began to trace.

'The track leading to the beach. As you can see, it goes some way from the house, passing along woodland, before starting the descent to the beach.'

'Well hidden from the other houses,' Müller observed.

'You can't see it at all,' Roth confirmed, 'from any of

those houses. You believe that's the way the killer got in, and out again?'

'It's the route I would use. Then I would walk a long way, perhaps through as much woodland as I could, before allowing myself to be seen. No one would know what my original direction had been. In a situation like this, and in weather like this, any vehicle would be too obvious. But people notice things, even when they think they haven't. You never know.'

'That's true enough,' Roth said. 'Harald had to go in via the back garden,' he continued, 'but he saw no footprints. Anywhere. We had very heavy snowfall yesterday, and the day before, of course . . .'

'And the killer used that to hide his tracks. The snow would have wiped them out instantly. All he had to do was listen to the radio and wait for the snow to fall.'

'Simple, and smart,' Carey Bloomfield said.

'He's been planning it a long time,' Müller said. 'Years.'

Roth looked from one to the other. 'I don't want to know what you're talking about, do I?'

'No you don't,' Carey Bloomfield said.

Roth gave a little nod, looking relieved. He folded the map and handed it to Müller.

'How many hotels and other holiday places in the local area?' Müller asked as he took the map.

'Hotels and other accommodation have been springing up like flies all over the island since the great rebuild began,' Roth answered, 'after the Wall came down. We're almost too popular for our own good. But there are none within the general area of Seeberg's house. There is one about two kilometres away, in an old fishing village. It's right on the seafront. It would be a convenient place to stop . . . if he did stop anywhere for the night. I could send someone . . .'

'No need. We're going in that direction anyway. Is it on the map you've given me?'

'No. But I was about to give you this one.' Roth had spread the second map. 'It's adjacent to the one you've got. The villa's on it, as is the hotel. I've ringed the villa.' He picked up a red marker pen. 'And the hotel is . . . here.' He ringed the location with the pen. 'You've got a great view of the little harbour from the bedroom window. The hotel itself is less than a kilometre away. It's called Hotel 1815 in honour of the year in which Rügen became Prussian, after centuries of Swedish rule. It's a very comfortable hotel, and only two years old. I would have recommended it, if you hadn't taken the villa.'

As with the first map, Roth folded it and handed it to Müller.

'Don't worry about getting into trouble over this,' Müller said. 'Any problems and Pappi will sort it out with the people in Bergen.'

'He would make me a very happy man.'

It was Berger who spotted them, a corridor away from turning into the one that would lead to Müller's and Pappenheim's offices, and the documents strongroom. They were deep in conversation, moving away from her.

'*Oh shit!*' she whispered to herself as she ducked into the first room available. 'He's not supposed to be here for a few days yet.'

The room was empty, without any windows, and seemed no bigger than a large cupboard. But it had a phone. She picked it up, and dialled Pappenheim.

'Chief?' she began, even before he had spoken. 'Trouble. He's back, and he's got another *Polizeidirektor* with him. In full uniform.'

'Shit!' Pappenheim said. 'You didn't hear that.'

'No, sir. I didn't.'

'Both in *uniform*?'

'Just the other *Direktor*. I've never seen *him* before.'

'Where are you?'

'In what looks like a cleaning cupboard. They're coming up the corridor that will lead into yours.'

'Alright. I'll take it from here. And Lene . . .'

'Sir?'

'Thanks.'

'My pleasure.'

In his office, Pappenheim leaned back in his chair and

drew luxuriously on his cigarette. He blew out a swirling cloud of smoke.

'Things,' he said, 'are about to get interesting.' He waited with remarkable unconcern for the peremptory knock on his door.

Nothing happened. When several long seconds had become a minute, Pappenheim frowned. Where had Kaltendorf and the unknown policeman got to?

Then he remembered.

'Shit! The goth is in the documents room!'

He picked up his phone. It was already too late.

At that very instant, Kaltendorf was punching in the access code.

Hedi Meyer, charging through the virtual sky in her F-16, turned round as she felt a sudden change in the air, and saw the last person she wanted to. She leapt to her feet, almost ripping the spider off her head. She stared aghast at Kaltendorf and his companion.

They stared right back at her; the unknown visitor with something close to amusement, Kaltendorf turning a dangerous shade of purple.

'*Who the devil are you?*' he barked.

'*Meisterin* Meyer, sir!'

'Is that a computer *game* you're playing on the taxpayer's computer? And what are you doing in here? This is a sensitive area. Only authorized personnel allowed. Who is your commander?'

'*Kommissar* Spyros, sir . . .'

'Does he know where you are? He is *electronics*. What are you doing in the documents strongroom?'

Hedi Meyer was getting fed up. She was also intensely annoyed by Kaltendorf's rude treatment of her before the unknown police director, and by the fact that he did not even seem to realize that she was the person who had killed the nasty electronic bomb that had been designed to rip his own daughter in half, just a few months before.

She lost it.

'*I am here sir, because I have permission to be here! I am working on something important for* Hauptkommissar

Müller . . . sir!' She said this at about one decibel below an absolute shout.

Kaltendorf stared at her in disbelief. It took him a while to get used to what had just occurred.

'Did you just shout at me, *Meisterin* Meyer?' he enquired with unnatural calm.

The unknown police director appeared to have a tiny smile on his lips. He seemed to be waiting for further developments.

Hedi Meyer, quivering with outrage, said nothing.

Kaltendorf stared at her. 'Well?'

She remained silent.

'Müller,' he said tightly. 'Müller's fault. Do you see?' he went on to his companion. 'Even the sergeants show disrespect. You stay here, *Meisterin*!' he went on to Hedi Meyer. 'I'll deal with Müller! Come on, Kristof,' he added to the police director.

They went out, leaving the outraged Hedi Meyer glaring at the closed door.

'Shithead!' she muttered. The phone began to ring. She picked it up. 'Meyer.'

'You sound tense,' Pappenheim said. 'Am I too late?'

'Yes, sir. I was just shouted at like a child, in front of a stranger; a *Polizeidirektor.* I'm afraid I shouted back.'

'You *shouted.* Hmm. I'll attend to it, Hedi. Continue what you were doing.'

'Yes, sir. Sorry, sir.'

'For what?'

'Shouting at him.'

'I didn't hear you shout.'

In the corridor a fuming Kaltendorf, followed by his strangely unperturbed companion, headed for Müller's office. When they got there, he did not knock, but shoved the door open.

'*Müller!*' he began, and stopped, eyes glaring round the office and focussing on the empty chair behind the desk. 'That man is *never* here!'

He stomped out, leaving the door ajar.

The police director looked at the Monet. 'The Magpie,' he

207

said. 'Intriguing.' He followed Kaltendorf, closing the door quietly behind him.

At Pappenheim's door, Kaltendorf barged in, coughing with loud exaggeration as he encountered what seemed like an impenetrable wall of smoke.

'Damn it, Pappenheim! Open a window!'

Pappenheim slowly rose to his feet as the two men entered. His windows, made opaque by his smoking habit, remained firmly shut.

The hitherto silent police director spoke. 'Aah!' he said. 'Nicotine heaven!'

Kaltendorf jerked his head round in shock. 'You *smoke*?'

'*Do I!*' The other dug into a pocket and pulled out two massive cigars. He offered one to Pappenheim.

'I don't normally touch these,' Pappenheim said, 'but on this occasion . . .' He took the cigar. 'Thank you, sir. I'll smoke it later.'

'Kristof Neubauer.' Neubauer held out a hand, which Pappenheim shook. 'Special Commission.' Neubauer bit the end off his cigar and carefully put it into the brimming ashtray. 'May I light off you?' He placed the cigar between his lips.

Pappenheim put the glowing end of his cigarette against Neubauer's cigar.

'Aah!' Neubauer sighed with satisfaction when the tip of the cigar began to glow like a tiny furnace. 'I've heard a lot about you, Pappenheim . . . and Müller too. Good team.'

'Thank you, sir,' Pappenheim said, grinning shamelessly.

Kaltendorf had listened to the exchange with an expression of increasing chagrin, and looked as if he felt he had wandered into a den of hardcore addicts.

'Müller!' he snapped at Pappenheim, making a bid for control. 'Where's Müller?' He coughed as he spoke, now having to deal with Neubauer's exhalations as well.

'Out, sir . . .'

'I know that!' Cough. '*Where* . . .' Cough. '. . . is . . . he?' Cough.

'On a case, sir.'

'Always the same . . . answer!' Cough.

'That's because it's always true, sir. You know the *Haupt-kommissar*. Pursues every case to the end.'

'I like that in a policeman,' Neubauer put in. 'We could do with more like him.'

'I'll be very glad to tell him you said that, sir.'

'You do that.'

Kaltendorf stared at Neubauer, as if seeing his colleague for the first time. 'Why don't I let Pappenheim show you around? We can . . . meet in my . . . office when you're done.' A fit of coughing seized him.

'I think you should get out of here, Heinz,' Neubauer said, winking at Pappenheim. 'This smoke is obviously too much for you. Say we meet in half an hour?'

'Yes.' Kaltendorf did not even try to hide his relief. 'Half an hour should do it.' He left the room in a barely controlled rush.

Neubauer glanced at the closed door. 'What a pisser.'

The first alarm bell went off in Pappenheim's head.

Smoker solidarity in a smoke-free zone was one thing. The denigration by a high-ranking police officer – and a stranger at that – of his equally high-ranking colleague to a subordinate several grades below, was imprudent, to say the least. Pappenheim did not believe that Neubauer had done so inadvertently.

Pappenheim gave none of this away as he waited to hear what would come next.

Neubauer took a draw on his cigar, removed it, briefly rolled it between finger and thumb, studied it for a fleeting moment, then put it back into his mouth.

'You two are famous,' Neubauer said.

'Famous, sir?'

'Oh very. And let's not stand on ceremony here, Pappi. We're old veterans. I'm Kristof.'

Alarm bell number two.

'Er . . . yes, sir . . . er, Kristof.'

Neubauer grinned. 'That's the spirit.' He came forward to sit on the edge of Pappenheim's cluttered desk. He gave the mess a cursory glance. 'Anyone seeing this desk would misjudge you, not realizing there's a keen brain hiding behind that camouflage. In his own way, Müller is also like that. He has a different kind of camouflage, of course. But, like you, he uses it to hide a razor-sharp brain. I like the irony of that magpie on his wall. And that model of the organ. Must confuse a lot of people.'

'I get the feeling . . . Kristof,' Pappenheim said, 'that this is leading up to something.'

The end of the cigar glowed like a fast jet on take-off. 'As I said. Sharp. What's it leading to? You just heard me say I'm with a Special Commission.'

'What kind of Special Commission?'

'We're experimental. Rather like you . . . created to target the more . . . unusual cases, somewhere between an intelligence unit and an investigative police force, but with rather more autonomy than you've got. Authority throughout the entire country. We're setting up on the outskirts of Potsdam.'

'A sort of FBI. But I thought we already had the *Bundeskriminalamt* for that.'

'The BKA still needs to be requested by the different states. Even you need to smooth things out before you can operate in different areas. We won't need to be requested, and we can take command in any state.'

'That won't go down well.'

'Exactly. Which is why we need the best people, capable of smoothing hurt feelings, as well as being excellent and unorthodox investigators. Europe is expanding. It's going to get very complicated out there in the big, bad world.'

Pappenheim stared at his visitor. 'You're *headhunting*?'

Neubauer winked. 'Kaltendorf believes I'm here on a visit. I really came to see you and Müller.'

'Have you known the Herr *Direktor* long?'

'Kaltendorf?' Neubauer sounded as if he considered Kaltendorf a lightweight. 'We've known each other for years. A political climber.'

Alarm bell number three was jangling.

If Kaltendorf and Neubauer had known each other for years, how come Kaltendorf was so astonished to discover that Neubauer smoked? Either Neubauer was a fake smoker, or he and Kaltendorf did not know each other as well as he'd said. Either way, the police director was lying, for reasons of his own.

Pappenheim's gut told him those reasons were not good ones.

'I'd hoped to find Müller too,' Neubauer continued. He gave another grin, this time conspiratorial. 'Is he really out? Or is he ducking from Kaltendorf and you're smartly covering?'

'He really is away.'

'Pity. When will he be back?'

'That's the thing,' Pappenheim said, blue eyes innocent. 'One never knows with him . . .'

Neubauer puffed some smoke from behind the cigar. 'But you do more than most, eh? Don't hide your light beneath a bushel, Pappi.'

Pappenheim did a fast weave. 'Shouldn't I be showing you around . . . just for appearances?'

Neubauer heaved himself off the desk. 'You're right. Kaltendorf is bound to check on us. Just to show willing, why not just take me to that amazing room with that nice young woman who shouted at him?'

'She *shouted*?' Pappenheim said, feigning surprise.

'Did she! Kaltendorf went purple . . . yes . . . that's the colour. Purple.'

'Good for her, but bad for discipline.'

'He blamed Müller,' Neubauer said with a wicked glint in his eye.

'He would.'

'Is she good at her job . . . that young woman? She's got spirit.'

'She's very good. As for spirit, she has plenty of that too.'

'Sounds just like what we're looking for.'

'If it's good people you're after, you would empty this place. We have an excellent crop. But they won't leave . . .'

'Good people . . . except Kaltendorf.'

Alarm bell number four.

'I think, Kristof,' Pappenheim said smoothly, 'we should head for the documents room.'

Neubauer leaned forward, jabbing his cigar into the full ashtray to extinguish it. As he ground it, a spill of ash formed a neat border on the desk.

Pappenheim watched, saying nothing as he pinched out his own cigarette.

Finally satisfied, Neubauer straightened. 'Now it's back into the poisoned air.' He gave a chuckle at his little joke.

'So what do you keep in that place?' Neubauer asked, studiedly casual as Pappenheim followed him into the corridor.

'All sorts of interesting things,' Pappenheim replied with apparent incaution. 'The other day, a real gem came into our hands.'

'Oh?'

'Remarkable thing. A diary.'

Neubauer was just able to stop himself from coming to a startled halt; but he was not quick enough to prevent Pappenheim from noticing.

'A *diary*? What is so special about it?'

'The fact that it is sixty years old, for one.'

'And for another?'

'It belongs to a *Scharführer*. Waffen SS. He died somewhere near Stalingrad. One Maximillian Holbeck. Quite a tale he has to tell.'

Pappenheim had positioned himself slightly back from Neubauer as he had spoken. He had quite clearly seen a nerve jump in Neubauer's left cheek when he had mentioned the diary's origins.

'And you've got it in there?'

'Alas, no. Müller has it. He's using it to help him on the case he's currently investigating. But it will be back when he's done with it.'

Neubauer suddenly glanced at his watch and came to a halt. 'My God. That late? While we were enjoying our smoke, time rattled on. Look. Can we skip the documents room for now? Let's talk later about the new unit I'm commanding. Tell Müller.'

'I will.'

Neubauer held out a hand. 'Nice to have met you at last, Pappi.'

212

'Nice to have met you, Kristof.'

They shook hands. 'I'll catch up with Müller later. Give Kaltendorf my regrets, but I must get back.'

'I'll do that,' Pappenheim said, eyes giving nothing away. He waited in the corridor until Neubauer had turned a corner. 'Pisser,' he added.

He hurried back to his office, grabbed a phone and punched a button. 'Berger,' he said with urgency as soon as she answered. 'Where's Reimer?'

'Right here, Chief,' she replied.

'That fancy uniform you saw . . . you two follow him. Set up a back-up team. Choose the best of the bunch and get them to tag you in a second car . . .'

'Weapons?'

'Anything you feel you might need. And hurry. Don't lose the bastard.'

'Chief . . . but he's a *Polizeidirektor* . . .'

'Why am I still hearing your voice?'

'I'm out of here.'

Pappenheim put down the phone, then reached into a drawer for spare magazines for his automatic pistol. He got his coat and went out again.

He stopped by the documents room.

'Miss Meyer,' he began as he entered.

She turned round. 'Sir?' She glanced at his coat. 'Going out?'

'For a short while. Anything else come in?'

'No, sir. Nothing new.'

'OK. Can you make me another copy of that seal?'

'Yes, sir. I've saved it on the hard disk.'

'Do that, please.' When she had done so he picked up the printout and continued, 'Now shut everything down and return to your department. Remain there until you hear from me.'

Eyes full of questions, she began to shut down the computer. Then she picked up her bag and stood up.

Her eyes were now studying him closely. 'You look anxious. Anything I should know about?'

'Nothing to cause worry. Just stay in your office.'

'Yes, sir.'

With a last, uncertain glance, she went out.

Pappenheim picked up the phone and selected an extension. 'Gieseler? Get Möhren. Both of you meet me by the documents room. Bring your pistols and your HKs. Make sure you're not short of ammunition.'

He hung up before the startled sergeant could say anything. He hurried out, shut the door, then changed the access code.

The two sergeants came trotting up a few moments later, wearing sidearms and carrying Heckler and Koch sub-machine guns slung across their chests. Both were tough-looking. Gieseler was a female officer.

'You two,' Pappenheim began, 'remain here until I get back.'

Gieseler looked curiously at him. 'What's going on, Chief?'

'Wish I knew. But let *no* one get past you to go in there.'

'No one? And the *Direktor*?'

'*No one*. If *Direktor* Kaltendorf turns up and bursts a blood vessel, you leave that to me. Your orders are to guard this room at all costs.'

'Yes, Chief. But no one except you, the *Hauptkommissar*, and the *Direktor* have the code.'

'I've just changed it, so only I have it. Any attempt at forcible entry will set off the alarms, but we don't want it to get that far, do we? And don't look so worried. It might not happen.'

'Yes, Chief.'

Pappenheim hurried away, leaving them staring after him.

Neubauer was on the phone as his chauffeur-driven Mercedes cruised the Berlin streets.

'They have the diary!' he said with urgent desperation.

'Are you certain?'

'Totally. Pappenheim gave details he could only have known from reading it.'

'Where is it now?' There was a cold tightness to the voice at the other end.

'With Müller, who is using it to help him with an investigation.'

'Müller!' This was said with an air of frustration. A long silence followed. 'You must get that diary,' the imperious voice in Neubauer's ear commanded.

'*How?*'

'You're a high-ranking policeman. Use your rank! *Order* them to give it to you!'

'You don't know these two. They did not get their reputation by being stupid. Pappenheim *fed* me that information. If we do as you suggest, it will only confirm what I'm almost certain he already suspects. He did not buy my line in bonhomie; nor the headhunting story for the new commission.'

'We got you that command. Earn it!'

'I tell you it can't be done that way!' Neubauer was beginning to react to the pressure. This had the effect of imprudently emboldening him. 'Even now, Pappenheim will be taking precautions. He's a clever policeman.' Neubauer glanced behind the car. 'I would not put it past him to have me followed. So we've been driving erratically for some time, to shake off any possible tail. So far, we seem to be clear.'

'Perhaps you're giving Müller and Pappenheim more credit than they deserve.'

'Even you can't believe that. How do you explain their knowledge of the seal?'

Another long silence followed.

'Then we *must* find out how they're getting their information. You must go back to . . .'

'You're not *listening*!' Neubauer was at the end of his tether. 'This is not the way . . .'

'Then we'll do it ourselves! You're out of a job, Neubauer!'

The connection went dead.

Neubauer stared at the phone, as if expecting it to speak to him.

In the driving seat, the chauffeur had listened to every word through an unobtrusive earphone. The device was completely hidden by the deliberately trimmed length of his hair. The last words were a signal he was now about to act upon.

He took his right hand off the steering wheel, reached for and pulled out a silenced pistol. In a sweeping motion, he

215

angled it to his right and slightly behind, zeroing on Neubauer. The action was so swift, Neubauer barely had time to register surprise before the pistol coughed twice at him.

Neubauer slumped sideways, two blooms of red staining his otherwise pristine uniform. By the time the gun was back in its hiding place, Neubauer was dead.

The Mercedes never left its course, nor did it change speed.

Berger and Reimer had followed Neubauer's chauffeur-driven car all over the city, it seemed to them; then it suddenly pulled into the side street of a quiet residential area.

'I can't see his head,' Berger said as she slowed down for the corner.

They had been positioned several cars behind, so as not to alert Neubauer.

'What?' Reimer said.

'His head. His head is not showing.'

'So? He could be reading something, or just leaning in a corner.'

The side street had been cleared of snow, but a low ridge of hard residue lined it on each side. The car danced slightly as it rolled over a patch.

'What the . . .' Berger said, staring ahead. 'It's stopping! Does he live here?'

'You're asking me . . .'

'That was a rhetorical question, Reimer.'

'Ah. That's what it was . . .'

'Driver's getting out . . . and . . .*walking* away! Call the others. Tell them to block this street at the other end. If he comes their way, they are to stop him.'

She turned the car broadside on, while Reimer quickly relayed the instructions and gave a description of the man.

Reimer finished speaking just as Berger began to get out. He followed, drawing his automatic pistol as he went. He began walking at an increasing pace behind the driver, who glanced round, and immediately started running up the street.

'There he goes!' Reimer called to Berger, breaking into a sprint.

She had drawn her own weapon, and began to run along the opposite side.

At that moment, the driver began to slow down, then came to an uncertain halt. He took another look behind him and saw Reimer, who had again slowed to a walk. The man looked about him, searching for a means of escape. His options were rapidly dwindling because, at that moment, Berger's and Reimer's two colleagues came charging in from the opposite direction. They too slowed to walking pace when they spotted Reimer and Berger.

'Don't move!' Berger ordered the driver. Her weapon was pointed at him.

The others had taken up crouch positions, weapons held two-handedly. It was a no-hope situation for the driver. Even so, he tried.

His hand went for his pistol. He was very fast; but he never made it. He had actually pulled it out when four guns roared at him, in the hitherto quiet street. He was hit each time, and he tumbled to the pavement, dying as he fell. The silenced automatic pistol clattered to the ground.

They approached him cautiously, weapons pointing. Reimer went down on one knee to feel for a pulse. He shook his head slowly.

As if from nowhere, people had begun to gather. One of the policemen glared at them. They backed away, but did not disperse.

'Bloody ghouls,' he said.

Berger had hurried back to the Mercedes. She looked in, and saw Neubauer.

'Shit!' she said, and immediately called Pappenheim.

'Pappenheim.'

'A bad one, Chief.'

'What do you mean?'

'The *Direktor*'s dead. Shot.'

'You?'

'No. The driver did it.'

'The dri— Where are you?'

She told him.

'Stay just long enough to keep the sightseers away until

217

the recovery teams arrive,' he told her, a sharp edge to his voice. 'I'll alert them. When they get to you, meet me outside Müller's house.'

'Right, Chief. Just me? Or the others as well?'

'Everyone.'

'Pity.'

'I heard that.'

Berger smiled, but said nothing.

'What happened to Neubauer's driver?' Pappenheim asked.

'Neubau— Oh, I see.' She glanced at the body in the car. 'The *Direktor*. Well, the driver's lying on the ground. I ordered him to remain still. Despite the four of us, he decided to go for his gun. He won't be shooting again in this life.'

Ten

Müller and Carey Bloomfield were on the road that led to the villa.

He had decided that, as the quickest route went via Pappenheim's holiday home, past the Hotel 1815, and then on to Seeberg's house, he might as well make a brief stop there.

It was a neat little two-storey place in gleaming white, with a filigreed balcony on the top floor. There was a short drive which enabled parking virtually at the front door; a small, neat garden at the back, and even a conservatory. There were views to the harbour on three sides.

'Hey . . .' Carey Bloomfield said, looking around as they entered. 'This is a cute place. Do you get the feeling Pappi – chain-smoking old rogue – is playing cupid? Don't answer that,' she added quickly, looking around some more. 'Lots of light, and a great view.'

'We can admire it later,' Müller said. He had brought the outdoor gear with him. 'We're staying just long enough for you to change into this. If—'

His mobile rang. He looked at the display.

'Pappi,' he said to her.

'Surprise, surprise.'

'Sorry,' he said. 'Excuse me. Won't be long. Yes, Pappi,' he added, going back outside.

'Where are you?'

'At your villa, on the way to Seeberg's house. Thanks, Pappi. It's very kind of you.'

'It's nothing,' Pappenheim said in a gruff voice. Then he cleared his throat to cover the awkwardness he felt.

'We'll enjoy it, Pappi.'

219

'So you should.'

Müller allowed himself a fleeting smile.

'Had an interesting visitor today,' Pappenheim continued. 'A *Polizeidirektor* Neubauer. I don't profess to know of every police director in the country, but . . .'

'Neubauer, did you say?'

'You know him?'

'I seem to remember the name, but that's from a long time ago. It can't be the same person. And anyway, I don't remember him as a policeman.'

'How long ago?'

'When I was twelve . . . Wait a minute. It's coming back. If it's the same person, he would be in his fifties now. Biggish man, very affable, smokes cigars. I remember he ruffled my hair. Pappi? Are you there? You seem to have gone quiet.'

'Where did you see this man?'

'He visited my parents . . . my father, to be precise. I think it was a few days before they went off on that flight. But I could be mistaken. I'm digging into the memory of a twelve-year-old boy.'

'Some twelve-year-olds can have long memories . . .'

'And a twelve-year-old has brought me here. I know. So what's this about Neubauer?'

'He's dead.'

It was Müller's turn to be silent. 'I thought you just said you saw him.'

'That was before he got shot.'

'Perhaps you should begin at the beginning, Pappi.'

Müller listened in silence to what Pappenheim had to say about Neubauer's visit and its aftermath.

'Someone obviously sent him,' Müller eventually said when Pappenheim had finished.

'No prizes for guessing.'

'Definitely no prizes. The question is, what could he possibly have done after he left you, to get him shot by his own driver?'

'Not guilty,' Pappenheim said. 'How about this . . .' he went on, 'the driver was already under instructions to take him out if he failed in whatever he had planned to do when he came in with the Great White . . .'

'Or if he refused to do it.'

'That too. Perhaps a little of what was left of the good policeman rebelled.'

'It got him shot for his pains. Von Graff does not like to be countermanded, as we know from Holbeck.'

'You seem to have made up your mind he *is* von Mappus.'

'More than fifty per cent, and rising.'

'You still have to explain the chess-playing Seeberg.'

'Hopefully, we'll have the answer soon. Where are you now? The office?'

'I was saving that. Outside your home.'

'*What?*'

'Just in case someone comes looking for a diary . . .'

'Whoever it may be would not be able to get in.'

'There are five of us here to make quite certain. Just to be sure, you understand.'

Müller smiled to himself. 'Alright, Pappi. Whatever you think best. Don't *you* get shot.'

'Don't be ridiculous.'

In his car near Müller's house, Pappenheim put his phone away.

'Neubauer met your parents a few days *before* their flight?' he muttered, deep in thought.

He frowned, puzzled by something.

'I intercept a note,' he continued, 'written to you by a person or persons unknown, accusing your father of being Romeo Six. Now it seems that Neubauer, *Polizeidirektor*, with connections to von Graff – who himself had connections with your cousin, former DDR Colonel of Police Dahlberg – and shot by his own driver, once came to your home when you were a boy. He even ruffled your hair. So what's *the* big connection? Was your father really Romeo Six?'

Pappenheim found the train of thought intensely disturbing. It made him doubly determined to ensure that Müller never got to know about the accusation from the unknown note-writer.

221

His phone began to ring. He got it out again. 'Pappenheim.'

'Your profile is ready,' the female voice said.

'Excellent!'

'Should I have it sent to our office?'

'No. I'll collect it personally.'

'Well, it's waiting.'

'Be with you as soon as I can. And thanks, Christiane.'

'Anytime.'

Pappenheim ended the call then contacted Berger, whose car was parked unobtrusively a short distance away.

'I've got to go off,' he said to her. 'All yours.'

'Right, Chief,' she confirmed.

'And be careful, Lene.'

'You know me. I'm always careful.'

On Rügen, Carey Bloomfield looked round at Müller as he returned.

'And what did Pappi have to say?' she asked. She had put on the weatherproof clothing. 'See? They fit perfectly.'

The lined trousers were white, and the pale-grey multi-layered jacket had a white hood. On her feet were sturdy boots that looked fit for any terrain.

'They certainly do,' he said in some surprise as he looked at her. 'I guessed correctly, after all.'

'You worry me, Müller.'

'Why?'

'You're getting to know too much about me.'

'You're getting to know a lot about me,' he countered.

'OK. Let's call it a stand-off. What about Pappi?'

'Well for a start, Kaltendorf's back earlier than expected.'

'Bummer.'

'I'll tell you the rest on the way. Ready?'

'As I'll ever be.'

Müller started the Cayenne and began to tell her about Neubauer as he reversed down the short driveway.

He was fairly detailed in repeating what Pappenheim had told him; but he did not tell her everything, especially the part about his boyhood meeting with Neubauer.

'Whoo!' she said when he had finished. 'Von Graff isn't

222

wasting any time. How high does this thing go? A director of police, for God's sake . . .'

'You've seen some of the people on the disc. A director of police is a minor rank to them, but necessary if your long-term plans include a wholesale usurpation. You've got to build up a base for keeping order.'

'State police.'

'Precisely.'

'Some people never learn. Do you think that special commission thing could be real?'

'It depends. To paraphrase you, there are special commissions . . . and then there are special commissions. You can hide a multitude of sins under that umbrella.'

'So his headhunting play was just hot air.'

'Yes. On the other hand, perhaps not. It would not be the first time that such people have tried to recruit individuals politically acceptable to the general public. Mix the good with the bad. It's a well-tried system in many authoritarian states. Democratic countries do that too, of course . . . but in a less inimical way.'

'You mean ruling by coalition.'

'Exactly. But what von Graff and his cronies are really trying to do, is grow a second skeleton – a shadowy one – that spreads far into the body politic. As it grows, it will eventually reach so deeply into the extremities of the body that removing it will cause almost as much damage as leaving it. Its marrow serves as a conduit for its poison. By then, it will be too late. So it has to be surgically removed early, before it can cause any real damage. It is an ongoing fight, Miss Bloomfield.'

'*Carey,* damn it, Müller!'

'The hotel.'

'*What?*' It was a restrained snap. She stared at him.

'Hotel 1815. Over to the left.'

She turned to look, without really seeing. 'What about it?'

The road skirted the seafront and here the covering of snow was very thin. He slowed down to turn into the hotel car park.

'I have an idea.'

223

He stopped and got out before she could say anything.

'Of course you do,' she said, watching him enter the hotel. She paused. 'Why am I suddenly so cranky, anyway. I can't still be jet-lagged.'

Müller went through the hotel lobby and up to the reception desk. The cafeteria, a little to the right, was almost empty: two couples, and a lone diner. One of the couples – elderly man and woman – had finished, and they got up to leave. The other couple, much younger, seemed engrossed with each other. The lone diner, a stocky man in a fisherman's sweater, was nursing a post-prandial coffee.

The receptionist gave Müller the usual bright smile. 'Welcome to the 1815, sir. How can I help you?'

'I was told a couple of friends would be staying here,' Müller began, loud enough to be heard in the cafeteria.

'What names, sir?' She began to look at her computer monitor, fingers poised to begin hitting the keys.

'The first is Maximillian Holbeck.'

'Max–i–mil–lian Hol-beck,' the receptionist went as she typed in the name.

Müller had taken a surreptitious glance at the cafeteria as he had spoken. He knew it was a very long shot; but he had nothing to lose, and he just might gain something.

He did.

For the barest moment, the young couple had frozen in astonishment; then control had taken over, and they had continued as if nothing had occurred. They did not even turn to look; but they were the only ones.

The elderly couple actually stopped on their way out, to glance at Müller with mild curiosity. Even the man in the fisherman's sweater looked up for a brief moment, before returning to his contemplation of his cup of coffee.

'I'm very sorry, sir,' the receptionist said with regret. 'He's not registered here. Perhaps he's at another hotel.'

'I was definitely told the 1815.'

She gave him a wide smile. 'I am glad he chose us, but there's no booking as yet. And the second person?'

'Rachko. Andrei Rachko. They're both very good friends.'

'Rach . . . how do you spell that, sir?'

Müller spelled it as she typed.

Then again, she shook her head. 'He has not yet booked either. I am so sorry, sir.'

'No matter. I'll try again.'

'Perhaps they'll be here by then.'

'Perhaps.'

'If they do get here before you, sir, who shall I say called?'

'Müller. *Hauptkommissar.*'

'Oh! It is trouble?' The receptionist's eyes had widened to their limits.

'No trouble. Can I leave a message?'

'Of course, sir.'

'Tell them I understand what happened.'

The eyes widened again. 'Is it a police message?'

'You could say that.'

'I'll see that they get it,' came the eager promise.

'Thank you very much.'

He got another beam. 'Always happy to help the police.'

God, he thought.

Müller left the hotel without a second glance at the young couple.

'Well?' Carey Bloomfield said as he climbed into the Cayenne. 'What was the idea? And did it work?'

He told her what had occurred.

'Do you think it really was him? *Rachko?*'

'I don't know if it is Rachko, or if there *is* a Rachko. I'm assuming. But I am not mistaken about their reaction. They were most certainly shocked to hear the names.' He started the engine. 'Now let's see what awaits us at Seeberg's house.'

She glanced at the hotel. 'You're not waiting to see what he does?'

Müller shook his head. 'No need. If I'm wrong. We won't see them again. If I am right . . . we shall. They know I've read the diary.'

In the cafeteria, Galina was staring at her brother in shock.

'*He knows!*' she whispered. 'No one could know about Holbeck unless he had read the diary. He even knows our name! *He's* got the diary, or he knows who has! And that message, 'Tell them I understand what happened'. That was to *us*, because he knows about grandfather!'

Rachko said nothing for long moments. When he finally spoke, he was strangely calm.

'Müller. I know about him.'

In Berlin-Wilmersdorf, Berger was beginning to wonder whether Pappenheim might have been mistaken about putting a watch on Müller's house, when a black car drew up before the entrance.

'Look at that,' she said to Reimer.

'I'm looking.'

There was no need to tell the others in the second car. They knew what to do.

As they watched, two men got out of the black car. Both wore special-assault-unit gear, and hoods. There were no identification letters on their backs.

'What the hell . . . ?' she began. 'A special team? Who from?'

'You're asking me? There's no ident—'

'It's a—'

'I know. Rhetorical question. Hey! What are you doing?'

Berger was getting out of the car. She had her pistol out.

The two men were now at Müller's door, and were doing something to it.

'Where are you going?' Reimer repeated in a sharp hiss. 'Those are colleagues!'

'Who says? And what are they doing at the boss's house? Cover me.'

'Jesus, Berger!'

But he got out and took up a position from where he could give her cover. With hand signals, he alerted the others in the second car, indicating they should also cover Berger. They left their car and took up covering positions.

The men at Müller's door were still unaware.

Berger was almost upon them when one glanced back. He tried to reach for his sidearm.

Berger had her gun pointing. 'I wouldn't,' she advised. '*Polizeimeisterin* Berger. Get away from there! Move!'

The second man had turned. Both straightened to full height.

'Go away, little policewoman,' the first said tolerantly. 'Don't meddle in things you know nothing about.'

'She must be Müller's lap dancer,' the other said.

They chuckled.

'Alright,' she said. 'I've warned you. Now you're under arrest. Turn around!'

'Do you think we should?' the first said. 'You never know these days with women.'

They sniggered.

'You really should go away,' he repeated. 'Pointing guns at colleagues . . .'

'I don't know you're colleagues. Identify yourselves, if you are.'

'You've had your fun, little girl,' the spokesman said, voice low and harsh. 'Now *go away*, and let us do our job before you get hurt.' The eyes behind the hood were merciless.

'You're the one who's going to get hurt.'

He sighed. 'That's it. I've had it with you!'

His hand dived for his weapon.

Berger's gun roared twice. The man, despite his body armour, was flung backwards. Berger had deliberately fired at both thighs where he was unprotected. They were crippling wounds. She covered the second man as running feet told her the others were racing up.

'You won't make it,' she told him.

He raised his hands quickly.

The man on the ground shouted, 'Jesus Christ! The little whore shot me!'

'Call me that again,' Berger snarled at him, 'and I'll stamp on your wounds! Give them bracelets,' she added to Reimer.

Reimer went up to the one who was still standing and whipped off the hood. Hard eyes glared at him.

'Don't look at me like that,' he said to the hard-eyed man. 'I don't know you well enough. Turn round, please. I have some jewellery for you.'

227

As he turned, the man cranked his head round to look at Berger. 'We won't forget this.'

But Berger was looking at something on Müller's door. 'Is that a bomb, you shithead?' She looked at the man.

'It's just a tiny charge,' he sneered. 'To blow the lock.'

'Reimer,' Berger said, 'cuff one hand to the door handle and leave the other free. Then move out of the way.'

Reimer did so quickly.

The door handle was not one of those that could be turned. Its splayed ends were immovably welded between two full-sized sheets of reinforcing steel within the massive wooden door.

The man stared at her. 'You're crazy. You're both crazy. It will blow my hand off!'

'Not if you remove that "little charge".' Berger stepped back, but still covered him with her weapon.

The man on the ground kept moaning.

'I need both hands!' the one with the handcuff insisted.

'Now you've got a problem.'

'You bitch!' he snarled, but he began to feverishly attempt to disarm the charge in time.

'Keep him covered,' she said to Reimer. 'I've got a call to make.' She moved further away, then called Pappenheim. 'We've got some trade,' she said as soon as Pappenheim had answered. 'Two . . . in special-unit outfits. Body armour . . . the whole kit. I shot one. No . . . just wounded.'

She told him about Müller's door, then paused to listen. 'No idea who they are, Chief. I asked for ID, but got no response. Alright. We'll wait.'

She ended the conversation and returned to where Reimer and the unknown men were. The charge on the door had been disarmed.

The man glared at her.

'See?' she said to him. 'Look at all the things you can do with one hand.' She grinned at him. 'Don't look so embarrassed. I'm sure you're not one of those. Some people are coming to pick you up,' she continued. 'When they get here, which will be soon, you'll be off our hands. If you have been impersonating police officers, you're in bad trouble.'

'You don't know what you're dealing with, lap dancer.'

Berger swung her pistol. It slammed against the side of the man's head. The blow rocked him and a drip of blood appeared.

'And *you* don't know what *you're* dealing with.'

Reimer stared at her. 'Are you *crazy*?'

'No,' she said, and walked away.

Rachko was outside the hotel, talking to someone on his mobile.

'Müller is on the island. He was right here in my hotel!'

'Müller, Müller, *Müller*!' the voice at the other end said in a fit of frustrated irritation. 'The man is a bane!'

'We need the boat.'

'It's already on its way. What did Müller do?'

Rachko told him.

'So he does have the diary,' the other said. There was a softness to the voice that was full of menace.

'He does not only have it. He has *read* it. He knows what happened.'

'A little knowledge can be a very dangerous thing . . . for some. Where did he go after he left?'

'I can make a very good guess.'

'Anyone with him?'

'He was alone.'

'The boat will be waiting as arranged.'

The connection was abruptly cut off. Rachko grimaced at the mobile, before putting it away.

'I know you're planning to double-cross me,' he said as he went back into the hotel.

Müller drew up before Seeberg's house and parked the Cayenne next to Kreuz's car. The policeman was outside, waiting.

Müller climbed out and went to Kreuz, hand outstretched.

'Müller,' he said as they shook hands.

'Kreuz.' Then Kreuz looked past Müller to see Carey Bloomfield climb out.

'Miss Bloomfield,' Müller said, 'Sergeant Kreuz.'

They shook hands.

'Sorry you had to wait here for so long,' Müller went on to Kreuz.

Kreuz looked sheepish. 'To be honest, I stayed outside as much as I could.'

'I don't blame you. Must have been a shock to find him like that.'

'Not one I would like to repeat for a long, long time, sir. I carried out a search of the whole place, but there was no sign of anything having been disturbed. Please come with me. I've left everything exactly as I found it.'

Müller locked the Cayenne with the remote, activating the alarm system. The Dragunov was safely out of sight in the luggage compartment behind the rear seats.

As they followed Kreuz through the house to the winter garden, Carey Bloomfield looked about her.

'He did very well for himself,' she remarked, 'your Herr Seeberg. A pauper's home this isn't.' They entered the conservatory. 'And the man himself,' she added, as Seeberg's head came into view.

They moved round to face the body from the front, touching nothing.

Müller stared at the wound in the throat, but made no comment.

Carey Bloomfield's expression mirrored exactly how she felt. 'Jesus,' she uttered softly in English. 'Sixty years end here.'

Not comprehending, Kreuz looked from one to the other, then decided not to ask any questions.

Müller looked closely at the razor, still without touching anything. He responded in the same language. 'The circle is finally complete, in this particular sense. The razor is back with its owner . . . perhaps.'

Müller studied the dried blood on the hand, the blade of the razor, and the floor. The rivulet that had run down the hand had missed the earlier spots of grandfather Rachko's own blood.

'Older blood,' Müller said.

Carey Bloomfield crouched forward to look. 'The grandfather?'

'Seems likely.'

'This is some revenge,' she said.

Müller straightened. 'How would you have behaved?'

'I know what you're thinking,' she said, standing upright. 'An immediate response, yes. But I'm not sure that as a grandchild I'd . . .' She let her words hang.

'Then again . . .'

'Then again, I can't say that I would not. If what happened to Rachko's grandfather had happened to mine, and my father had witnessed it as a boy . . .'

'And then passed the task on to you because he was unable to continue for whatever reason . . .'

Carey Bloomfield thought about it. 'When I think of assholes like von Graff, I get your point. So now what?'

'If the man I saw in the hotel is Rachko the third, I have no option but to arrest him, whatever my own private feelings.'

'Life is hell. He did the world a service.'

'I'm not so certain.' Müller was frowning as he studied Seeberg's body. 'Notice anything?'

She followed his gaze. 'Notice what?'

'Keep looking.'

Müller took a pair of gloves out of a pocket, and the familiar small plastic bag. Very carefully, avoiding touching any blood, he prised the opened razor out of the dead hand. He closed the razor with extreme caution, then placed it into the bag, which he sealed. He gave the bag to Kreuz, then removed the gloves. He put them into a separate bag, and handed that to Kreuz.

'I'll take them from you later,' he said in German.

'Yes, sir.'

Müller turned to Carey Bloomfield. 'Found it yet?' he asked, switching back to English.

'I don't . . .' She paused, staring at Seeberg's face. Even in death, she could now see the resemblance. 'My God. He looks like von Graff! They could be brothers!'

'Now you do see the problem.'

'But if this isn't von Mappus, then von Graff . . . could . . . be . . .'

231

'My gut has been banging away like mad, pushing me away from what seemed to be the correct path to take.'

'But Rachko believed this to be his man. He's been tracking him for God knows how long.'

'He was steered here.'

'By whom?'

'That,' Müller said, 'would be an enlightenment.' He stared out across the garden, then back to the body. 'His last view. The snow, and the distance. Appropriate. Rachko deliberately chose this way to do it.' He looked at the chess set. 'Is this your game?' he asked Kreuz, switching once more to German.

The sergeant shook his head, looking puzzled. 'I've been wondering about that. When we last met for a game, the positions were different when we stopped. I had a good chance of winning. I was surprised to see this, because it looked as if he tried to move the pieces to different positions. But he has never cheated once, in all the time we have played.'

'He still lost,' Müller said. 'But not to you.'

He walked over the low barrier of snow and went into the garden. He walked up to the gate and stood there, staring out to sea. After a while, he heard Carey Bloomfield come up behind him.

'This gate,' he said, 'is almost like the one in *The Magpie*.'

'It's just a gate, Müller.' She stopped next to him.

'Perhaps.'

'And the answer's not out there on the water.'

'It could be. I've been watching a speck. It's growing; very slowly, but definitely.'

She squinted into the distance. The day was not as bright as the hopeful weather announcer had said it would be, but neither was it gloomy. Eventually, she spotted the moving dot on the horizon.

'Could be a fishing boat.'

'Could be,' Müller repeated, 'but I doubt it. I must get down to the beach. If . . .'

The sound of the mobile cut him off.

He quickly got it out. 'Yes, Pappi.'

232

'Where are you now?'

'At the scene. The wound is exactly as described by Holbeck. It's uncanny. I believe I may also have found our killer.' Müller explained what had happened.

'That was a smart move,' Pappenheim said approvingly. 'You were lucky he chose that particular hotel.'

'One always needs luck. But I believe a certain imperative drove him to stay there. It's sufficiently far away from Seeberg's house to avoid suspicion. And the little place itself, as you know, is no longer the busy fishing port it used to be. The holiday intake is as yet not fully into its winter swing, whatever that is. Plenty of deserted, out-of the-way beaches from which to catch a boat. It was a good place to pick.'

'So? Is it von Mappus?'

'The way you've just said that, Pappi, is raising the hairs along my spine.'

'So it should. I've got the profile.'

'Go on.'

'Von Graff's matches exactly the one marked VM. *He* is von Mappus, just as you suspected.'

Müller felt a stab of heat go through him. 'My God,' he said, so softly Pappenheim almost missed it. 'A judas goat.'

He was vaguely aware that Carey Bloomfield was staring at him.

'Who is?' Pappenheim prompted.

'One of the six men from Stalingrad. The VG. Villem Grootemans.'

'You get ten out of ten. The bastard set up his own comrade.'

'Pappi, Grootemans even looks like von Mappus. The resemblance is quite . . . eerie.'

'Plastic surgery?'

'I thought that at first. But no, this is as nature intended.'

'Bad luck for Grootemans.'

'Bad luck indeed. Although he must have been paid quite generously for the impersonation. He was definitely a rich man.'

233

'Didn't help him in the end, did it? He got his throat cut. Just as it didn't help Neubauer. *He* got shot for his pains.'

'Playing with von Graff – von Mappus, as we must now call him – is a dangerous business. Now there's a *true* killer. One can only guess at his real tally during the past sixty years.'

'Well he's definitely interested in you. You had visitors to your palatial home. Two hard men, kitted out like our special-assault colleagues, tried to take on that castle drawbridge you call a door.'

'And?'

'They got stopped of course. Berger was in command of the team that took them.'

'Good for her. Were these men colleagues?'

'Sort of.'

'*Sort* of?'

'Let's file them under Neubauer.'

'Ah!'

'They're ex-colleagues now, and will be facing some stiff jail sentences.'

'Serves them right, the idiots. Von Mappus again?'

'Oh, definitely. He's been burrowing deep into the system, Jens. Anyone's guess how far he – and others like him – have got.'

'His days will soon be over,' Müller said.

'And Rachko?'

'I'll have to take him in.'

'Poor bastard. One has to feel sorry. All those years and he gets the wrong man.'

'It's a hard life.'

'Don't we know it.'

Müller looked out to sea. The speck was perceptibly bigger. 'Alright, Pappi. Thanks for keeping things watertight. Anything else comes up . . .'

'I'll let you know.'

As he ended the call, Müller turned to Carey Bloomfield. 'How much did you pick up?'

'Pretty much the whole thing, from your part of the

conversation.' She glanced back at the house. 'So, von Mappus has managed to escape again.'

'Not if I can help it.' Müller, too, looked back at the house. 'The penultimate member of the Stalingrad six. The last of the five. Von Mappus killed them all, one way or another. Now, he's the *true* last of the six.'

'Where from here?'

'Norbert Roth can handle it. As far as he's concerned, Seeberg was the victim of an assault by someone he surprised in his home. That will be the story.'

'And Rachko?'

'I've got to stop him from making it to that boat. Coming?'

'Do I have a choice?'

'Of course not.'

'A girl likes to know these things, you understand.'

Müller called Roth. 'All yours, Norbert. Send your recovery team in. Seeberg surprised an intruder.'

'That's the story?'

'That's it. Any problems, refer to us in Berlin.'

'OK. Fine. I'll tell poor Kreuz he has to hang on a bit longer.'

'I'll tell him. You get your people organized.'

'Will do.'

They walked back to the house and Müller gave the sergeant the bad news as he retrieved the two plastic bags.

'And all I wanted to do was play some chess,' Kreuz said ruefully.

The Cayenne was heading away from the house.

'You'll need the Dragunov,' Müller said to Carey Bloomfield. She looked at him. 'I will? Why?'

'I'll need you to give me cover. I believe that Dragunov was intended for use on Rachko. It's a feeling. The man who died in the accident might actually have been the one meant to do the job. I also believe it possible that the boat will not be taking Rachko back. When I am down on the beach I want you up on high ground, keeping both Rachko and the boat in your sights. But do *not* shoot Rachko . . . unless it seems absolutely likely that I would be unable to defend myself.'

'And is it likely?'

'Is what likely?'

'That you might be unable to defend yourself?'

'Is there a needle in there somewhere?'

'Four questions in a row! Wow! We're doing well. You know, Müller, if I were given to uncharitable thoughts – which I'm not – I could begin to think that you got me this outdoor outfit just for this.'

'As I myself do not harbour uncharitable thoughts,' he countered, 'I got this as a precaution, in case we ended up trekking across country in pursuit. I did not want you to get frostbite.'

'It's an answer.'

Out to sea, the 16-metre high-speed, offshore sports cruiser made its way towards the rendezvous at an easy pace. Powered by twin 700PS Volvo D12s, it could hit 36 knots at full blast. In gleaming white with black side flashes, it was a sleek example of maritime art. Its sleekness belied its passenger capacity. It could sleep four with ease, and could carry eight.

There were just three people aboard.

The road had widened briefly, bulging at either side. Müller pulled over and stopped. He got out the map of the area around Seeberg's house and spread it across the steering wheel.

'This section of the road moves away from the coast for about three kilometres,' he said. 'We'll be past where I want to go by the time it heads back towards the sea; and from here we're about one and a half kilometres in a straight line from the spot I'm aiming for. I want to get there before that boat is close enough.'

'So what do we do? Walk?'

Müller studied the undulating white landscape to his left. A vast, open field greeted his eyes. 'Take us too long in this. Luckily, we don't have to walk.'

He turned the wheel to the left and began to drive off the road. At first he did so cautiously, testing the ground beneath the snow for firmness. It was solid. The Cayenne

236

raised itself on its air springs, and let its four-wheel-drive system go to work.

'I hope there's no swampy ground underneath all this,' Carey Bloomfield said. 'Somehow, I don't think even your wonder toy can beat a swamp.'

'It would depend on how deep the swamp,' Müller told her as the Cayenne charged through the snow and up a steep slope.

Carey Bloomfield took a quick glance behind. The rear view was a sea of white. To the front was open sky, minus the comforting view of terrain.

'When we took off in the Echo,' she began with as much calm as she could muster, 'the pilot did one of those homesick-angel lift-offs. You know, straight up, runway below the tail. I looked back and there it was, mother earth and nothing else. I get that feeling now. Hope it's not a cliff on the other side.'

'Don't worry.'

'Who's worried?'

The Cayenne breasted the rise, then launched itself down the other side.

'No cliff,' Müller said.

'Hah!'

They came to a mainly flat expanse that spread into the distance, and the Cayenne raced across it towards woodland, churning snow in its wake. At the edge of the wood, a gentler slope came into view. The trees in one section had grown in a pattern that formed a natural avenue, rising to the summit. It was unnervingly reminiscent of a ski jump.

Müller drove up it as fast as he dared and came to a halt at the top. He left the engine running.

While not a cliff in the strictest sense of the word, the ground dropped away steeply enough to make continuing sufficiently hazardous, even for the Cayenne. The crest was plainly a favourite viewing point, for the outlines of two benches were evident beneath their thick covering of snow, a short distance back from the screen of trees.

'Can't beat gravity, huh?' Carey Bloomfield said, leaning forward in her seat to peer out.

'This is where you get out.'

'Hey . . . it was a joke . . .'

'Oh that. You did not offend me. I mean this is where you position yourself with the rifle. Look through the trees.'

She peered for a few moments. 'The boat! It's coming this way . . .'

He nodded. 'Rachko may already be on the beach. I've seen a way to get down; over to the right, just behind us. There's a sort of trench-like depression that should get me there. The screen of trees should also give you good cover. I am quite certain they'll have a pair of binoculars on the boat. Essential equpiment on the water.'

'OK . . .' she said, and began to get ready. 'This is where I get to freeze.'

'You shouldn't. That gear is very thermal.'

'I trust you. You're a doctor.'

'I've got the joke,' he said with a tolerant smile.

She raised the hood of her jacket, picked up her bag and climbed out. Müller joined her and went to the back to remove the Dragunov, which he handed to her.

He glanced westwards, to his right. The weak sun was curtained by some hazy, high-altitude cloud. It gave the day a surreal light.

'Sundown up here at this time of the year is between fifteen forty and fifteen forty-three. We've got plenty of light left, allowing for twilight. Don't forget to wear your mittens,' he reminded her. 'They have an internal glove. If you've got to fire, just pull the mittens – they're on straps – and . . .'

'The gloves will enable me to fire the weapon without touching the metal parts. We're not at the north pole, Müller. And I do know how to handle weapons in sub-zero conditions.'

'Of course.'

He took a small unit out of a pocket. It was no bigger than a packet of cigarettes, and half as thick. Attached to it by a short cable was an earphone-microphone combination.

'Put the main unit in a breast pocket of your jacket,' he told her, 'then attach the earphone-mike. It's a two-way unit, person-to-person only. No one else can hear us. It's eavesdrop-proof.'

'Looks kind of home-made,' she said as she took it.

'One of the goth's inventions. It works very well indeed.'

'The goth, huh?'

'Another needle?' When she did not comment, he added, 'Will you be alright?' He shut the rear door of the Cayenne.

'Müller, I'm a major. I've got me a big gun in my bag, and a long-range firestick in this one. What do you think?'

He looked at her for a long moment, as if pondering upon something to say. 'Just be careful,' he said, and went round to climb back behind the wheel.

He started the Cayenne, turned it round, and headed back down the slope towards the depression he had seen.

'Sure,' she said, as the Cayenne disappeared in a flurry of snow.

Eleven

M üller discovered that the depression hairpinned down to the pebbly beach much more steeply than it had at first appeared.

He negotiated it carefully, not overspeeding, but not being particularly slow either. He allowed the Cayenne to dictate the pace. It tipped, settled down again, sometimes on two wheels only, at other times all four biting reassuringly into the snow that covered the hard surface. Snow billowed around it as it went.

Then the gradient levelled out and the Cayenne gathered speed as it arrived at the beach.

Müller glanced to his right. No one. He glanced left. *Rachko*. Alone, and in the clothes Müller had seen in the hotel, except that Rachko now wore an all-weather jacket. Rachko did not appear to be in a particular hurry. The boat was still some way out.

From the shore, a glistening platform went some distance out to sea. The Baltic, at least this close in, had frozen over. Müller wondered how thick the ice was, and how far this apparent solidity extended.

'Hello,' he said. 'Can you hear me?'

'Loud and clear,' Carey Bloomfield replied. 'Hey. This works.'

'I did tell you.'

'Don't be so smug, Müller. So?'

'Rachko's here.'

'Where?'

'Up ahead. He seems in no hurry.'

'Has he seen you yet?'

'He has not turned around to look . . . but he must have heard the Cayenne.'

'That's staying cool. Where's the boat?'

'Still some way out. But the sea around here is frozen.'

'You're kidding.'

'Not completely frozen over,' Müller explained. 'But the ice reaches some distance out. The boat must be trying to find a way through. That will depend on the thickness of the ice.'

'It is strong enough to walk on?'

'It looks it, close to shore. However, it could be very thin further out. And there's something else: Rachko has come alone.'

'So where is she?'

'Possibly back at the hotel, hiding out here somewhere, or on her way off the island. No one's looking for a woman.'

'Maybe he doesn't trust whoever's picking him up.'

'I would say this is most likely . . . if von Mappus is the one sending the boat. Only von Mappus could have steered him to Grootemans . . . which brings up a lot of intriguing questions. Ah . . .'

'What? What?'

'Rachko has stopped and is looking back at the Cayenne. He's just standing there, making no move to run. I'm not sure he can see me properly . . . as yet.'

'Watch yourself, Müller.'

'Worried?'

She made no reply.

Müller smiled to himself as he drew closer to Rachko, who still made no move to avoid him.

Then he saw something in Rachko's right hand, pointing down.

Carey Bloomfield had unpacked the Dragunov and had carefully prepared it for firing, as she had been taught.

She had found herself a good position and lay prone, well hidden by the screen of trees, but still giving her a wide field of vision. She had secured the hood of her all-weather snugly about her head, and though she lay within a trough she had scooped, she felt no dampness from the snow.

'You were right, Müller,' she said to herself. 'This gear is nice and warm.'

She switched on the Dragunov's optical sight, then looked through it. She focussed on the Cayenne, following it until she could see Rachko. He filled the scope. The one vertical and two horizontal dashes which formed the wide T, with its range and height markings to the left of the bottom leg, put his height at 1.82 metres. She moved the rifle until she found the boat. The four-fold magnification gave her a good image. She focussed on the head of the man at the helm. Then she switched back to Rachko.

'Can you see him now?' came Müller's voice.

'I've got him.'

'Don't shoot unless I tell you.'

'Sir, yessir.'

'Ha ha,' he said.

As Müller drove on, Rachko stood his ground. Müller drew right up to him and stopped.

Müller climbed out of the Cayenne and shut the door. He did not take out his own gun. Both men looked at each other from a distance of about two metres.

'*Hauptkommissar* Müller,' Rachko began. 'I know much about you.'

'I am surprised, and flattered,' Müller said. 'And, after the hotel, you are now aware that I know about you . . . at least, about the story behind you. Your German is very good.'

'I had a good teacher.'

'Yes. I know. Your father, who learned it from your grandfather.'

'I did learn some from him,' Rachko said, 'but I perfected it in Germany. The DDR, of course.'

'Of course.'

'Why are you here, *Hauptkommissar*?'

'You know why.'

'In the hotel, you said you understood.'

'I do understand. It is all in the diary.'

'The diary.' Rachko spoke of it as he would an heirloom. 'If you understand, then you know I did the world a favour, and avenged my grandfather, and my aunt; and . . . though this may surprise you, Sergeant Holbeck.'

'It does not surprise me.'

The arctic eyes studied Müller. 'Max Holbeck died saving my aunt, Galina. He placed himself between her and the bullets from von Mappus. Holbeck had given my father the diary, and had told him to run and find somewhere to hide. Then my aunt entered the house. Soon after that, von Mappus entered. My father could not see exactly what happened from where he was hiding, but he heard the firing. He heard my aunt scream, just once. Max Holbeck made no sound.

'My father peered through a crack and saw von Mappus take a small camera from Holbeck's body. Holbeck had fallen on my aunt, still protecting her, even in death. Then my father ran away to hide in the woods, and heard von Mappus leaving. From there, he saw a soldier – a big man – fire on the house with his machine gun, after von Mappus spoke to him. Then he threw grenades. It had been the last house that had not yet been burnt. Now it had joined the others.

'Long after the soldiers left, my father went back to the village. He found my grandfather lying where he had been killed. He picked up the razor and vowed to use it to kill von Mappus in exactly the same manner in which he had killed my grandfather. Then he gathered what food had been left unspoiled and began walking. The soldiers had taken the village horses they could use and shot the others. My father eventually met up with some partisans. He became respected for his fighting. He killed many soldiers, operating behind the enemy lines. All the time, he was searching for von Mappus; but he never found him. He finished the war as a junior lieutenant, and not even sixteen. The village was rebuilt. The burnt remains of Max Holbeck and my aunt are buried next to each other. He has a place of honour in our village.

'My father stayed in the army. He went to Korea as an advisor and was wounded by splinters from an artillery shell. One hit him where he always carried the diary. It went right through . . .'

'So the blood on it is his,' Müller said.

Rachko nodded. 'While he was being attended to in the field hospital, the diary disappeared. He got very angry. He was a major at the time and he yelled at the people in the hospital. But they had no idea what had happened. I am astonished it came into your hands, after all these years.'

'I cannot tell you how it came to me, because I don't know. I can only suspect that it came from an intelligence source.'

'It would make sense. My father always said he suspected that Army Intelligence, the GRU, kept it. Why would someone in our army intelligence send it to you?'

'I have no idea,' Müller said.

'I think you do, knowing what I know about you.'

'Would you care to explain?'

'No.'

On the boat, von Mappus was looking through his binoculars. His sudden intake of breath came in a sharp hiss when he saw Müller with Rachko.

'*Müller!*' he said through gritted teeth. 'Damn that man!'

He lowered the binoculars to let them hang from the strap around his neck. He hurried down into the cabin, pulled open a deep drawer and took out a rifle.

It was another Dragunov SVDS.

Rachko glanced at the earphone and mike that Müller wore. 'You've got people watching us.'

'Yes.'

'So, if I shoot you, they will shoot me.'

Müller glanced at the pistol Rachko held, which was still pointing down. 'Yes.'

Rachko nodded, as if confirming something to himself. 'Do you know what Rachko means?' he asked suddenly.

'Judge.'

'I am impressed. I am Zima Andreivitch. Do you know what *that* means?'

'Andreivitch is from your father – son of. I have no idea what Zima could mean.'

'It means winter. My father gave me the name. You could say I have been named the winter judge. I carried on when he could not. The wounds he had received in Korea eventually killed him.'

'I am sorry. From what little I know of him – from the diary, and now from you – he was a very courageous man. Now you believe you have passed judgement upon, and executed von Mappus, in the name of your grandfather, and in place of your father.'

'Yes. I joined the KGB. I applied for, and got sent to the DDR. I felt this would help me find von Mappus. In the course of my work I met von Graff, who was in the police, and he promised to help me trace von Mappus. We met from time to time, during the course of my . . . duties. I learned that Von Graff had himself been Waffen SS. In the days after the war, the rulers in the DDR turned a blind eye. They needed people like him.'

'How could you bring yourself to work with a man who had been a member of the same organization as von Mappus?'

'I would have dined with the devil himself, if that would have helped me get to von Mappus. I also wanted to find Max Holbeck's camera, with all its evidence.'

'You know, of course, that von Graff will double-cross you.'

'I am sure of it. That is why Galina . . . she's my sister . . . is not here. My father gave her my aunt's name. My mother agreed to it. So . . .'

'Where is Galina?'

Rachko looked at Müller warily. 'Gone. I thought it safest for her.'

'So you intend to confront von Graff. Then what?'

'I used to be KGB, *Hauptkommissar*. I am not a defenceless chicken.'

'And von Graff is a former General of Police, with a long, long history . . .'

'I know the kind of creature he is.'

'I am not sure you do, Zima Andreivitch Rachko,' Müller said.

Rachko stared at him. 'What do you mean?'

Müller glanced past the bonnet of the Cayenne and out to sea where the boat, much closer now, was nudging at the

245

edge of the ice. It was breaking through the thin surface with ease.

'The boat will stop when the ice gets too thick. You will have to walk out to it, if the ice will support you. I don't think von Graff will let you make it.'

'He must. He wants the camera, and I have it.'

'You have made a mistake,' Müller said. 'You were fooled, because von Mappus himself had no idea where the camera was; or he knew, and wanted you to get it, knowing you would kill someone he wanted to get rid of, without any suspicion falling on him. Von Mappus hates leaving witnesses alive, even when he has had need of them. He even tried at first to steer me off; then when that did not work he tried a little heavier persuasion.'

Rachko was looking at Müller as if at someone who has suddenly gone mad. 'What are you talking about?'

'The man you killed up at that house, the man who called himself Seeberg, was a stand-in for von Mappus. A double, if you like. You killed one of the men who came to your village in the winter of 1942, but it was not von Mappus. You killed Villem Grootemans. I know that for a fact, because we have the DNA profiles of both. I think von Mappus gave Grootemans the camera for safe keeping . . . but Grootemans didn't completely trust him and hid it well, as insurance. That did not help him in the end.'

Rachko was opened-mouthed. He looked distraught. 'I *failed*? After all this time? After all these *years*? You are lying!'

'Why should I lie? What reason could I possibly have?'

Rachko looked from Müller to the boat, and back again. 'If this is true . . . then . . . then I'll still get him. He's on the boat. He's wants me to personally give him the camera.'

'You won't survive the meeting.'

'Are you going to stop me?'

'I have to.'

'As I said before, I did the world a favour.'

'You committed a major crime, in this country . . .'

'Why would you want to protect someone who—'

'I most certainly do not want to "protect", as you call it,

246

anyone like that. But I am a policeman. I have a duty, and even though I may sympathize with your motives, I cannot . . .'

'What do you know, Müller? Nothing! What would you do, if someone killed your father . . .'

'My parents are both dead. Plane crash.'

Carey Bloomfield had listened to the conversation in growing wonder, awestruck by the implacable desire for revenge that had spanned two generations.

When she'd heard that von Mappus could himself be on the boat, she had moved the rifle to cover it. She had looked through the scope and there he'd been, looking at Müller and Rachko through binoculars.

Then he had disappeared below deck.

She now waited, still focussed on the boat, for him to return.

'I know,' Rachko said.

Müller stared at him. '*You . . . know?* You know what?'

'I know your parents are dead. I know how they died. I discovered the details in a file when I was with the KGB.'

Müller felt a strange heat go through him. 'What . . . do you mean? What file?'

'A man called Neubauer . . .'

'*Neubauer?* How do you know about Neubauer?'

'What you believe *you* know, Müller, is a lie. Neubauer visited your parents a few days before they went on a flight.' Rachko spoke quickly, as if he felt time was running out. 'Your parents were killed, Müller. Neubauer had something to do with it, and so did von Mappus. I don't know who gave the order . . .'

Rachko paused as he saw the shock in Müller's eyes, and the sudden paling of his face. As if coming to a decision, he reached into his jacket and took out a small package. He put it into Müller's hand. He had to close the hand about it as Müller stood there, staring at him.

'The camera,' Rachko said. 'It will be safe with you. Use what is in there in the best way you think fit, and in the interests of your country.' He gave a tired smile. 'Time to go.'

*　　*　　*

On the boat von Mappus again had the binoculars to his eyes. He watched in horror as Rachko passed something to Müller.

'*The camera!*' he shouted. '*He's giving him the camera! The treacherous Bolshevik! No one cheats me! Turn the boat!*' he ordered. '*Turn the boat! I want a firing position!*'

He let go of the binoculars as the boat began to turn so that its stern would point towards the shore.

Carey Bloomfield was herself still in a state of shock over Rachko's revelations about Müller's parents.

'My God,' she murmured softly. 'Poor you, Müller. I'm so sorry.'

Then her attention was distracted by the boat's movement. She shifted the rifle to cover it, again sighting through the scope.

'What the hell's going on?' She watched as the stern began to come round.

Then she saw von Mappus, and what he carried.

'*Jesus!*' she said.

'*Müller!*'

Müller heard the yell in his ear, and that startled him out of his shock. He stared down at the small package in his hand, as if trying to remember how it had got there.

'*Müller, damn it! Wake up! Sniper, sniper, sniper!*'

The words registered just as something slammed into Rachko's chest. A bright, expanding flower of red liquid erupted from the point of impact. Rachko's arms were flung wide. The gun went sailing out of his hand in a sweeping arc to fall with a hissing thud on to the pebbles. His body followed.

At last, Müller galvanized himself and leapt for cover behind the Cayenne.

'*Shit, shit, shit!*' Carey Bloomfield swore.

She rapidly swapped the magazine already fitted to the Dragunov for one with armour-piercing incendiary rounds.

Then she swiftly adjusted the scope to the image of von Mappus.

His height was given at 1.80 metres. He made no attempt to hide, clearly not expecting that he was also within the sights of a sniper.

'Just stay there,' she breathed. 'Just long enough . . .'

Von Mappus was sweeping with the rifle, trying to locate Müller.

'A little longer . . .' Carey Bloomfield remarked softly.

She fired.

The conical muzzle brake cut down the flash, ensuring that her position had not been betrayed, in case she missed.

She did not.

She watched through the scope as von Mappus was pitched backwards by a round with a muzzle velocity of 830 metres per second ripping into his heart.

'One for the *Untermensch*,' she muttered.

Immediately, the boat seemed to rise out of the water as the man at the wheel opened the throttles in an attempt to get away.

'Oh no, you don't,' she said.

Already sighted on the stern, she fired three, evenly spaced shots.

The incendiary rounds slammed into the boat, and ignited the fuel. A violent bloom that would rival a sunset spread out across the cold waters, followed a moment later by the thunder of the explosion as the boat disintegrated in an expanding fireball that sent dark smoke boiling upwards.

'Wooo!' she said. 'Did I do that?'

Müller heard, and saw, the destruction of the boat. He knew what Carey Bloomfield had done.

He scrambled towards Rachko, who was trying to speak as the life ebbed out of him.

'Save . . . save Galina,' came Rachko's voice in a low sigh.

'My parents,' Müller asked. '*My parents*. It is true? Is what you said true?' Rachko's eyes tried to focus. His mouth moved. No sounds came out of it. Then, very slowly, the head nodded.

And Zima Andreivitch Rachko died.

'Rachko! *Rachko!* Don't leave me with this!'

Müller stared at the body for a long time, as if waiting for a response. Then he slowly rose to his feet, absently putting Holbeck's Minox into a pocket.

He went round to the seaward side of the Cayenne, sat down on the pebbles and leaned against the front wheel. He stared out to sea and began to slowly throw pebbles across the ice.

He was still doing that when Carey Bloomfield arrived, Dragunov safely packed away.

She looked down and, without speaking, carefully placed the encased rifle on the ground. Then she sat down next to him. She turned her gaze out to sea. A pall of smoke was still rising from the wreck of the boat.

Hesitantly, as if afraid to do so, she reached out to place a tentative, comforting arm about Müller's shoulders.

He kept on throwing pebbles across the ice, but he did not pull away.

They were still sitting there when the police helicopter arrived.